Papa Schimmelhorn p[...]
The motors screamed; th[...]
each other; flashes and [...]
rent the air; the blue ray [...]ed, turned a savage purple, and, moaning hideously, drowned the
statuette in its dark light.

Mavronides took a quick step backward, making a protective sign. Meister Gansfleisch squirmed
aside. Only Papa Schimmelhorn and the Princess
held their ground.

For five full minutes, during which he stood
with his eyes fixed on his cuckoo watch, the sound
and fury maintained their crescendo. No one could
hear the small voice of the cuckoo when the time
came. He pushed the off-button. Gradually, the
purple ray thinned and paled; the din subsided;
the electrical discharges died away.

The statuette was still there on the plate. It had
not moved. But it was no longer dull and leaden.
It gleamed. There was no doubt, no doubt at all,
that it was now of purest gold.

pushed the big red button.

he page scratched against

lowing balls of lightning

the darkness

REGINALD BRETNOR

SCHIMMELHORN'S GOLD

A TOM DOHERTY ASSOCIATES BOOK

SCHIMMELHORN'S GOLD

First printing: June 1986

A TOR Book

Published by Tom Doherty Associates
49 West 24 Street
New York, N.Y. 10010

Cover art by David Mattingly

ISBN: 0-812-53239-2
CAN. ED.: 0-812-53240-6

Printed in the United States

0 9 8 7 6 5 4 3 2 1

For T. R. Fehrenbach, who wrote so informatively about *The Gnomes of Zürich*,
and for my old friend Alan L. Harvie, who first suggested that Papa Schimmelhorn should work for them.

CHAPTERS

I.

The Gnomes of Zürich

It certainly was not malice aforethought that led Papa Schimmelhorn to apply his genius to the (more or less) Black Arts. Having solved, to his own satisfaction and for the most practical purposes, such abstruse scientific problems as time travel, the manipulation of small black holes, shuttling to and from alternate universes, and the restoration of an entire planet's stolen manhood, the suggestion that he might have to be concerned with magic would have seemed utterly absurd to him.

Indeed, at least in the very early stages, he exercised no choice in the matter. The first critical decisions were made by a solidly established Swiss banker and by Mama Schimmelhorn, who respected solidly established Swiss banks and bankers as profoundly as she did her church and Pastor Hundhammer, who was also peripherally involved. (She, of course, did not know that Fräulein Philippa von Hohenheim, of whom she had never heard and of whom she would strongly have disapproved, would be intimately associated in the enterprise.)

It all started when Anton Fledermaus, the Schimmelhorns' grandnephew, delivered a shipment of bullion to Dr. Gottfried Rumpler, president and owner of G. Rumpler & Co., the most prestigious of all Swiss private banks, on Zürich's Bahnhofstrasse. He really was no longer Little

Anton, the pudgy, pimply lad whose parents had thankfully deported him to the Schimmelhorns' tender care some
years before. He had matured: his complexion was now
fresh and clear; much of the culture of Eton and Oxford
had rubbed off on him (though a bit indirectly), to say
nothing of the good manners of such aristocratic Chinese
as Horace Pêng; his sturdy frame filled his magnificently
tailored Italian silk suit to perfection. Now, facing Dr.
Rumpler across the latter's overly modest desk, he basked
in the reflected glory of his employers, Pêng-Plantagenet,
Ltd., the world's greatest conglomerate, and in his own
self-esteem as their Director of Special Services, a position
that involved such chores as escorting several million Swiss
francs' worth of gold from Hong Kong. Like all good
Swiss, Little Anton regarded Dr. Rumpler with immense
respect. He saw a tall and massive man in his mid-fifties,
with thick graying hair, a noble nose, a deep voice, and a
strict military bearing; and he did his best to conceal his
own pleasure at the realization that the Herr Doktor had
sized him up and appeared to regard him quite as respectfully.

"May I say, Herr Fledermaus," declared Dr. Rumpler,
"that it is most gratifying to me personally, and of course
to G. Rumpler and Company, to have for a client Pêng-
Plantagenet, known and esteemed throughout the world."
He inclined his head graciously. "And I only hope that
you, on your part, will find our services and your association with us completely satisfactory."

Purring, Little Anton assured him that it was quite certain
that they would, and he followed up this statement with an
extremely apt and learned quotation from Confucius, which
was very well received. Then Dr. Rumpler proceeded to
question him on such matters as the gold market in the Far
East, and jade collecting, and—with a conniving chuckle—
on whether the girls of Hong Kong were still as beautiful
and, well, *obliging* as they had been when he had visited
the city some years earlier. Little Anton, fully informed on
all these subjects, gave him even more information than he

had expected, and at the end of half an hour their acquaintanceship had ripened into camaraderie. Dr. Rumpler announced that they were truly kindred spirits; he canceled two appointments; brushing aside Little Anton's rather feeble protests, he invited him to dinner.

"You will meet my dear *petite amie*," he told him, "and also I will ask Fräulein Ekstrom, my secretary whom I am sure you noticed—"

"The blonde girl?" asked little Anton eagerly.

"The same! How do they say in English? We will have a ball!"

Finally, after a guided tour of the bank's vaults, and of their bullion bars, newly minted sovereigns, nostalgic United States double eagles, and shining krugerrands, together with Miss Ekstrom they rode off in Dr. Rumpler's chauffeur-driven Citröen. They picked up Brigitte, his *petite amie*, who giggled and tickled him and called him Rumpli, and were taken to the Rumpler mansion, a model of unpretentious luxury. There, over a superb dinner of many, many courses, Little Anton was plied with fine wines and liquors, with the very welcome attentions of Miss Ekstrom, and with sparkling conversation, into which, of course, a great many very astute questions were unobtrusively sandwiched by the Herr Doktor.

In spite of the fact that everything was going to his head, Little Anton recognized these for what they were, and fielded most of them subtly and politely; and when they got too pointed and too probing, he dextrously changed the subject and told them all about his great-uncle, now well into his eighties, of his undiminished sexual vigor, and his inventions, and how on the conscious level he was really almost stupid—a foreman in a cuckoo-clock factory—but that subconsciously he was a scientific genius, about whom even the great Jung had published several learned papers.

"My friend," exclaimed the banker, "you are not *joking?* Do you *really* mean that your great-uncle, this Papa Schimmelhorn, can solve all these problems? And that the famous Dr. Jung himself has studied him?"

Little Anton assured him that it indeed was so; and then his host was strangely silent for a while, though Miss Ekstrom filled the gap quite satisfactorily. All in all, Little Anton had a bang-up time, and when he left Zürich next day in Pêng-Plantagenet's imperial-yellow private jet, Miss Ekstrom kissed him a warm good-bye at the airport.

It had not taken Dr. Rumpler very long to recover his aplomb and once again take an active part in the conversation, but at Little Anton's recital of the Schimmelhorn accomplishments he had been hit by an idea so wild, a dream so appealing to the hearts of all Swiss bankers, that it had taken all his manly fortitude to conceal his intense excitement. After he went to bed, he could not rest; his mind was whirling, and even after he managed to go to sleep he kept rolling over and muttering to himself, to the point where his *petite amie* actually prodded him awake and threatened to go home immediately. They rose at daybreak, and presently he left her sulking and pouting over breakfast and was driven directly to the bank. There he paced up and down all morning, sometimes pounding his fist into his palm, sometimes frowning down at Bahnhofstrasse without seeing it.

"Perhaps," he muttered, "perhaps it is a mad idea—but what if what the young man said is true? *Ach*, why not?"

After an hour or two of this, he sat down decisively and made several discreet phone calls to people of influence and prestige, some in Switzerland, some elsewhere in Europe, and one or two in the United States. Then he waited impatiently for them to bear fruit, absentmindedly transacting a few hundred thousand Swiss francs' worth of business in the meantime. He had his lunch sent in from his favorite restaurant, ate only half of it, and told Miss Ekstrom, who had come in late and a bit breathless, that he expected important phone calls and was not to be disturbed.

The calls came in at intervals all afternoon. His contacts were unable to confirm all of Papa Schimmelhorn's scien-

tific triumphs, but by three o'clock he had heard enough to
recognize that Little Anton had told him nothing but the
truth—and to realize that perhaps his idea was not so mad
after all. Very practically, he sat down to consider ways
and means, and he began to see that there would be many
difficulties in the way, for what he had in mind was
definitely out of the normal run of conservative Swiss
banking practice. Knowing that he would have to have
assistance, he tried to think of people who, because of
Papa Schimmelhorn's proclivities and the highly sensitive
nature of the project, might be suitably qualified.

One name kept coming up—Fräulein von Hohenheim's—
and every time he thought of it, he shuddered. He wrestled
mightily with his banker's conscience, with his entire
Züricher cultural and religious heritage, but his idea had
seized him so effectively that they didn't have a chance.
Presently he called Miss Ekstrom, and told her to put in a
call and ask the Fräulein whether she could see him on a
matter of important business, either at the bank or at her
own offices—that afternoon, if possible.

Miss Ekstrom obeyed him with raised eyebrows, and
returned shortly with the news that the lady could give him
a few minutes of her time if he was sure the matter really
was important and if he would arrive in precisely half an
hour.

Dr. Rumpler, unused to such cavalier treatment, especially from a woman, ground his teeth and told Miss
Ekstrom to say that he'd be there.

Twenty minutes before the appointed time, he summoned chauffeur and Citröen to drive him the several
hundred yards down Bahnhofstrasse, so that at least he
would arrive in seemly state, but it was with considerable
uneasiness that he entered the small building whose plain
bronze plaque read simply, SCHWEIZERISCHE FRAUENBANK,
P. v. Hohenheim, Präsident. Shuddering at the very thought
of this arrogant feminine invasion of a field always completely masculine, he allowed a lean and hatchet-faced
female clerk to lead him, grumblingly, to the confrontation.

Fräulein von Hohenheim was seated at her desk, and she did not rise to greet him. At his polite salutation, she merely gestured at a chair.

Uncomfortably, he sat down. She was a splendid figure of a woman, with magnificent Minoan breasts, great, dark Minoan eyes, massive coils of bronze-black hair. Arabs inevitably wore their dark glasses when transacting business with her; and now, looking at her, Dr. Rumpler too could not help mentally undressing her—first perhaps the Parisian suit, then ever so gently the Celliniesque golden necklace at her delightful throat, then— But at that point, she caught his eyes and held them with her own—and he was forcibly reminded of a time when, touring Mexico, he had peered into the icy depths of a black well reputed to be bottomless, into which for centuries the native clergy had thrown the virgins whom they sacrificed. He also realized that she undoubtedly knew exactly how his mind had been engaged, and blushed like a Victorian schoolboy.

"To what do I owe the honor of this visitation?" she asked him then, in a voice that was deep, beautifully modulated, and as cold as the eyes that had transfixed him. "In the past, we have transacted all our business less directly."

"That is correct," he answered, starting to perspire. "But the matter I wish to discuss with you, my dear Fräulein, is of so confidential a nature, and holds out prospects of so vast a profit, that I must be more than ordinarily frank. You are, I believe, the only person who can help me." He swallowed hard. "You too are a Swiss banker. You are singularly accomplished and astute. I know, for instance, that you have three Ph.D.'s—one in Economics, one in Business Administration, and one, from a university very little known, in more arcane sciences. I also know—and believe me, this is even more important— that your full name is Philippa Theophrastra Bombast von Hohenheim, and that you are descended from, and named after, our own great Swiss, Philip Theophrastus Bombast von Hohenheim, better known to the world as Paracelsus, the so-called Golden Doctor, the prince of alchemists, whose talent and whose interests you have—er, some people *say* you have—inherited.''

She frowned, and Dr. Rumpler shuffled his feet and shifted in his chair. "It seems to me, mein Herr," she said, "that you have gone out of your way to learn perhaps too much about me."

"Bear with me, dear lady!" he pleaded. "Only be patient. Listen to me, and you will understand."

"Very well. Continue."

"Everything I tell you will, I'm sure, be held in complete confidence? That is—"

Fräulein von Hohenheim did not deign to answer him. *Mein Gott*, what a male chauvinist *schweinhund!* she thought. Without a word, she managed to convey the message that she had been grievously insulted.

He blushed again. Then, hesitantly at first, he told her the whole story of Little Anton's visit, and all about Papa Schimmelhorn's genius and accomplishments, and how he himself had checked on their validity. During this recital, he kept watching her expression for some hint of how she was reacting to it, and every once in a while he interjected an apology: "You understand, dear Fräulein, that while this is difficult to believe, I am assured . . ." or "I know definitely that this Schimmelhorn has carried out a scientific task for Pêng-Plantagenet, but Herr Fledermaus would not tell me what it was."

Gradually, as he watched her, her countenance began to lose something of its severity; her eyes betrayed a growing interest. Her very active mind was busy sorting out the data, evaluating it, drawing deductions from it. Long before he had finished, she had fathomed precisely what he had in mind, and had approved of it.

He stopped. For the first time, she smiled at him, sending delicious little shivers up his spine. "And so, Herr Doktor Rumpler," she said sweetly, "because this person Schimmelhorn has performed these wonders, you think it might not be too difficult for him to do what my great ancestor once did—to turn lead into gold?''

"But—but you have read my mind!" he cried.

She smiled again. "Not at all. I have simply drawn the logical conclusion. What other scientific problem could so excite the interest of the most eminent of Swiss private bankers? Why, were this to succeed, the greatest international bankers would be mere pygmies by comparison! And now I'm sure you'll tell me that it is a great good fortune for the world that such a secret should fall into Swiss hands—and ours especially—because we are so responsible?''

Dr. Rumpler, who had been about to express these very sentiments, declared that he had not thought of it, but that it indubitably was true.

She laughed aloud. "Well," she declared, "you will be glad to know that I, Philippa Theophrastra Bombast von Hohenheim, agree with you. I agree that this Papa Schimmelhorn may very well find us the secret of the alchemists, and I agree that it would be wonderful for us to get it. But before we get down to business, I must tell you more about myself.''

She leaned forward, fixing him once again with her eyes. "While I am not the direct descendant of the great Paracelsus, for he left none, he was my collateral ancestor. I have inherited all his surviving papers, which the world does not even know exist—yes, all his records—*and much more*. I assure you, there is no true dividing line between science and alchemy, between alchemy and magic. I myself have repeated many of his experiments. I *know*. You were wise to come to me, *mein Herr*.''

"You honor me." He bowed. "Yes, and I also came to you because of your reputation for practicality, for astuteness. You understand how delicate—and, yes, how perilous—this project is. If we undertake it, we certainly can never run the risk of having Papa Schimmelhorn do his work at home or even here in Switzerland—''

"Ah!" she broke in. "So you have heard of my retreat?''

"Fräulein, I have heard you own a little island in the Mediterranean. Such a place would be ideal for our purposes. The man Schimmelhorn could devote himself to his, er, studies and pursuits without distraction—and without being spied upon."

"Yes," she said, "I have such an island. It is near Crete. Like this"—she touched her necklace—"it was my heritage from my mother, who was of Grecian ancestry." Once more, her eyes were fathomless. "Of very *ancient* Grecian ancestry. There I have—well, call it a chateau. In it, I have set up the world's finest alchemical laboratory, under the greatest of all living alchemists—and I can make all Paracelsus's papers available to Schimmelhorn. You say that, even though he cannot comprehend much of what he reads or hears, his subconscious absorbs it and translates it into practical processes and devices?"

"That is correct. That is what Herr Fledermaus has told me. Even after he has succeeded, Schimmelhorn cannot really understand what he has done or how he did it—so much so that once he's finished all his interest's gone, so he never can repeat a process."

"For us, Herr Doktor, once should be enough." Her teeth, as she smiled, were white and strong; and Gottfried Rumpler closed his eyes momentarily, imagining how passionately—

"Now I shall ring for cognac," she informed him, "so we can drink to our association and success." She pressed a button. "But first there is the little matter of percentages."

Dr. Rumpler, shaken out of his brief daydream, forgot the fifteen percent he had originally intended to suggest, and when she told him that, in her opinion, a fifty-fifty partnership would be only fair and equitable, he could not find the courage to haggle with her.

A stout young woman entered, bearing a tray with a Baccarat decanter of superb cognac and two glasses. Fräulein von Hohenheim filled them. She raised hers to her lips. "To *gold!*" she said, her eyes suddenly afire. "To all *our* gold!"

For another half-hour, they discussed ways and means, agreeing that each of them separately would secure all the information possible about Papa Schimmelhorn—especially regarding such matters as his astonishing virility—and that they would then decide what their initial approach to him would be.

That night, Gottfried Rumpler slept alone, and all night long he dreamed that he was chasing a naked Philippa von Hohenheim through endless labyrinths of solid gold, and never catching her.

II.

Papa and Mama and the Steeple

Dr. Rumpler's carefully composed letter reached New Haven two weeks later. It was late on a lovely April afternoon, and Papa Schimmelhorn was innocently occupied in his basement workshop, discussing the project on which he was engaged with his old striped tomcat, Gustav-Adolf, who was watching him suspiciously from the top of a large TV. He was stylishly attired in very tight blue jeans, with an equally adhesive brass-buttoned jacket, all of which set off the massive muscles of his legs and shoulders to best advantage, contrasting dramatically with his huge white beard and the scarlet cockatoos ornamenting his viridian sport shirt.

He was pleased with himself. Amid the usual loot and clutter of the bench was an opened cardboard carton colorfully labeled JUNIOR ELECTRONIC EXPERIMENTERS KIT, AGES 9–12, from which he had cannibalized any number of components; and in his hand he held a digital wristwatch of Japanese manufacture, to which he had just finished doing things.

"*Ach!* Only look, Gustav-Adolf!" he exclaimed proudly. "Imachine! A veek ago, I know noding aboudt micro-vot-you-call-'ems, und lidtle electronic chippies, und now I haff made something no vun else has made. It iss true, Gustav-Adolf. I am a chenius!"

One of the many cuckoo clocks hanging on the wall

over the bench whirred, opened its little doors, and emitted a large cuckoo to announce that it was half-past four; and Gustav-Adolf, who resented any bird neither warm nor edible, muttered "*Murrow!*" disgustedly.

Papa Schimmelhorn laughed. "Don'dt vorry, now ve haff something bedder." He exhibited the watch. Just under its display, there was a little rectangle which had not been put there at the factory. "Look!" he cried out.

He pressed a button. The rectangle lit up—and on it there suddenly appeared, brilliantly, a tiny cuckoo. It opened its infinitesimal beak. Melodiously, it sang out four times—*Cuckoo! Cuckoo! Cuckoo! Cuckoo!* And then twice more.

"*Ja!*" said Papa Schimmelhorn. "Four times for der hour, und tvice for die qvarter-hours. Der vorld's first cuckoo vatch—but you haff seen noding yet." He stepped over to the TV and turned it on. A ginghamy young housewife was happily displaying a super toilet-bowl cleanser to her admiring children.

He stepped back again. He pressed another button—and instantly the small family had vanished, and in its place the cuckoo had appeared, enormously magnified, in full color, and complete in every detail. Its song filled the room.

Cuckoo! it caroled, four times and then twice again, and once more after that. "Ha!" crowed its inventor. "Der hour, der qvarter-hour, efen der minute—chust like a fine Shviss vun-minute repeater vatch made maybe by Audemars Piguet oder Patek Philippe. Listen, Gustav-Adolf, it iss vunderful—like vot's-his-name landing on der moon! You haff nodt met lidtle Clothilde in der chewelry shop, lidtle Tilda Blatnik—*ach*, such a predty pussycat, vith a cute lidtle bottom, round like so"—he cupped his enormous hands—"und red hair, I think maybe eferyvhere." He heaved a huge and hungry sigh. "It iss too bad der day after tomorrow Mama und I vill fly to Shvitzerland for dot vedding. But shtill maybe iss enough time. Vhen Tilda sees der cuckoo vatch—nodt efen X-rated!—I tell you she vill—"

He had been about to tell Gustav-Adolf how, after vainly trying any number of amatory techniques, the sheer magic of the cuckoo watch would at last enable him to vanquish Ms. Blatnik's maiden modesty, but at that point, upstairs, the doorbell rang.

Mama Schimmelhorn, he knew, was off attending a meeting of the Ladies' Auxiliary of Pastor Hundhammer's church. "Probably it iss chust die Moonies," he grumbled. "But ve must go und see."

He bent down for Gustav-Adolf to jump onto his shoulder, and together they made their way to the front door.

It was the postman, a hulking, shaggy youth with tiny eyes and an air of absolute exhaustion.

"Letter fer yuh, Pops," he mumbled.

"Und vhy nodt drop it in der shlot?" Papa Schimmelhorn retorted. "Maybe you are too tired, *nicht wahr?* Chunior, how many times I haff to tell you? Nefer vill you haff vinegar unless you chase die predty pussycats! Ho-ho-ho!"

The postman only stared at him sadly. "It's registered," he said. "Yuh gotta sign a pieca paper fer it."

Gustav-Adolf glared at him and hissed, and Papa Schimmelhorn, frowning, signed the receipt and took the envelope. He looked at it and saw that it was from his native land. "Der Rumpler Bank," he muttered, watching the postman slump off down the street. "Dot name I haff heard. But vhy? Maybe I owe somevun in Shvitzerland money?" Then the more cheerful thought came to him that possibly some countrywoman, cherishing tender memories out of the past, had named him in her will.

He went back in, sat down in the parlor under the two ancestral portraits of himself and Mama Schimmelhorn in ceremonial Chinese robes acquired in his transdimensional tour for Pêng-Plantagenet, and opened the letter with his pocketknife.

Dear Herr Schimmelhorn, (he read)

Some time ago, your extraordinary scientific genius

and accomplishments—of which, my dear sir, every true Swiss is justly proud—were brought to our attention.

Because we, here at G. Rumpler & Co., were preparing to initiate an extremely daring and innovative research project to which your talents seemed almost miraculously well suited, we took the liberty of confirming the favorable reports we had received. Needless to say, our expectations were more than fulfilled.

As I am sure you know, the Rumpler Bank is the most substantial of all Swiss private banking institutions, and we would be honored and delighted if you would consent to join in our exciting and challenging program. Your title will be Chief Executive Director and Administrator of Research, and you will be given every facility you may require: an idyllic place in which to work, any and all necessary books and instruments, the most capable technical assistants, and a friendly and in *every* way attractive staff.

Because the project is of an extremely important and secret nature, and because the resources it requires are not generally available, it will be necessary for you to work overseas, though not on the continent of Europe, and I will ask you to inform *no one* (except of course your wife). We can very tactfully make the necessary arrangements for a leave of absence from the Luedesing Cuckoo Clock Factory, where you are so valued an employee.

We will, I assure you, be generous. On your acceptance, a retainer of 75,000 Swiss francs will be paid into your numbered account here at our bank, and this will be yours whether you succeed or fail. Then, when you do succeed—as I am personally sure you will—the sum of *at least* one million Swiss francs, and possibly much more, will be yours.

In addition, you will have had the satisfaction of

performing a memorable and outstanding service for
the land of your birth and your countrymen.

Please be assured, dear Sir, of our highest personal
and professional regard and our sincere wish that you
will soon be associated with us.

The letter was signed, very respectfully and cordially, by
Dr. Gottfried Rumpler, Präsident, G. Rumpler & Co.

Papa Schimmelhorn read it through once, frowning; he
read it through again; finally he slapped the paper contemptuously. "Such nonsense!" he exclaimed. "Crazy
bankers, alvays they are der same, even die Shviss—
business, business, business, money, money, money, und
funny titles—Chief Grand Executive Adminishtratings! Bah!
I tell you, Gustav-Adolf, I do nodt need. I haff mein goot
chob at Heinrich Luedesing's. I haff mein nice Stanley
Shteamer vith der antigrafity from die Chinesers. Und now
I haff a lofely cuckoo vatch vich goes also on TV—und
soon, oh-ho-ho-ho!—predty lidtle Clothilde!"

"Mrreo-ow!" agreed Gustav-Adolf emphatically, which
meant *You tell 'em, chum!* in Cat.

Papa Schimmelhorn scratched him around the ears. He
scrunched Herr Doktor Rumpler's letter into a ball and
tossed it with its envelope into the wastebasket under
Mama Schimmelhorn's little desk. "Und now," he said,
"ve haff vun more dry run vith der vatch before ve make
our date vith lidtle Tilda."

Back in the workshop, chuckling, he tried the cuckoo
watch again several times, on each occasion finding it
even more perfect than before. Then the phone called him
upstairs again.

"*Ja?*" he answered it.

"You dam' well right, *ja!*" It was his neighbor to the
south, a retired policeman. "Schimmelhorn, what th' hell
you doin' bustin' up my ball game with your goddam
cuckoo? You got a license from the Audubon Society or
something? It's on every channel—and don't you go denyin'
it—I know it's you!"

Genuinely astonished, Papa Schimmelhorn mumbled an apology: he was sorry; he vould make adchustments . . .

His neighbor hung up, grumbling unintelligibly; and instantly the phone rang again. This time it was his neighbor to the north, fat Mrs. Clausewitz, who disapproved of him and was a teatime crony of his wife's. She too was indignant; no one should be permitted to interrupt her favorite doctor-nurse show right in the middle of a tensely emotional operating-table scene, especially not with cuckoos, and she would see that Mama Schimmelhorn heard all about it, and—

Papa Schimmelhorn listened to her without interrupting, not wanting to make matters worse; he didn't even realize that Mama Schimmelhorn had come home until he heard her authoritative step at the front door.

He bade Mrs. Clausewitz a quick good-bye, and called out, "How nice! Mama, you are home!" trying to sound delighted and not quite making it.

Ominously, she did not answer. He looked up. Tall and forbidding in her black hat and stiff black dress, her hands hefting her rigid black umbrella, she looked at him like a female Torquemada contemplating an especially juicy heretic.

He tried again, with a feeble smile. "You—you come home early, *ja?*"

"In der lifing room!" she ordered, gesturing with the umbrella.

He obeyed reluctantly, Gustav-Adolf following him.

"*Und sit!*"

He sat. So did she. Gustav-Adolf promptly abandoned him and jumped into her lap, purring.

"*So!*" she hissed. "Now you vill tell me all aboudt Miss Clothilde!"

Papa Schimmelhorn shuffled his feet, smirked, and tried to pretend he didn't understand.

"Don'dt lie! Dirty old man! Her Papa, Herr Blatnik, tells der Catholic priest, who tells der rabbi, who tells his vife, who tells Mrs. Hundhammer in der chain shtore. *Ach*, you should be ashamed! At more than eighty years . . .''

She went on to recite the long tale of his infidelities, hitting only such high spots as naked dancing girls at the 1915 San Francisco Exposition, a female Viennese string quartet, and a dozen others.

She snorted. "Maybe on Beetlegoose I make a bad mistake—bedter I had sent you to der vet! *Shnip!*" She made an appropriate gesture. "How can ve go to Shvitzerland to der vedding—my own grandniece, Minna Schwegelheimer, to such a nice young man, vith all der family in church? Vith such an old goat I vould be ashamed!''

Papa Schimmelhorn hung his head abjectly. "Maybe— maybe I bedter shtay here in New Hafen und take care of Gustav-Adolf?" he suggested hesitantly.

"Ha!" she cried. "To shtay up late at night, und chase die predty pussycats, und molest poor Fräulein Blatnik? Nefer!" Her eyes narrowed. "Don'dt vorry—somehow this time I fix.''

And at that point, her glance took in the wastebasket. "Vot iss? A letter vith Shviss shtamps? Vun of your naked vomen writes to you?''

Lamely, he mumbled that it was just an ad.

She looked at him scornfully. With her umbrella handle, she hooked the basket to her. She lifted out the envelope. She stared at it. "*Der Rumpler Bank!*" she exclaimed in awe. Then she retrieved the letter, smoothed it out, and read it, first to herself and then aloud.

Smiling cruelly, she looked up at him. "So it iss chust an ad? Vell, this time, chenius, you oudtshmart yourself. It iss a help-vanted ad, and now you haff der chob! To der telephone, *dummkopf*. Ve phone Herr Doktor Rumpler right avay.''

"But Mama!" Papa Schimmelhorn protested plaintively. "Already I haff a goot chob with Heinrich, und ve haff enough money, und I haff infentions I am vorking on, und—''

"*Shudt up!*" she ordered, fire in her eye. "Maybe *you*

haff enough money, but *ve* do nodt. All day, die Ladies'
Auxiliary talks about how ve raise enough to build der new
shteeple for der church. First Pastor Hundhammer makes a
speech, und tells how efery oder church except maybe der
synagogue has a fine shteeple, und makes us all ashamed.
So you vill vork for der famous Rumpler Bank, und do
maybe something useful inshtead of time machines, und ve
can build a shteeple taller than die Presbyterianists' oder
die Methodisms'. It iss settled.'' She aimed the sharp end
of the umbrella menacingly. ''To der telephone, oder in
der shortribs I giff der bumbershoot! Ve call collect. I
listen on der oder line so no monkeyshines.''

Papa Schimmelhorn, blackmailed on the one hand by
the scandal of little Clothilde, and also fully aware of the
reality of the umbrella threat, squirmed, heaved an enormous sigh, and made his way to the hall telephone, while
his wife, glaring at him and followed dutifully by Gustav-
Adolf, went off to pick up the other in her sewing room. A
momentary impulse to try and trick her by pretending that
it was too late in Zürich was instantly checkmated by her
warning that Dr. Rumpler's letter had gifen also his home
phone, und nodt chust der office.

Papa Schimmelhorn called the overseas operator. He put
in his call collect, listening to his wife's approving murmurs. The phone in Zürich rang and rang, finally awakening
Dr. Rumpler from a sound sleep next to his *petite amie*.
When the operator mentioned Papa Schimmelhorn, he came
fully awake abruptly, shushed his girlfriend, and accepted
the call as cordially as he would one from any prosperous
oil sheik in the once Trucial States. He was delighted that
Herr Schimmelhorn had called. No, certainly not, it never
was too late; he had simply been discussing high finance
with a friend.

Obediently, Papa Schimmelhorn informed him that he
was accepting his most generous offer, and would do his
utmost to please his new employer. And what, he asked,
might be the nature of his assignment?

Dr. Rumpler informed him that the urgent need for

secrecy precluded any discussion of it until he actually reported in for duty, but he could promise him faithfully again that, where working conditions and assistants were concerned, he could have anything he might require. "Absolutely *anything!*" he chuckled.

At that point, Mama Schimmelhorn coughed. It was a rather shrill, rasping cough, somehow full of menace, and her husband hastened to explain. It was just Mama, who had heard so much about the famous Rumpler Bank and the Herr Doktor, and who would like to meet him if only over the telephone.

Dr. Rumpler had, of course, been briefed on Mama Schimmelhorn, and he was taken aback only for an instant. He congratulated her on having so eminent a genius for a husband, ignored her muttered "*Ach*, dot old goat!" and made much of the high quality of the technical assistance and research facilities he was providing at such vast expense. He sighed. It was a shame, he said, that the pressure of work would leave no time at all for relaxation, but he would see to it that Papa Schimmelhorn got lots of rest and was properly nourished.

Mama Schimmelhorn was mollified. She asked how long Papa might be away, and was informed that this was unpredictable, but that judging by his past performances it should certainly not be more than a few weeks. And when did the Herr Doktor plan to take delivery?

"My personal jet will pick him up the day after tomorrow, as early in the morning as possible. Is that agreeable to you, Frau Schimmelhorn?"

She told him that it was perfectly agreeable, that that was the exact date of her own planned departure for Minna Schwegelheimer's wedding, and—seeing a chance, not only to save a dollar, but to continue the supervision of her husband for a while—suggested that maybe she could ride along.

Dr. Rumpler hesitated, but only for an instant. Her goodwill would undoubtedly be worth the detour to Switzerland. Papa Schimmelhorn groaned, but agreed. With everything arranged, they terminated the call with many expressions of mutual esteem.

"Vell!" exclaimed Mama Schimmelhorn triumphantly, as she came back into the living room. "For vunce, I go avay withoudt vorrying about naked vomen! With a great Shviss banker like der fine Herr Doktor iss no time for foolishness—eferything iss business." She chuckled good-humoredly, and sat down; and Gustav-Adolf, with a throaty "*Mro-ow!*" leaped back into her lap.

She petted him. "You are a goot cat, Gustav-Adolf," she informed him, "vorking hard all day and at night efen, catching mices, nodt like some people ve know—" She sat up suddenly. "*Donnerwetter!* Almost I forget! For you I haff a present, a nice present from Mrs. Laubenschneider." She rummaged in her black, beaded reticule. "She iss vot you call Pennsylvania Deutsch, und knows all aboudt hexes und shpells, und now she has made mein Gustav-Adolf a fine collar for die fleas."

"A *collar?*" scoffed Papa Schimmelhorn. "For Gustav-Adolf? Nefer! He vould nefer vear."

"Nonsense!" She brought the collar out. It appeared to be woven out of several colors of silk thread, horsehair, and very fine silver wire; and at least a dozen hex signs were very cleverly woven into it. "See, Gustav-Adolf, all die lidtle signs Mrs. Laubenschneider puts in? They shcare avay die shpooks und defils, und nodt chust fleas."

She held it temptingly in front of Gustav-Adolf. He investigated it, at first suspiciously, then with greater interest. Then suddenly, with a great "*Mrr-r-ow!*" he pushed his huge chops through, and sat there purring loudly while she made the final finicky adjustments.

"See how proud?" she simpered. "He knows it iss a medal for vorking hard und catching all die mices."

Regretfully but wisely, Papa Schimmelhorn shelved his plans for the seduction of Miss Blatnik, and decided to save his cuckoo watch for some more favorable occasion. He spent the following day preparing for his journey and listening to Mama Schimmelhorn's practiced homilies on Dirty Old Men who persisted in chasing invariably naked women vhen they ought to be thinking of going to Heafen vhen they died. She varied this theme only twice, first to reprove him for shtealing the JUNIOR ELECTRONIC EXPERIMENTERS' KIT, AGES 9–12, which was to have been her birthday present to a young relative named Willy Fledermaus, and then to argue that he vas foolish efen to think of taking Gustav-Adolf with him. Gustav-Adolf, she declared, should stay at home, catch mices, and be fed by Mrs. Clausewitz. However, Mrs. Clausewitz herself scotched that idea effectively by phoning, accusing Papa Schimmelhorn of sending cuckoos to sabotage her TV programs, and then, when Mama Schimmelhorn seemed unable to understand, screaming hysterically that *she* had put him up to it.

So Papa Schimmelhorn tucked three fresh catnip mice into his luggage and stowed Gustav-Adolf's flea-und-hex collar in his jacket pocket, while his wife put a catbox and a large sack of kitty-litter into a huge net shopping bag, explaining that these were for Gustav-Adolf on the airplane; and early next morning a trim de Havilland jet picked the three of them up at the airport and, despite Gustav-Adolf's swearing and muttering, took off immediately, Papa Schimmelhorn traveling with the British passport once arranged for him by Pêng-Plantagenet.

Presently, Gustav-Adolf settled down on one of the plane's luxuriously cushioned chairs and devoted himself to tearing one of the catnip mice apart, rolling on it, and uttering cries of feline ecstasy. Mama Schimmelhorn rummaged in a small valise, took out something purple she was knitting, and let the clicking needles punctuate her interminable moral disquisitions.

As for her husband, he managed to conceal his disappointment to find, not two or three pretty pussycat stewardesses, but only a plump, pink, and very swishy steward. For a time, he consoled himself by staring at the clouds and recalling happier journeys, like his flight to Hong Kong, when he had been so ably entertained by the lovely and ingenious Misses Kittikool and MacTavish. Once in a while, he sighed. Then, absentmindedly, he tried to amuse himself by trying out his cuckoo watch—until he realized that his wife had stopped her knitting.

"*Und so!*" Transfixing him with an icy eye, she tapped her umbrella handle threateningly. "So poor Mrs. Clausewitz maybe vasn't crazy after all? *Ach*, you chust vait—"

At that point, the copilot came back to complain that something electronic was interfering with the navigational instruments.

A long and deadly silence followed. The steward served lunch. Time dragged on. The steward served high tea. Time passed even more reluctantly. Contemptuously, Gustav-Adolf used the catbox, kicking litter all over the rich carpeting.

The steward served supper, and Mama Schimmelhorn opened up a package of fresh liver she had brought along for Gustav-Adolf. She ate her dinner grimly; Papa Schimmelhorn ate his despondently; Gustav-Adolf gobbled his liver and yelled for more. The steward started cleaning things away.

Then the voice of the pilot came over the intercom, informing them in French that in ten minutes they would be landing at Lucerne.

"Luzern!" exclaimed Mama Schimmelhorn. "Dott is because Minna liffs so close. It has been arranched by der goot Herr Doktor, who iss a chentleman, und nodt like you."

She bustled about, getting her things together and giving her husband a running lecture about how he must do *eferything* der Herr Doktor told him to. "Ha!" she added as an afterthought. "If he has goot sense, he locks you in der vault at night!"

The steward helped them with their safety belts; the plane touched down; the door opened; the gangplank was extruded. Almost at once, an extremely precise little man came aboard, pinch-nosed, spectacled, and as neat as any Swiss banker's confidential ledger. He introduced himself

as Herr Grundtli, bowed to Mama Schimmelhorn who was
tremendously impressed, and announced that a limousine
was already on the runway to take her directly to the home
of Miss Minna Schwegelheimer. Then he insisted on helping her with her bags and boxes.

Papa Schimmelhorn watched dolefully as she gave him
a final frown of warning, kissed Gustav-Adolf good-bye,
and disappeared with Herr Grundtli through the door, followed almost immediately afterward by the steward. He
watched her get into the sumptuous limousine. He watched
until the limousine had vanished. "Und now vot?" he said
lugubriously. "Gustav-Adolf, maybe she iss right. Maybe
Herr Grundtli vill lock us in der vault at night." At the
prospect, a tear bedewed his bright blue eye, and he was
still feeling sorry for himself when Herr Grundtli reappeared, clearing his throat politely.

Papa Schimmelhorn looked up. He started. His mouth
fell open. Herr Grundtli suddenly looked much more human than he had before. Besides, he was not alone.

Behind him stood two of the prettiest pussycats Papa
Schimmelhorn had seen in many a day.

Proudly, Herr Grundtli introduced them as Emmy
Hoogendijk, of Amsterdam, and Niki Aramanlis, originally from Istanbul, Miss Hoogendijk very pleasingly round
and pink, Miss Aramanlis much taller, dark, and very lush
indeed.

Instantly, Papa Schimmelhorn's vital juices began to
flow. His bushy eyebrows jumped; his whiskers quivered.
His fears vanished into thin air. He bounded to his feet
and, making sure his modish denims displayed his muscles
to the best advantage, swept them a courtly bow.

The pretty pussycats stared at him in amazement, and he
hastened to put them at their ease. "*Ach!*" he cried out. "I
haff read your minds! You haff expected chust a poor old
man, vithoudt vinegar? Ho-ho-ho!" From his jacket pocket
he took two chocolate bars, rendered slightly flexible by
the warmth of his emotion, and proffered them. "Emmy

und Niki, I show you maybe a goot time you do nodt expect!''

Looking a little dazed, Emmy and Niki took the bars, which he obligingly peeled for them. They nibbled with small, sharp, white teeth. Papa Schimmelhorn put an arm around each of them.

"Our employer," Herr Grundtli told him *sotto voce*, "arranged to have them here. He wants your journey to be as pleasant and, er, *relaxing* as possible." Then he left the aircraft again.

Within five minutes, the pretty pussycats were cuddling up to Papa Schimmelhorn, running their nimble fingers through his beard, sitting on his lap, petting Gustav-Adolf, and generally doing their best to keep Herr Grundtli's promise, while he amused them by demonstrating the cuckoo watch and letting them feel his bulging muscles. He did not even notice the reappearance of Herr Grundtli, now accompanied by Gottfried Rumpler, who had driven up very discreetly in an unobtrusive Fiat.

Herr Grundtli coughed, and instantly the pussycats were on their feet and, smiling respectfully, hastening back to the aftercabin.

"Don't worry," he declared, seeing Papa Schimmelhorn's disappointment. "They'll be right back as soon as Herr Doktor Rumpler here"— he bowed to his employer—"has briefed you on the task ahead of you."

Papa Schimmelhorn stood up. He looked at the stalwart Rumpler figure. Beaming with pleasure, he declared that never had he realized how wrong he was, believing that all bankers were as dry as sticks, thinking only of plus and minus and who owed what to whom! He could see that the Herr Doktor was, like himself, full of vinegar—that he understood what kept a man young despite his years. He gestured at the aftercabin and winked.

Dr. Rumpler returned the wink. "Herr Schimmelhorn," he chuckled, "there's more to Swiss banking than meets the eye."

Herr Grundtli seated them, and joined Emmy and Niki, leaving them alone.

After expressing his delight at having so great a genius to solve their problem for them, and swearing him once more to complete secrecy, Dr. Rumpler lowered his voice conspiratorially, and told him what his task would be. "We want you to find out how to turn lead into gold," he declared. "That is all."

Papa Schimmelhorn laughed aloud. Maybe, he said, it would not be too difficult. Maybe not even as hard as time travel or antigravity. Already, in his head, his subconscience was beginning to churn promisingly. And it would be such a good joke, would it not? All the lead pipes, and fishing sinkers, and all the bullets in the guns! Affectionately, he slapped Gottfried Rumpler on the knee, and the Herr Doktor chuckled with him, rather artificially.

"Fräulein von Hohenheim, my associate in this enterprise," he said, "owns a lovely island just off the coast of Crete, where she has already installed alchemical laboratories under the direction of Meister Gaspar Gansfleisch, the greatest living authority on the subject. He will work closely with you, and assist you. If you need anything, you will only have to ask. Of course, because I and my associate are very much in the public eye, I will not be in direct touch with you, but if she can do so unobtrusively, she will fly down to look things over every two weeks or so."

Papa Schimmelhorn enquired a little worriedly whether Miss Hoogendijk and Miss Aramanlis were coming too, and Dr. Rumpler promised him that they were.

Smiling warmly, he arose. "Now I must go," he said.

Papa Schimmelhorn leaped up. He embraced him in his mighty arms. "*Ach*, you don'dt need to vorry!" he boomed out in English. "Mr. Banker, you will have your gold!"

"You will stay in Lucerne tonight," Dr. Rumpler told him. "Tomorrow you will fly to Athens and to Crete, where you will be met and taken to the island. I am sure you will succeed!"

They parted on the very best of terms, and presently another limousine drove quietly up—and that night, at the Lucerne Hilton, Papa Schimmelhorn slept cozily between his pretty pussycats, comfortably exhausted by his efforts and dreaming as he drifted off that he could hear both of them (as well as Gustav-Adolf, now curled up at his feet) purring happily.

III.

Meister Gansfleisch

The magnitude and difficulty of the problem facing him troubled Papa Schimmelhorn not at all. He gave no thought to the thousands of brilliant and determined minds who, over the centuries, had tackled it without success. Turned over to his subconscious, it left him completely free to devote all his attention to his hobby. He scarcely noticed when, next morning, the plane took off; when they changed to a smaller aircraft at Athens, his sole concern was to make sure that Miss Emmy and Miss Niki weren't left behind; and finally, when they landed at a minor Cretan airport, he didn't even bother to enquire where it was.

A tall, craggy, middle-aged Greek was waiting for them. He greeted Herr Grundtli, twirled a fierce moustache, and flashed menacing black eyes at both pretty pussycats, who giggled. The customs officers, deferring to him, passed them without delay, not even troubling to open the huge Schimmelhorn carpetbag or to ask whether Gustav-Adolf had had his rabies shots.

A worn taxicab was waiting for them in the Mediterranean sunlight; and, as the Greek opened its door, Herr Grundtli bade them farewell, saying that business compelled him to return to Switzerland. "However," he said, "you are in good hands. Herr Mavronides is Fräulein von

Hohenheim's majordomo. He will see to it that you have everything you want.''

"Herr *who?*" exclaimed Papa Schimmelhorn.

"Mavronides," replied the Greek. "Sarpedon Mavronides."

Papa Schimmelhorn reached out and pumped his hand. "Ho-ho-ho!" he shouted. "I vill call you Zorba—it iss more easy to remember!''

Herr Mavronides smiled. "It is good that you speak English," he declared, "because we shall use no other language on the Prin—on *her* island. It is my duty to take you there, and explain everything, and introduce you to Meister Gansfleisch, with whom''—for an instant he looked very dubious—"you will be working. As for the name Zorba, I am not offended. I too have seen the motion picture.''

He waited until his guests had climbed in, then jumped into the front seat with the driver. The tortured transmission uttered one hideous protest, and they were off. One arm round Emmy, and with Niki sitting on his lap, Papa Schimmelhorn stuck his head out of the open window and sniffed the breeze winnowing his beard. "Chust shmell der air, Gustav-Adolf!" he cried ecstatically. "Goats und chickens und garlic und I think maybe orange blossoms—how romantic!''

Gustav-Adolf, in the rear window, meowed appreciatively. "You betcha," he said in Cat. "The mice round here oughta be real juicy.''

Herr Mavronides looked back over his shoulder. "Meister Gansfleisch," he declared a little hesitantly, "he will not be pleased that you have brought a cat.''

"Und vhy?" asked Papa Schimmelhorn. "Maybe he belongs to der Autobahn Society? Gustav-Adolf only vunce in a vhile catches birds, because he gets die feathers in his teeth.''

"He's a *very* sweet cat!" said Niki loyally, and Emmy vigorously nodded her agreement, as befitted members of the local Papa Schimmelhorn fan club.

They continued on through the outskirts of the city, and the taxi turned to follow the shoreline of a bay, Papa Schimmelhorn commenting enthusiastically on the sights and sounds and smells they were encountering, and sometimes listening to Mavronides's careful orientation lecture.

"The reason we shall speak only English," Mavronides informed him, "is this: all the servants descend either from Greeks whom Miss von Hohenheim's family saved from the Turks, or from Turks saved from Greeks. Then there are some, like myself, who have been with her family for—forever. You understand? That is why all are so faithful and obedient and would defend her to the death. Also her island of Little Palaeon, to which we go. Turkish is spoken, also Greek, and she has taught many of them German. But I am the only one with English. So, because your work is secret, we must speak that tongue."

Papa Schimmelhorn, distracted by the amatory calisthenics of two donkeys in a nearby field, asked for a replay of this information, which Mavronides gave him very patiently.

"You will have your own rooms," he then informed him, "you and your so-charming friends." His eyes flashed, and he twirled his moustache again; and Papa Schimmelhorn began to suspect that, under his majordomo manner, he might be a man after his own heart. "There you will be served your meals, except perhaps when the Prin—when Miss von Hohenheim is here. Then, perhaps once, she may invite you to eat with her. In no case"—he shuddered visibly—"will you have to eat with Meister Gansfleisch."

Papa Schimmelhorn frowned. "*Ach*, Herr Zorba," he enquired, "this Meister Gansfleisch iss nodt a nice man, *nicht wahr?*"

"I have said too much already," replied Mavronides. "Now I must say no more. Soon you will judge him for yourself. In any case, you will be with him only when you work together. At other times, he does not like to be with human beings, only with his familiar, whose name"—he made a sign against the evil eye—"is translated as Twitchgibbet."

"Ooh, how *exciting!*" Niki squealed. "Just like *The Exorcist!*"

"Vot iss, der familiar?" asked Papa Schimmelhorn. "A shpook maybe? Oder a goblin?"

"I will say no more. You will see."

Papa Schimmelhorn shrugged. *Vell*, he thought, *votefer, me und Gustav-Adolf, ve are nodt shcared.* And he turned his attention once again to the landscape.

The taxi had turned into a cobbled street skirting a stone seawall, and now it pulled up at a little jetty where a spick-and-span motor cruiser awaited them. They boarded it, were greeted ceremoniously in Turkish by Fräulein von Hohenheim's weatherbeaten pilot, and put to sea. The boat rounded a headland into the gentle swells of the blue Aegean, and they beheld the island of Little Palaeon three or four miles ahead of them. Papa Schimmelhorn, promptly forgetting all about Meister Gansfleisch and his familiar, devoted his attention to the seagulls circling overhead, one of whom he identified positively as the original Jonathan Livingston, and to a brace of porpoises following them off the starboard bow. He tickled Niki intimately, pinched Emmy's plump, pink posterior, and promised them both that that very night he would take them shvimming in der lofely vater—vith no vun looking they vould nodt haff to vear efen bikinis.

The boat rounded a miniature lighthouse at the end of a stone breakwater and entered its protected little bay, where a few fishing boats were riding at anchor; a few others were beached drying their nets and sails, and a number of gnarled fishermen and leathery fishwives were unhurriedly attending to their chores. The pilot pulled up to a tidy little pier, and they disembarked. Mavronides lifted their luggage into a red Japanese station wagon driven by an enormously fat Levantine, seated them in it, and they set off down the fishing village's single cobblestoned street.

"This person," Mavronides said, pointing at their driver,

"is called Ismail. Miss von Hohenheim obtained him from an Arabian who did business with her. He had made him into a—a harem employee. You understand?"

Papa Schimmelhorn groaned sympathetically, indicating that he understood only too well. His two pretty pussycats squealed. Ismail grinned at them with astonishingly white teeth.

"But now he is not unhappy," added Mavronides.

The village well behind them, they passed through one or two neat olive orchards and a number of green fields where fat sheep and goats were grazing, and more love-sick donkeys disporting themselves. Little Palaeon was a small island, but low hills near one end hid Fräulein von Hohenheim's residence from them until their car had reached the crest. Then suddenly it stood before them in all its strange and forbidding dignity.

"Is it not beautiful?" exclaimed Mavronides, offering it to them with an expansive gesture.

And indeed, though any architect would have been sorely put to determine all the periods, styles, and cultures that had contributed to its construction through the centuries, it did have a character and a beauty all its own. A close examination would have revealed that its foundations rested on ancient limestone and marble, that much of it, including at least two walls and two grim towers, had been inherited from a Crusaders' keep, and that the rest had been added on by several generations of princely Renaissance scholars and eighteenth-century *virtuosi*. More marble adorned its lavishly carved facade; marble and porphyry had been fashioned into an Italianate bell tower. They drove through great gates into a flagged courtyard and halted before a flight of marble stairs leading to two majestic doors of massive bronze sculptured with intimate episodes from the lives of the Grecian gods and goddesses, with which Papa Schimmelhorn was immediately enchanted.

Servants bowed them in, and Mavronides escorted them into the great beamed and paneled hall. There, suits of armor stood their silent guard; ancestral portraits, swords, and battle-axes adorned the walls; ancient banners hung in brilliant, contrasting lights and shadows from tall mullioned windows.

And there Meister Gaspar Gansfleisch waited. He uncoiled as they entered. He was extremely long and thin. His skin was gray and hairy, and somehow he seemed to have too many arms and legs, as though he might have had more than a touch of tarantula in his ancestry. His clothing looked as though it had been made for him by an amateur tailor in a small German provincial town during an especially dreadful war.

Mavronides presented them. Meister Gansfleisch fixed them with a beady, baleful eye. He bowed very formally. He smiled, and his teeth reminded Papa Schimmelhorn of a possum to whom he had once been introduced.

Gustav-Adolf, crouched on a broad Schimmelhorn shoulder, looked at him and growled disgustedly.

Papa Schimmelhorn shushed him, and told him he must nodt growl at der nice man who was going to vork vith him. "It iss nodt goot manners," he declared. "He cannodt help it vot he looks like." He added that he was sure he and Meister Gansfleisch were going to haff a shvell time togeder.

The Gansfleisch smile disappeared; his brows drew down. In a high, dry, grating voice, he recited that he welcomed Herr Schimmelhorn, whom Fräulein von Hohenheim had informed him was very talented. He had every hope that they would work well together. Mr. Mavronides would show them to their quarters presently, and make them comfortable, and he himself would see Herr Schimmelhorn in the laboratory immediately after breakfast.

"*Das ist gut,*" said Papa Schimmelhorn. "I too vant to get to vork. But"—he laughed—"all der time to say 'Meister Gansfleisch'? Maybe iss bedter I chust call you Gassi."

"I am first among the alchemists of Europe, of the world!" stated Meister Gansfleisch frigidly. "You will please address me by my name and title."

"Okay," replied Papa Schimmelhorn agreeably. "Only I do nodt mind it if you call me Papa."

His remark was ignored. "Where did you study alchemy?" demanded his new associate.

"I haff nodt shtudied. I am chust a chenius," Papa Schimmelhorn told him modestly.

Meister Gansfleisch made a strange, dry, whinnying sound, and Gustav-Adolf growled again.

There was a long, cold silence. Finally, "Well, we shall see," Meister Gansfleish said. "But"—he stared at Gustav-Adolf, twisting his hands in agitation—"that cat I do not want to see again. For me, it is impossible to practice the hermetic art with cats. You must keep him in your quarters, and he must *not* get loose. Do you understand?"

Papa Schimmelhorn shrugged. "Okay," he said, "but I think poor Gustav-Adolf vill nodt be happy."

Meister Gansfleisch turned on his heel, and left without another word; as he left, Niki let out a frightened squeak. "*Look!*" she whispered. "Look at his *coat pocket!*"

They looked. A head protruded from the pocket, a head with small, red, glittering eyes, the head of a huge black rat.

"*Gott in Himmel!*" gasped Papa Schimmelhorn. "Vot *iss?*"

"That," answered Mavronides, "is Twitchgibbet, his—his familiar." Again, he made a sign against the evil eye. "Sir, it is not a creature one would wish to anger."

"*Mein Gott!* Rats in der pocket! No vunder Gustav-Adolf growls. Vith Meister Gassi I tell you vot iss wrong. Chust look at him! He nefer efen saw Emmy und Niki here! He has no vinegar. All his life maybe he nefer chases predty pussycats. Imachine! Chust sitting with his rat und maybe playing with himself." Sadly he shook his head.

"Please pay no attention to him," said Mavronides apologetically. "I assure you that he was trying very hard to be polite to you. As you can see, there is a sourness in him—it is not his nature to be polite."

Again, Papa Schimmelhorn shrugged. "Vell, anyvay,

vith rats inside der pocket bedter I put der flea collar on Gustav-Adolf right avay.''

He fished the collar out, and Gustav-Adolf good-naturedly permitted Niki to slip it on over his whiskers.

Actually, in his judgment of Meister Gansfleisch, Papa Schimmelhorn had done the alchemist a grave injustice. The man was a true ascetic. For twenty years and more, he had been dedicated to his pursuit of the arcane arts and sciences—in a crassly materialistic age when patronage was hard to come by. A former rajah had supported him penuriously for a few years, and then, finding that no progress had been made toward his enrichment or the restoration of his onetime powers and prerogatives, had unceremoniously turned him over to the Government of India as an impostor. He had drifted from here to there, once falling so low as to concoct aphrodisiacs for a Syrian doctor practicing in El Paso. Finally, five years before, he had entered the service of Fräulein von Hohenheim—with whom he had immediately fallen wildly and hopelessly in love, so much so that secretly he had spent a great deal of his time seeking an elixir that would turn him, if not into a handsome prince, at least into a figure virile and dynamic enough possibly to excite her interest. Then, after each vain effort, he had returned to his normal alchemical pursuits, desperately seeking some astounding breakthrough, some success so stupendous that it might excite, if not her love, at least her gratitude.

Now, in the privacy of his own chambers high in the southern turret of the Crusaders' keep, he ate his solitary dinner, scarcely tasting it, and conversing sporadically with Twitchgibbet who, crouching on the tablecloth at his right hand, was gnawing a steak with a much heartier appetite.

Twitchgibbet represented one of his rare triumphs; he had summoned him with a series of dark rituals prescribed in a medieval grimoire stolen from a Romanian library, and had bound him to his service with fearsome incantations. He had realized at the time that he had not summoned up a fiend of high rank or tremendous power—indeed, in the Hellish hierarchy, Twitchgibbet didn't rate any higher than a Pfc—but he had proven useful. Not only was he company during Meister Gansfleisch's most lonely and despairing moments, but he served as watchdog over his master's treasures, prevented the servants—especially the female servants—from pestering him, and was extremely helpful in the minor operations of the magic arts. As his conversational ability, in his rat body, was distinctly limited, he also usually was a good listener.

Meister Gansfleisch's quarters were almost monastically austere. Two paintings only hung on the stark walls: one of Paracelsus, the other of some nameless Arabian sorcerer with frightening eyes. There was an enormous fireplace with an alembic in it; there were ancient tomes bound in alum-tanned white pigskin, in calf and vellum, and one or two (reputedly once in the library of Elizabeth Bathory) in human skin. Books were piled on the mantelpiece, on chairs, in a dark, towering bookcase. At the window stood a long brass telescope through which he occasionally observed the stars. Two iron strongboxes held the most precious of his paraphernalia: manuscripts dating back to the Golden Age of alchemy and to the Dark Ages preceding it; a bronze key—which not even the Fräulein knew that he had pilfered—to one of the most dreaded doors on the island; and—most valuable of all—a genuine homunculus named Humphrey, originally brought into being by Doctor John Dee during the reign of the first Elizabeth and passed down from one alchemical hand to another over the intervening centuries. He had, reputedly, been created from a formula devised and recorded by the great Paracelsus himself,* and the jar in which he was

---

*HOMUNCULI
"Human beings may come into existence without natural parents. That is to say, such beings grow without being developed and born by a female organism; by the art of an experienced spagyricus (alchemist)."—*De Natura Rerum*, vol. i.

imprisoned was kept securely in the larger strongbox. He was a secret Meister Gansfleisch had carefully kept from Fräulein von Hohenheim, for he suspected that the homunculus still knew much that he had not been persuaded to reveal: how to confect the Universal Solvent, how to devise the Philosophers' Stone, perhaps even a recipe for eternal youth, any one of which (he rather forlornly hoped) might soften the Fräulein's heart.

Meister Gansfleisch pushed his plate away; he stared at his untouched wine glass. "What shall we do, Twitchgibbet?" he groaned, striking his pallid forehead with both palms. "What *can* we do? The Princess is determined. She believes this miserable Schimmelhorn is a true genius, and—and I'm afraid she may be right! You can see the man's an *innocent!* He does not lust for power. He yearns after no riches. He knows nothing of hatred, envy, jealousy. Therefore he is *dangerous*. Besides"—he shivered—"he has a *cat*."

"The *generatio homunculi* has until now been kept very secret, and so little was publicly known about it that the old philosophers have doubted its possibility. But I know that such things may be accomplished by spagyric art assisted by natural processes. If the sperma, enclosed in a hermetically sealed glass, is buried in horse manure for about forty days, and properly 'magnetised,' it begins to live and to move. After such a time it bears the form and resemblance of a human being, but it will be transparent and without a corpus. If it is now artificially fed with the *arcanum sanguinis hominis* until it is about forty weeks old, and if allowed to remain during that time in the horse-manure in a continually equal temperature, it will grow into a human child, with all its members developed like any other child, such as could have been born by a woman; only it will be much smaller. We call such a being a homunculus, and it may be raised and educated like any other child, until it grows older and obtains reason and intellect . . ."

Quoted by Franz Hartmann, M.D., *The Life of Philippus Theophrastus Bombast of Hohenheim* . . . London n.d., p. 256.

Twitchgibbet's little eyes flashed like glowing coals. He showed his yellow teeth. "Now don't you worry, boss," he squeaked. "Ain't never been no cat I can't turn inside out. You just say the word!"

"No, no! The Princess simply wouldn't stand for it—at least not now." He began pacing up and down distractedly. "Remember—she herself has terrible powers! For centuries, her family has guarded rites and mysteries even I dare not understand. No, I must endure the unendurable. I must give this peasant all the assistance he requires."

"Couldn't you just pretend?" suggested Twitchgibbet helpfully.

"It would not work—*she* would know instantly."

"Or maybe, boss, you could sort of trade me in on somebody more powerful. It's like I told you when you snatched me—all you gotta do is sign the contract."

Meister Gansfleisch knew very well that, in order to secure the services of any higher-ranking demon, he would have to sell his soul like his more reckless predecessor, Faustus. "*Never* say that to me again!" he snapped. "The subject is forbidden."

"Okay," squeaked Twitchgibbet. "It's your funeral. Go ahead, give him all the help he wants, if you gotta, but keep on digging in your books—maybe you'll find a gimmick that'll clobber him. Also, how's about getting Humphrey out of storage and asking *him*? There's no good having a homunculus unless you use him."

Meister Gansfleisch moaned. "Humphrey is very old and frail. Besides, I would have to tell him what is going on, and I fear to do so because he hates me, and the only hold I have over him is the threat to withdraw his sustenance. If he thought he could work my ruin, even that might not suffice. No, if I am to get any aid from Humphrey, it must be cleverly, by subterfuge. There you can help me. Even though it gives you pleasure, you must stop tormenting him when you are guarding him. And sometimes you must whisper to him that I mean him well, that—that I'm suffering pangs of conscience for the way I've treated him."

"Well, maybe it's worth a try," muttered Twitchgibbet dubiously.

For another hour or two, the alchemist kept up his pacing, pausing occasionally to wring his hands or to look up some hopefully helpful passage in his books. As he paced, he addressed a monologue, sometimes to himself, sometimes to his familiar, and sometimes, imploringly, to the absent Fräulein. Finally, he stopped decisively and phoned her home in Zürich.

"What do you want, Gaspar?" she demanded. "Mavronides has already told me that Schimmelhorn and his friends arrived safely, and I happen to be busy."

Gaspar Gansfleisch apologized profusely. Never, he averred, would he have called had he known that he was interrupting her; surely she knew that her convenience was always foremost in his thoughts; was he not her ever-devoted servant? But—but he had felt she ought to know. Schimmelhorn had come there *with a cat.*

"*And what of that?*" His employer's voice was glacial.

"It—it is impossible to conduct spagyric operations with cats in the vicinity, as—as I'm sure you know."

The phone's response was a deadly silence.

"B-besides," said Meister Gansfleisch lamely, "I—I am allergic to them."

"Don't be absurd! You will ignore this cat. You will make no attempt to harm it. You will, if necessary, take it up on your lap and make much of it. You will continue to do so until I arrive there, probably in a few days. Is that clear?"

Before he could declare that he would obey her to the letter, the phone went dead.

By now, the sun had long since set; a fine half-moon had risen. Meister Gansfleisch staggered to the window and stared out at the sea. For a moment, he stood beside his telescope; then the thought came that contemplation of some far nebula, some distant galaxy, might bring him solace. He bent down and peered into the eyepiece. But he did not behold the glory of the heavens. He had left the telescope aimed at the moonlit beach, at the warm, sparkling, gentle surf.

And there, in the bright circle of his vision, rising like Father Neptune from the sea, was Papa Schimmelhorn, wearing only his beard, muscles, and those other adornments with which nature had endowed him. He had an arm around each of his two nereids, and he was very obviously enjoying life.

Meister Gansfleisch turned from his instrument with a hoarse sob, and that night, for the first time in many a year, drank down a powerful sleeping draught of his own decoction.

At daybreak, Papa Schimmelhorn awakened, marvelously refreshed by the various exertions in which he had indulged. He stretched luxuriously in his vast four-poster bed. Affectionately, he patted a sleek, dark head and fondled both aspects of a pink behind. His accommodations, though they were in the other turret of the keep, were by no means as uninviting as Meister Gansfleisch's, having been expensively redecorated by a sybaritic eighteenth-century ancestor of the Fräulein's, who had filled it with rare erotica. Rich tapestries and magnificent Italian mirrors graced the paneled walls; Boulle desks and dressing tables, fantastically curved and inlaid, were everywhere; Capo di Monte and Meissen figurines simpered from the shelves of dainty cabinets, and there were secret compartments here and there if one cared to look for them. A lush modern bathroom held not only all the ordinary facilities, but also an antique porcelain sitz bath, adorned with nymphs and satyrs, which Mavronides had provided as Gustav-Adolf's catbox. Finally, in a place of honor where he had placed it after unpacking his carpetbag the night before, there stood a small color TV Papa Schimmelhorn had brought along to make sure that he'd be able to demonstrate his cuckoo watch to all and sundry.

Glorying in the sunlight, he helped his companions shower; appreciatively, he watched them dress. He and they ate a hearty breakfast, served by two giggling servant girls. Then Mavronides was at the door to lead him down to the laboratory where he and Meister Gansfleisch were to work together.

Kissing his pretty pussycats, and telling them to take good care of Gustav-Adolf, he let himself be led away, the cuckoo watch singing out the hours and minutes as they strode through a dark, portrait-lined corridor and down a curving flight of stairs.

The laboratory was still in the keep, but on the floor below the turrets. Mavronides said nothing until he came to a huge oaken door reinforced with iron. There he stopped. "Please pay no attention if Meister Gansfleisch is offensive," he said in a low, tense voice. "It will be noise, nothing more. I shall tell you something—in her own right, the Fräulein is a Princess. She knows many ancient secrets. Always he will obey her—he would not dare do otherwise. And she has given him strict orders. Later I will tell you more."

"Don'dt vorry, Herr Zorba!" Papa Schimmelhorn slapped him cheerfully on the back. "If he does nodt behafe, maybe I let Gustav-Adolf catch him. Ho-ho-ho!"

Mavronides knocked sharply on the door three times. They waited. Presently there came the sound of bars being pushed back, of a great key turning. Slowly and heavily, the door swung open.

Meister Gansfleisch stood there, looking much the worse for wear. Instead of his best suit, he was now attired in a stained black robe with strange devices on it. He glared at his visitor with bloodshot eyes, and made no response to Papa's booming, "Goot morning, Herr Meister Gassi. Maybe you haff nodt shlept all night? Vell, after ve vork togeder a lidtle vhile, I promise you haff lots more vinegar!" He shrank away as Papa Schimmelhorn moved into the room, and as soon as Mavronides departed he made haste to triple-bolt the door.

For a moment, they stood there looking at each other, Papa Schimmelhorn shaking his head sadly. Then, with an effort, the alchemist began his orientation lecture.

"It is my duty, Herr Schimmelhorn," he declared, "to—to show you everything in this laboratory. You will understand that it has a long and very interesting history—"

"Maybe iss bedter I sit down," said Papa Schimmelhorn, pushing aside a flagon full of a murky greenish fluid to make room on an ancient tabletop.

"If it pleases you to do so," Meister Gansfleisch frowned. "*I* shall stand. This laboratory was established more than three hundred years ago by a direct ancestress of Fräulein von Hohenheim's, who was herself an able alchemist and thaumaturge. That was on her mother's side, where she is descended from a Paleologus, from the family of the Emperors of Byzantium. So, on both sides, she comes from alchemists. Her father, Professor Ulrich Bombast von Hohenheim, inherited all the books and manuscripts, even the laboratory equipment, of his famous relative, of whom even you may perhaps have heard."

"*Ja,*" said Papa Schimmelhorn. "I haff heard. I read inside his books when I am vorking for Pêng-Panflageolet und die Chinesers. His shtuff did nodt make sense."

"*Did not make sense?*" Meister Gansfleisch almost screamed his outrage. "Do you realize whom you are criticizing? *Paracelsus,* the genius of a thousand incomparable discoveries, in alchemy, in medicine, the first man to prescribe the mercury treatment for syphilis!"

Papa Schimmelhorn snickered. "Maybe I am chust lucky. Imachine—all my life I nefer catch!" He shrugged. "You must be patient vith me, Meister Gassi. Vhen I say die books of Para-vot's-his-name do nodt make sense, I only mean to *me*. You must undershtand, it iss chust like Herr Doktor Jung has told me—I am a chenius only in der subconscience; I am nodt shmart in der IQ."

The alchemist managed to control himself. "Very well," he said. "I shall show you everything with which we work. Also, I shall try to explain in simple words. First, regard the furnaces . . .''

Papa Schimmelhorn did his best to listen attentively. *After all, he told himself, it iss for Mama und der shteeple, und here vhen I do nodt vork I am haffing a goot time, so ve let Herr Gassi talk, und vhile my subconscience maybe finds how to make der gold I think about my predty pussycats.*

In front of him, Meister Gansfleisch paced up and down, his hairy forearms waving like mandibles as he pointed out furnaces and crucibles, tongs, bellows, pincers; as he explained ingots of unknown metals, great glass flasks and flagons holding mysterious and presumably potent liquids, jars of rare and odorous unguents; as he elucidated cabalistic symbols graven on bronze mortars and pestles, the titles and contents of tomes and notebooks inherited from Paracelsus and his successors; and finally, though disapprovingly and with reluctance, as he pointed out a variety of modern gadgets added by the Fräulein, starting with neon lights overhead and finishing with what Papa Schimmelhorn, harking back to his days as a janitor at the Institute for Higher Physics, thought might be an electron microscope.

The lecture continued through the morning, interrupted only occasionally when Papa Schimmelhorn could not resist asking his cuckoo watch the time. On these occasions, Twitchgibbet always stuck his ugly black head out of a pocket of the robe, bared his teeth, and glared at the intruder angrily, demonstrations to which Papa Schimmelhorn invariably replied by doing his best to look like Gustav-Adolf and making fierce faces while Meister Gansfleisch wasn't looking.

At noon, Mavronides knocked on the door again to announce luncheon, and Papa Schimmelhorn returned thankfully to his quarters for two hours of well-deserved rest and recreation, of which he made the best use possible. Then, for the balance of the afternoon, he went back to the laboratory to endure more of the same, paying as little heed as possible to his mentor, and amusing himself with his watch and by surreptitiously teasing Twitchgibbet. Every once in a while he would ask questions suggested by his subconscious, some of which Meister Gansfleisch ignored, some of which he contemptuously answered in words of one syllable, and one or two of which appeared to send him into a momentary state of shock, as though by asking them Papa Schimmelhorn had violated alchemical security.

At the end of the working day, the alchemist was utterly exhausted. When Papa Schimmelhorn thanked him, affirming that he himself had been having lots of fun and was looking forward eagerly to tomorrow's session, he replied curtly that he wasn't at all sure about tomorrow: trying to explain things to someone totally unable to understand had been too wearing; he had a headache; also there were several critical experiments he had in progress . . .

Papa Schimmelhorn told him not to worry. Winking, he said that there were one or two little experiments of his own he wanted to work on with his pretty pussycats. "Maybe," he suggested eagerly, "if ve vork efery *oder* day, it iss enough?"

Meister Gansfleisch hurried him to the door, where Mavronides was waiting, bolted it hastily after him, and collapsed onto a workbench. For a few minutes, he just sat there breathing heavily, then poured himself a terrible draught from a beaker kept in a locked cabinet. His eyes rolled; he shuddered; he straightened his thin shoulders, onto one of which Twitchgibbet had climbed.

"Am I or am I not Europe's greatest alchemist?" he asked rhetorically. "So! Am I man—or mouse?"

"That's a good question, boss," squeaked Twitchgibbet, gnashing his teeth. "But just wait till you hear what that old bastard did to *me*."

"But what *could* he do to you?"

"He could make cat-faces at me every time your back was turned. Boss, ain't it bad enough we can smell that damn cat of his all the way through this stupid castle? Do we gotta hold still for him treating me like I was just any kind of rat? Okay, you said it—are you man or mouse?''

''Get back into my pocket!'' snapped his master.

''But, boss—''

''Do not argue! I shall do my best.''

He rose. He poured himself another stiffener from the beaker. He left the laboratory by a secret stairway and ascended slowly to his own rooms. Presently, he mustered up the courage to put another call through to Zürich, and to report the day's events to his employer.

Though she did not interrupt him, he felt the temperature drop rapidly while he was talking. Yet finally he informed her that in his opinion (which was, as she knew, an expert one) Papa Schimmelhorn was a menace, not only to himself, but to the art and science of alchemy, to her project, her castle, her servants, the reputation of her family, and everything she held most dear. Furthermore, he was lazy—now he wanted to work only every other day. He urged her, indeed he begged her, to send him back to the United States immediately.

''*Is that all?*'' the Fräulein demanded.

He admitted that it was.

''Then,'' she said, in a voice that reminded him of a striking cobra, ''you will continue to do exactly as you have been told, my little Gaspar. If Schimmelhorn does not wish to work every day, you will work with him when he wants to. He will tell you what he wants to know, and you will teach him. And you will be *very* nice to him. Listen carefully. If, when I return to Little Palaeon, I learn that you have not obeyed me to the letter, *I shall have you placed inside the Labyrinth, you and that unpleasant rat of yours, and left there*. Both of you know what that will mean. Do not dare to trouble me again!''

The phone clicked decisively, but for a time he just sat there staring at it.

''Twitchgibbet,'' he whispered, ''our question has been answered. Where *she* is concerned, I am a mouse.''

''Me too,'' Twitchgibbet squeaked back. ''But, hey

boss, couldn't I just get in touch with, like, some of the higher-ups down below? There's plenty of 'em could even fix what she's got in that there Labyrinth.''

Meister Gansfleisch did not answer him. He replaced the phone. He went down his secret stairway again, fetched the beaker back with him, and spent the next few hours finishing its contents. His despair did not dissolve, but it did recede into the background of his mind; and Twitchgibbet, listening to him, was pleased to see that fear, anger, and resentment were at least starting to generate dark plans and desperate expedients.

Not once during the evening did the alchemist put an eye to his brass telescope—which was probably just as well, for had he done so he might very well have witnessed an interesting experiment Papa Schimmelhorn and Niki carried out behind a moonlit hummock on the beach while Emmy fanned them lazily with an eighteenth-century French fan of painted silk and fretted ivory, borrowed for the occasion from the collection of the Fräulein's sybaritic ancestor.

IV.

Shopping Lists

While these events were taking place, Mama Schimmelhorn, Papaless and free of care, was enjoying herself thoroughly at the nuptials of her grandniece. It pleased her to see that only one of her husband's relatives, his respectable cousin Alois, noted for his artistry on the bassoon, had been invited; it pleased her even more to be treated as an absolute oracle in all matters involving men and marriage, presumably because of her long experience and endurance; and she was delighted to be able to shake her head and hold a finger to her lips importantly when anyone asked her what Papa Schimmelhorn was up to. True to her word, she did no more than hint delicately that secret dealings of great moment were involved, carefully satisfying no one's curiosity. More than a week went by before she rather reluctantly phoned Dr. Rumpler and asked him to arrange her passage home.

This he did without demur. Fräulein von Hohenheim had briefed him on Papa Schimmelhorn's progress, carefully deleting all reference to Meister Gansfleisch's anxieties—not because she especially wanted to delude him, but simply because she felt that, as a mere man, it was no affair of his. Indeed, despite the alchemist's two harried calls, she was in no way apprehensive. Even without resorting to the powers and prestige she had inherited, she had never failed to handle any man effectively and expeditiously, and now she saw no reason to anticipate that events would take any course other than the one she had ordained. In Zürich, she went about the usual business of her prosperous Schweitserische Frauenbank, laughing to herself at the thought of how thoroughly she had breached the hitherto male bulwark of Swiss banking, and taking time off occasionally to make discreet enquiries about stocks of lead that could be purchased to advantage.

For Papa Schimmelhorn, the time passed pleasantly. Now, during each session with Meister Gansfleisch, he knew he could look forward to a whole day of fun and games, without so much as a frown from his mentor or a squeak from Twitchgibbet. This did not mean that he forgot his obligation to Dr. Rumpler, to Mama, or to Pastor Hundhammer's steeple. On the contrary, he spent each of his free mornings lying luxuriously in bed, dallying absentmindedly with his pussycats, and boning up on the various learned works he had brought with him in his carpetbag, some dating back to his employment with Pêng-Plantagenet, others hastily selected by his subconscious from the New Haven Public Library shortly before his departure: two favorite volumes of the 11th edition of the *Britannica*, the instruction manual that had come with Willy Fledermaus's JUNIOR ELECTRONIC EXPERIMENTERS kit, various works of Niels Bohr and Erwin Schrödinger which consciously he didn't understand at all, a biography of Nikola Tesla in iambic pentameter, a copy of *Asimov's Guide to Shakespeare*, and assorted books on the theory of numbers, chemistry in ancient China, and UFOs as a source of air pollution. Some he read; others Niki and Emmy read aloud to him; and he could tell, by his consequent feeling of self-satisfaction and well-being, that his subconscious was being immeasurably enriched.

After each such morning of intensive study, Mavronides, at his behest, would bring a loaded picnic basket, and would accompany them on explorations of Little Palaeon, its flora, its springtime-drunken fauna, and its ancient ruins. Only one area appeared to be taboo—an enormous mound at the island's end, bordered by groves of trees and crowned with more ruins, which Mavronides avoided like the plague—and in this Papa Schimmelhorn was totally disinterested.

The island's inhabitants—at first deeply suspicious of him—finally took him to their collective bosom after he had made friends with all their children, demonstrated his cuckoo watch, told them wonderful stories (with Niki and Mavronides interpreting) of his adventures in time and space, and quite jovially thrown over his shoulder two unwise young men who thought they could outwrestle him. Even their initial disapproval of his evening skinny-dipping with his pussycats vanished after he saved a reckless grandson of Mavronides from drowning and then, to make sure the boy had learned his lesson, paddled his dripping bottom in front of everyone. They soon found out, too, that Meister Gansfleisch was actively antagonistic to him. Nothing more was needed to make him *persona grata* where the Fräulein's retainers were concerned.

As for the alchemist, he was in despair. He found each session more frustrating than the preceding one. Papa Schimmelhorn listened to his recitals and his explanations—then asked him questions that were completely meaningless, or simply sat there playing with his cuckoo watch. Finally, as if that weren't bad enough, he began asking for the loan of rare old books, some in Greek, others in Arabic, others in ancient versions of the more common modern tongues. At first, Meister Gansfleisch put him off, or spoke hastily of other matters, doing his best not to display resentment. But Papa Schimmelhorn persisted, and one day Gaspar snapped, "It would be useless! You can read neither Greek nor Arabic!"

Papa Schimmelhorn admitted his ignorance cheerfully. "*Nein*, I cannodt read der Greek," he said, closing his eyes dreamily. "*Aber* Miss Niki can, und she vill read to me in bed. So nice! Und for der Arabic, I send for Ismail."

"I-I-Ismail?" sputtered the alchemist. "The—the eunuch? He can't read!"

"Ja, ja! He has taught himself. Imachine—vithoudt lead in der pencil, vot else can he do? It vill be chust like Douglas Valentino und der Sheik from Baghdad."

He went on to say a great deal more about the imagined joys of harem living, and how sad it was that poor Ismail had been so cruelly deprived of them. Then he related in great detail how, after he and Mama had been kidnapped by a spaceship from a woman-dominated planet, he had managed to restore the lost virility of its downtrodden men, and he wondered sentimentally whether, through the exercise of his genius, he might not be able to perform a similar service for the unfortunate Ismail. At this point, seeing that his remarks were distressing his companion, who was gnashing his teeth and clenching and unclenching his gray, bony hands, he considerately changed the subject. He was, he asserted heartily, becoming deeply interested in alchemy, about which Meister Gansfleisch was so well informed, and now he could hardly wait to get into Herr Paracelsus's private papers.

"Maybe ve shtart today?" he said enthusiastically. "If der old langvidge iss too difficult, ve sit right here und you can read aloud to me, und explain eferything so I undershtand."

"The papers of the great Paracelsus?" Meister Gansfleisch cried out hysterically. *"Never!* I—I mean, not yet. You are not yet ready, Herr Schimmelhorn! It would be too— too dangerous. Instead I—I shall let you take some of the books you have requested. Yes, yes."

He began pulling books from shelves and loading them into Papa Schimmelhorn's waiting arms, while Twitchgibbet, from his pocket, glared balefully.

"You must take great care of them," he warned, glaring just as balefully. "I will let you have even one in Arabic, and *I* shall tell Ismail exactly how to handle it. It is a book of power, very rare—a book that frightens even me! There must be certain ceremonies, rituals, before you read it, while you are reading it, even afterwards. I shall tell Ismail.''

"Don'dt vorry," Papa Schimmelhorn assured him. ''Ve do nodt need. Alvays mein subconscience tells me vot to do. I vill take care, chust like vith die books from der New Hafen library. I efen put avay so Gustav-Adolf does not sit upon. Anyvay, predty soon now—maybe after ve read der Paracelsus shtuff—I shtart building der machine.''

"The *machine?*" screamed Meister Gansfleisch.

"*Natürlich,* mein machine to make der gold from der lead oudt.''

"But—but, you—*you ignoramus!* You can't make gold with a *machine!* Look, look, *look!*" Frantically he waved at the cluttered paraphernalia of his laboratory. "*That* is how we make gold. The Philosophers' Stone, the Arcanum, the—the—''

"*Nein,*" Papa Schimmelhorn told him pleasantly. "Mein subconscience now iss planning der machine. You cannodt undershtand—it iss too deep for you. But you vill see!''

Moaning, Meister Gansfleisch hastily finished the loading of the books, dropping two or three of them. Then, muttering to himself in an unknown but vituperative tongue, he hustled his unwelcome pupil to the door. It was late, he croaked, too late to work any more that day.

"*Auf wiedersehen,*" said Papa Schimmelhorn, making a cat-face at Twitchgibbet as the door shut behind him; and he walked off jauntily with his load.

Inside the laboratory, the alchemist paced frantically up and down for several minutes. He sought the solace of his refilled beaker. He sat, and drank, and paced again. He groaned terribly.

"*A machine!*" he kept repeating. "*A machine!* He is an idiot! A madman! Gold cannot be made with a machine! Why cannot the Princess understand the danger? Twitchgibbet, oh Twitchgibbet, how on earth can I *stop* him?''

Twitchgibbet, who had left his pocket as soon as they were alone and climbed up his gown to his shoulder, spoke into his ear.

"You told me not to give you any real *good* advice," he squeaked, "so I'll just remind you—you're a sorcerer. Why don't you fix that cat-lovin' bastard like them Arabs went and fixed old Ismail? Hey, that'd put a crimp in his subconscience!" Twitchgibbet actually cackled. "Hey, wouldn't it!"

Abruptly, his master stopped his pacing. A flicker of hope showed momentarily in his dull eyes. "I—I'm sure I *could*," he said. "Perhaps not, well, surgically, but the result would be the same."

Then, just as suddenly, the flicker died. "No, no," he declared dismally. "It cannot be. The—the Princess . . ."

Twitchgibbet said something so rude and intimate about the Princess that his master instantly ordered him back into his pocket. Then, despite his deep depression, and without consciously intending to, Meister Gansfleisch began looking over his shelves of jars and bottles, ewers and flagons, seeking some vicious distillation, some subtle essence, that might have the recommended effect on his adversary.

Actually, Papa Schimmelhorn had been oversimplifying when he described the device now being born in his subconscious as a machine. Certain mechanical elements would, he knew, have to be incorporated in it—gears of brass and steel which he proposed to get out of old washing machines and clocks, strangely shaped eccentrics on which even stranger crystalline structures would be mounted, several large flat springs which could be conveniently wound up, and one or two pumps and pressure tanks whose functions were unclear to him. However, it was also to contain highly sophisticated components derived from Willy Fledermaus's electronics kit, and any number of indescribable elements having their origin not only in European, but also in Chinese alchemy and thaumaturgy.

His sessions with Gaspar Gansfleisch had contributed to it; so had his far more pleasant and effective cram sessions with his pussycats. Later that day, as he lolled luxuriously among his cushions with his head on Emmy's commodious lap, listening to Ismail intoning the Arabic of the ancient volume, then translating it into Turkish for Miss Niki, who did her best to render it in English, he congratulated himself on the unique form his genius had assumed.

Chust imachine! he told himself. *Vithoudt any vork at all, like die* Arabian Nights *vith der djinn inside der bottle!* And for a while he dallied with the notion of putting his subconscious to work on the bottled genii problem. It would be so nice to have a djinn who could bring him pretty pussycats from anywhere without even having to use a time machine. . . .

Ismail, smiling broadly, read the formulas and incantations in a high, soft, pleasant voice. Chuckling occasionally, he translated them. Niki listened attentively. Once in a while, she blushed; more frequently, she shuddered or uttered exclamations at the ingredients and procedures specified. Still, she did not give up, and even though her English version probably left much to be desired by way of accuracy, it satisfied Papa Schimmelhorn, who had full confidence in the ability of his subconscious to sort out any errors or omissions.

"*Ugh!*" She shivered. "I just can't see how moldy toads brewed in a slave's skull with spoiled hasheesh and rats' brains and—and all the rest of it—can bring the corpse of 'an unclean infidel' to life—or why anybody'd *want* to!"

"I do nodt undershtand it either," said Papa Schimmelhorn, stroking her thigh consolingly. "But Meister Gansfleisch says reading it maybe helps me in my chob. This efening ve go schvimming und forget all aboudt."

He let Ismail continue for perhaps an hour. Then he announced that there was now enough for his subconscious to work on for the day. For a while they just sat around listening to Ismail's X-rated stories of what went on in the almost-royal harem where he had spent his boyhood and his youth, and to Papa Schimmelhorn's tales of his adventures, scientific and extra-marital. Poor Ismail was particularly intrigued by his account of how, with mutated catnip, he had restored the lost virility of an entire planetful of men.

"Effendi," he asked wistfully, "do you—do you think this magic herb, if I could procure it, could do anything for *me*?"

And Papa Schimmelhorn had promised him that indeed it could—even though, considering the gross nature of his handicap, it might take longer than it usually did.

"But don'dt you vorry, Izzy. Vhen I go home to New Hafen I send you some. Ho-ho-ho! I tell you, I think efen on a shnake mein catnip vould grow balls like a bull!"

Ismail looked disturbed. Glancing apprehensively over his shoulder, he assured his would-be benefactor that he would be quite satisfied with much more modest equipment. Then he bowed himself from the room, pausing only to whisper that, if Papa Schimmelhorn could indeed repair the damage, he would willingly be his slave for life.

"How stranche!" Papa Schimmelhorn exclaimed. "Vy vas he shcared vhen I talk aboudt der bull? Sometime I ask Herr Zorba, who maybe knows."

And at dinner he did indeed put the question to Mavronides—to his astonishment evoking a very similar reaction. Stuttering nervously, Mavronides replied that perhaps a bull had attacked poor Ismail when he was small—who could say? Or maybe, having taken Papa Schimmelhorn too literally, he was just frightened at the prospect of having his lost organs replaced by anything so enormously conspicuous—what man would not be dismayed at the idea? Then, hastily, he changed the subject, muttering that there were more important things to talk about. Did Herr Schimmelhorn and his young ladies like the cooking? Were they comfortable? Was Meister Gansfleisch now being more cooperative? And so on.

Papa Schimmelhorn did not press the point, but his

curiosity was piqued. At his next session with the alchemist, he brought the subject up, he thought, quite subtly.

"Vhy iss, Meister Gassi," he enquired, "dot eferybody here iss maybe shcared of bulls? I say to Ismail only—"

He had no chance to finish. It was as though he had without warning administered a stiff drink containing a small depth bomb.

The alchemist leaped up, his thin hair flying, his eyes widening hideously. With Twitchgibbet squeaking from his pocket, he stood there tense and trembling, waving an angry forefinger under Papa Schimmelhorn's nose.

"Never! Never! *Never* mention bulls again in my presence!" he screeched. "This is the castle of the Princess, the priestess! I am her servant! You—you *baboon!* You simpleton! Here nobody dares to speak of bulls so lightly!"

Panting, suddenly exhausted, he sat down again; and Papa Schimmelhorn wisely dropped the subject. *Ach,* he told himself, *so maybe dot iss vhy he has no vinegar! Maybe somebody cuts off, like vith poor Ismail, und so he is chealous of die bulls. Only—* he frowned thoughtfully— *dots iss nodt der trouble vith mein friend Zorba. Vell, maybe it does nodt matter. . . .*

As a matter of fact, Mavronides's nervousness had not been due solely to Papa Schimmelhorn's question about bulls. For several days, he had been getting more and more worried about Meister Gansfleisch. Various members of the Fräulein's staff had reported seeing the alchemist pacing up and down on the castle parapets, making dramatic gestures of defiance and despair, and talking— sometimes pleadingly, sometimes with an unwonted ferocity, and always in an alien tongue they could not understand— either to himself or to Twitchgibbet. He had also been observed standing in an embrasure of his turret and shaking his fist at the turret opposite, occupied by Papa Schimmelhorn and his pussycats.

Sarpedon Mavronides was in a quandary. He was, of course, intensely loyal to the Fräulein; he had also become fond of Papa Schimmelhorn, to say nothing of being indebted to him for saving his grandson's life. Meister Gansfleisch's behavior had always been eccentric; now, in his opinion, it had become nothing less than dangerous. For another day he fretted over it, trying to decide what to do. Then he phoned Fräulein von Hohenheim in Zürich, gave her a brief but detailed résumé of events, stated that he simply didn't know what to do next, and begged her to return to Little Palaeon right away.

The Fräulein was annoyed, for she had hoped to stay in Switzerland, where she had more than enough business to keep her occupied, at least for a few more days. However, Mavronides had served her all her life; she knew that his judgment usually could be trusted. She promised him that she would arrive early on the morrow, and that she would promptly put an end to any nonsense Meister Gansfleisch might be contemplating.

"Don't worry about it, Sarpedon," she ordered. "That damned Gaspar needs stepping on, and hard. Obviously, he is jealous of Herr Schimmelhorn—and for more than one reason, I imagine. Well, I'm going to tell him he has one more chance—and *only* one. Otherwise—to the Labyrinth."

Her tone, as she said it, sent shivers down Mavronides's back.

"Yes, my lady. Thank you, my lady," he said meekly.

She hung up. She phoned Gottfried Rumpler, told him that next morning she would set off on her first Schimmelhorn inspection, and requisitioned his jet for the flight to Athens. He did not question her, merely expressing the polite hope that everything was progressing satisfactorily, and when she said good night he drifted off into a daydream in which he and she disported themselves like the less restrained sort of classic nymphs and shepherds by the blue Aegean. . . .

When she arrived in Crete next day, Mavronides and Ismail were waiting for her. Papa Schimmelhorn, they explained, was still abed, studying with his—well, his young ladies. By the time she reached the castle, her many questions had been answered and her picture of people and events filled in. It was not favorable to Meister Gaspar Gansfleisch. Papa Schimmelhorn, she was informed by both of them, was a tremendously cheerful, invariably kind old man, who was polite to everyone, especially nice to children, good to cats, and strong as an ox, his only fault being his ardent and wonderfully active interest in Miss Niki and Miss Emmy.

At the castle, her retinue waited ceremoniously to welcome her. She smiled at them, singled out her two personal maids, and, with Ismail carrying her hand-luggage, went up to her own apartments.

"I shall change into something more suitable," she proclaimed as she left. "Then I shall have my lunch. Afterwards, Sarpedon, I shall transact business over the phone. Then, at four o'clock, bring Gansfleisch to me in the Great Hall."

"Shall I prepare the Throne?" asked Mavronides.

"Do so," she commanded. "And be sure to have your two burliest footmen next to it. Oh yes, and have them go with you when you fetch him down. Tell them to frown at him and to ignore anything he may try to say."

"Yes, Highness," whispered Mavronides, bowing deeply.

Promptly at four, having obeyed her orders to the letter, he and the two glowering footmen led Meister Gansfleisch before the Throne which, gilded, carved, and canopied appropriately in cloth of gold, stood on a dais at the far end of the Great Hall, where she let him wait, mumbling, twitching, and shuffling his feet, for more than twenty minutes.

Finally, she swept in. She was indeed suitably attired. Her gown, of cobalt blue adorned with pearls and intricate gold lace, had been fashioned by one of Italy's foremost and most expensive couturiers, very much after the fashion of the sixteenth century; Lucrezia Borgia might have worn it. It displayed an amazing decolletage, allowing her beautiful Minoan breasts a perilous degree of freedom; its cinctured waist emphasized the flowing lushness of her hips. Around her perfect throat, she wore the golden necklace that had caught Dr. Rumpler's eye, and on her head, above her great, glowing Minoan coils of hair, a severe tiara of emeralds, diamonds, pearls, and platinum.

Having taken everyone's breath away, she ascended to the Throne. Holding up a hand for silence, she frowned down at the unfortunate alchemist. Lucrezia herself could not have done it better.

"*Speak*," she said.

His mouth working, he looked at her fearfully, hungrily. "P-Princess," he croaked. "Wh-who has denounced me?"

She said nothing. Her expression did not change.

"Princess!" he shrieked. "I have been several years in your service. Never, never, have I given you cause to doubt me. Have I? *Have I?*"

She only regarded him contemptuously.

"Princess! *Princess!*" There was desperation in his voice. "I have done my best to teach this—this person Schimmelhorn alchemy's most precious secrets. *It is impossible!* He is a moron! He—he thinks you can make gold with a *machine*. Look! *Look!*" He pulled a paper from his pocket and waved it wildly. "*This* he has given me—*a shopping list!* He wants *me*, Meister Gaspar Gansfleisch, to shop for him—to buy this—this *trash!* It is unbelievable! Listen— 'the gears from a seven-speed French bicycle, a small, X-ray device of the kind once used in shoe stores, eight square meters of copper wire netting (the finest possible), a Swedish sewing machine with electric motor (used is okay), three mercury-vapor lamps (used also is okay), and—and—' "

His voice broke, and the Fräulein interrupted him. "Do not read any more," she ordered. "All you need to do is buy it for him. I am sure he knows what he is doing."

"But, Princess!" cried the alchemist. "That is not all. You do not *understand*. He—he is a monster—a—a sex maniac. He spends his time debauching those poor young girls, not just at night in bed, but in the evening, in the bushes, on the beach! I myself have watched them through my telescope—''

One of the footmen snickered.

"At over eighty years! It is indecent. It is *demoniacal!* Your noble ancestor, Paracelsus, himself said that sexual indulgence always prevents success in alchemy! Now, do what you will, but I must warn you. If you persist in using Schimmelhorn, you must first do to him what the Arabs have done to Ismail. Otherwise, through his lust and ignorance, terrible forces may be set free. You yourself will be in fearful peril. You, Princess, are descended from great Emperors, ancient Kings, priests and priestesses who have handed awful secrets down to you over many centuries—secrets you are sworn to guard!'' Meister Gansfleisch was gibbering now, and Twitchgibbet was squeaking horribly in his pocket. "You yourself are a priestess! Y-you must choose! You—''

She silenced him with a lifted hand. "Listen, Gaspar," she said, and her voice had a cutting edge like a headsman's axe, "all you say is true. I *am* a princess and a priestess. But''—pausing, she leaned forward to fix him with her eyes, the eyes that had made so profound an impression on Herr Doktor Rumpler—"but that is on one side only. On my father's side, I am a Swiss, with the famous Paracelsus in my family. I am a Swiss first—and a Swiss banker *first and foremost*. Never forget *that*. Do you understand?''

He uttered a dry sob.

"Now, as a Swiss banker, I doubt very much that you can make gold. As a Swiss banker, I have every reason to believe that Schimmelhorn can. So, as a Swiss banker, I will give you one more chance to work with him without making trouble, to do his shopping, to assist him in every way. *Otherwise*''—she paused to let her words sink in—"otherwise, I shall again be the princess and the priestess, and you will end up in the Labyrinth.'' She gestured to Mavronides. "Take him away.''

She waited until the whimpering Meister Gansfleisch had departed. Then, "Bring me this Schimmelhorn," she commanded, "and perhaps you had better bring his young women with him."

Mavronides hesitated. "Highness," he said apologetically, "it may be impossible to bring him down immediately. He—he may be engaged in his favorite, er, exercises. In that case, he—well, he might have to dress."

She smiled thinly. "Very well. Bring them to my apartments in one hour exactly."

Mavronides had been quite right in his estimate of Papa Schimmelhorn's activities. He knocked tactfully on the door, waited until it was opened just a crack by a giggling Emmy, announced that they had been summoned by the Princess, and told them he would call for them.

When he arrived, all of them were ready, Niki and Emmy discreetly garbed in their best Parisian tailorings, Papa Schimmelhorn wearing his form-fitting jeans, huaraches, a vermillion shirt emblazoned with cactuses, burros, and sleeping Mexicans, and his cuckoo watch. On his shoulder, on this special occasion no longer confined to quarters, rode Gustav-Adolf; in a brown paper bag he carried one of his own very special cuckoo clocks, which he had brought tucked away in his carpetbag. It boasted a trio of cuckoos, who not only sang out "Cuckoo! Cuckoo!" but actually, against a Matterhornish background, yodeled the hours melodiously. "*Ach*, Gustav-Adolf," he declared, "for die Fräulein-Prinzessin it iss a fine present. She can listen vhile she sits und sews und vatches qviz shows or reads die lidtle Gothic nofels like Mama."

Somehow, never having asked anyone for a physical description of Fräulein von Hohenheim, and because he knew that she vas a person of some authority, he had formed a mental picture of her as a woman of mature years, perhaps somewhat younger than his wife, possibly a shade less determined in her attitudes, but probably with a very similar view of men, manners, times, and opinions.

As they walked beside Mavronides, down staircases and through one corridor after another, he rehearsed what he would say when he was introduced. Like his grandfather, who had guided many a crowned head into the Alpine vastnesses, he would first bow—gracefully but independently as befitted a true Swiss—then he would murmur, *Küss die hand, Serene Highness*, and if she offered him her hand, would keep his promise as aristocratically as any archduke.

Unhappily all these good intentions came to naught. They entered a section of the castle that looked like an especially florid Venetian palazzo with a touch of Neueschwannstein; they marched down a final corridor lined with portrait busts on pedestals, with beautifully nude statues from classical antiquity, with glorious tapestries. They came to a great polished door, on which Mavronides rapped discreetly. It opened instantly, and he urged them forward.

"The Princess Philippa Theophrastra Paleologus Bombast von Hohenheim!" he proclaimed.

Papa Schimmelhorn beheld a drawing room which could easily have been designed and decorated for Lola Montes by her infatuated king—but he did not see it. Before him, in the full light of the tall windows, reclining on a First Empire chaise longue, still garbed in her throne-room finery, and with her astounding cleavage displayed to best effect, was the Fräulein.

He halted in his tracks. For a moment, words failed him. Then, "*Mein Gott in Himmel!*" he said, more to himself than to the world. "Such a *beaudtiful* pussycat!"

He didn't even feel Mavronides kick him in the shins; nor did he hear his companions' little gasps of astonishment. He simply stood there goggle-eyed, grinning foolishly as the Princess rose and flowed toward him.

"*Ja, ja!*" he murmured, doing his best to X-ray her attire. "Herr Doktor Rumpler vas so right! There iss more to Schviss banking than meets der eye."

The Fräulein appeared not to hear. Instead, she was regarding Gustav-Adolf. "He truly is a handsome cat,

Herr Schimmelhorn," she said. "But I don't think he would appreciate your calling him beautiful or a pussycat." She reached up and rubbed Gustav-Adolf's chin, and he responded with a passionate *mrrrow* that expressed his master's feelings perfectly. "Come, you and your pretty friends must sit down with me, and we shall talk after we have been properly introduced."

Papa Schimmelhorn said nothing; Mavronides had kicked him in the shins again. They were led forward; they were seated on three First Empire chairs; the Fräulein, all Princess now, questioned them: were they comfortable? had her staff provided them with every comfort and necessity? and did they not consider the climate of Little Palaeon simply wonderful? Niki and Emmy replied enthusiastically, thanking her for her gracious hospitality, and Papa Schimmelhorn, still bedazzled, did the best he could with nods and chuckles and mumbled incoherencies. Finally, when she abandoned small talk to ask him about his work, catching Mavronides's now steely eye upon him, he managed to inform her that eferything was going beautifully; that *ja*, he could vork vith Meister Gassi, who vas nodt much help, alvays making shtinks in pots und shmokes in fires; that he was nodt vorried efen aboudt that because in der subconscience he vas a chenius. Still not quite in gear, he demonstrated the workings of his cuckoo watch, explaining that no vun else could haff infented it, and then presented the yodeling cuckoo clock.

"Serene Highness," he explained untruthfully, "I haff made it chust for you. Maybe you hang it by der bathtub so der lidtle cuckoos can all see—" He broke off, chuckling to himself and actually blushing at the picture in his mind's eye.

The Fräulein signed to a handmaiden to take the clock. She thanked him for his consideration, commending him for his cleverness; she told his pretty friends to take good care of him because, after all, he was a genius. Mavronides took him by the elbow, and turned him round.

"Good-bye, Herr Schimmelhorn," said the Fräulein. "*Auf wiedersehen.*"

And, "*Auf wiedersehen,* Serene Highness," called Papa Schimmelhorn. *Philippa Theophrastra Bombast von etcetera,* he thought as Mavronides propelled him through the door. *Maybe vhen ve know each oder a lidtle bedter I chust call you Philli.*

As they returned, Mavronides explained to him that never before had he seen the Princess so gracious, so condescending, so slow to take offense. Indeed, Papa Schimmelhorn had been honored above the commonalty of men. Truly, it was beyond his understanding, and he warned him not to take advantage of it, not to be in any way impertinent.

Papa Schimmelhorn slapped him on the back. "Herr Zorba," he declared, "she iss nice to me because I am a chenius." But quite a different idea occurred to him. *Maybe,* he told himself, *maybe she iss chust like oder vomen und sees dot I haff plenty of vinegar. . . .*

Meanwhile, the Princess had turned from the door to her handmaiden. "By the Gods of Greece!" she exclaimed. "By all the Satyrs! By the Minotaur himself!" She burst out laughing. "Niobe, I thought that Gottfried Rumpler was the ultimate male chauvinist *schweinhund!* Compared to this old goat, he is just nothing. This Schimmelhorn is *unbelievable*—he is a male chauvinist *überschweinhund!* It's lucky for you he has those two little trollops with him—otherwise he'd probably have you running clear around Little Palaeon! Did you see the way he leered at you while he was in the room?"

"At me, my lady? He wasn't ogling *me.*"

The Princess frowned. Her laughter died. "He *must* have been," she stated. "He is a peasant. He never would have dared to look at *me* that way!"

She returned to the chaise longue. "Niobe, bring me a decanter of fine brandy and a glass."

She waited until Niobe poured. Then she smiled as she

gazed down into the brandy-breather—a smile like the coming of the Second Ice Age.

"Let him play!" she murmured. "Even with Niobe if he wants to. If he can indeed make lead into gold, what does it matter?"

V.

The Princess and the Peasant: Overture

It did not take long for Niki and Emmy to notice that Papa Schimmelhorn was no longer his usual ebullient self. Now he seemed completely unaware of their existence or of Mavronides's presence except when he was more or less forcibly reminded of it. On their way back to their quarters in the keep, he actually had to be steered around several corners. Occasionally, he would close his eyes, smile secretly, and lick his chops. Even Gustav-Adolf, perturbed, more than once rubbed his whiskers against his master's hairy ear and uttered a querulously questioning *meow?* Mavronides, however, was not concerned. Initially, he had been worried by the first Schimmelhorn reaction to the Fräulein, but afterwards, like her, he had concluded that, since any such effrontery was unimaginable, it must have been Niobe—indubitably a pretty pussycat—who had stirred his gonads. He spoke reassuringly to Niki and Emmy. Papa Schimmelhorn, he told them, was after all an impressionable old gentleman; once the initial impression had subsided, everything would return to normal—and anyhow they shouldn't let little Niobe, a mere serving wench, the distraction of a moment, disturb them.

They were relieved. When Papa Schimmelhorn's strange mood continued, when during supper he merely dallied with his food, staring vaguely into unknown distances and answering their efforts at communication with nothing more than vague murmurs, they finally gave it up, assured each other that given an hour or two he would once more be his old ardent self, and told him that they were going for a walk along the beach, perhaps to swim, perhaps to gather seashells.

They left him to his reverie, but it was not a peaceful, contemplative one. For a time, he tried diligently to give his talented subconscious full rein, for he knew that even then it was doing its best to design the complicated device that, it had indicated, would infallibly turn lead into gold; specifically, it was trying to determine the precise shape and proportions of a structure to be made of nice, clean, wire coat-hangers, on which a horribly complex crystal was to be grown. With a green felt pen, Papa Schimmelhorn tried to trace its intricacies on a piece of brown wrapping paper. However, his inner voices kept interrupting him. One of these, small and cautionary, kept telling him that a Fräulein-Princess was definitely a no-no, and that he should be satisfied with the two lovely pussycats Fate had already blessed him with. The only trouble was that this voice sounded very much like Mama Schimmelhorn's; it seemed to have a sarcastic bite to it, while the other voice, very definitely his own and speaking with a glandular insistence, kept telling him that all women, whatever their social station, were alike. It reminded him of a Belgian baroness with whom he had once enjoyed a hectic fortnight, and of an interesting dark lady whose claim it was that her ancestors had belonged to Dom Pedro's Brazilian nobility. The cautionary voice would whisper he should be ashamed—*ach*, such a dirty old man!—while the other would tell him forthrightly that, as der poet Rudyard Tvain had written, Chudy O'Grady und der Herr Oberst's lady vere all sisters vhen der undervear came off.

Finally, after enduring a couple of hours of this moral wrestling, with a great sigh he let himself be persuaded that a walk along the shore, and perhaps a refreshing swim, might solve his problems. He stripped down to a

gaudy pair of green, pink, and yellow polka-dotted shorts
and his huaraches, donned a terry-cloth bathrobe, and set
off, instinctively retracing the way that led to the Princess's own apartments. It vould do no harm, he told
himself, chust to valk by her door. . . .

As he approached it, he realized that his heart was
beating somewhat faster, that his breathing was deeper,
that the roots of his whiskers were tingling. He paused, the
door before him.

It was, though very slightly, open.

Just so might an amorous lady have left her door open
as an invitation to a lover. Just so, in fact, had any number
of doors been left, at one time and another, for him.

The cautionary voice mumbled its feeble argument. It
didn't have a chance. He pushed the door a little farther.
He tapped on it very gently. No one answered. There was
not a sound. He entered. The room was empty, but across
its vast expanse another door stood open an inch or two,
invitingly. He tiptoed massively across the splendid Persian
carpet. He peeked in.

The Princess was sitting in front of a carved and gilded
Florentine dressing table. Her back was to him. She was
brushing her glowing hair, now freed from its restraints.
And she was, he saw, magnificently naked.

He drew his breath in sharply. He knocked very lightly
on the door.

"Come in, Niobe," called the Princess over her shoulder. "Come in, girl—don't just stand there!"

And, "*Peek-a-boo! I see you!*" bellowed Papa Schimmelhorn coyly.

The Princess whirled to face him. Brushing her hair
aside, she stood. . . .

Papa Schimmelhorn stared at her. For a moment, he just
stood there goggling, gasping like a suddenly stranded
fish. Never, never in all his long experience, had he
beheld so lovely a display. His cautionary voice guttered
feebly and winked out.

"*Ach*, Serene Highness! *Ach, meine* predty lidtle Philli—

ach, Herr Gott, how *beaudtiful!''* He threw his arms wide, as though to embrace the world. His robe fell open, revealing not just his brawny chest and vivid polka-dotted shorts, but also the astonishing degree of his impressionability. *"Wunderschön!* Listen, lidtle Serene Highness, oudtside iss shpring, und all die predty shtars, und ve can chase each oder down der beach, und—ho-ho-ho!—maybe sometimes catch, und also shvim togeder vith die porpoises, und—"

He saw that, very slowly, she was advancing on him. For the first time, he raised his eyes from her more startling attractions to her face. Indubitably, it was not the face of one who shared the pretty idyll he had been describing. Her black brows were drawn down to form an absolutely terrifying Medea-mask; she was as pale as death itself; her incongruously red mouth was working, uttering words in a language he could not identify; hoarse words, harsh words, words like high-pitched rip-saws, they obviously were not endearments.

He shuffled his feet uneasily. Uncomfortably, he rewrapped his unfortunate robe.

She kept advancing. Agitatedly, he retreated, one pace, then two. "B-but, Serene Highness," he mumbled. "I haff made maybe a mistake, *ja?* It vas chust you are so—"

Now her strange words inundated him, drowning out his own. She halted. She pointed a dreadful finger at the door. And Papa Schimmelhorn finally looked into her eyes. As Herr Doktor Rumpler had done in Zürich, but much, much, much more profoundly, he shuddered.

Muttering that he was sorry, that he begged her pardon, he backed toward the door. "Okay," he said, "I know vhen I am nodt vanted! I go avay. It vas chust I am so full vith vinegar—ha-ha! Now I go to vork hard und maybe make der lead into der gold."

Somewhere in the background, the yodeling cuckoo clock cheerfully sang the hour.

An instant later, he was in the corridor, the door shut tight behind him. Still shaken, he began to stagger off—

but Papa Schimmelhorn was nothing if not resilient. By the time he reached the next turn in the passage, he was beginning to feel sorry for the Fräulein, who simply didn't know what she was missing. *So sad!* he thought. *Maybe iss something like vith Herr Doktor Freud, in der subconscience. Vhen she iss lidtle somvun shcares her, maybe vith a shnake.* The thought cheered him. *So perhaps tomorrow she vill nodt be angry. But it iss a shame—such a vaste, und such a predty pussycat efen if she iss die Prinzessin.* He shrugged. *Ach, vell, is plendty fishes in der sea.*

Fifteen minutes later, he and Emmy and Niki were happily chasing each other down the beach, and sometimes catching, and even going swimming with the porpoises. When finally he went to bed between them, he had filed the episode away as one more among the many missed and wasted opportunities of a long and active lifetime.

The Princess, needless to say, did nothing of the sort. For a time, she paced her bedroom floor tempestuously, cursing in the unknown tongue and promising herself that Papa Schimmelhorn would suffer cruelly for his insolence. She tried to think of cruelties savage and exquisite enough. She reviewed those used by the inventive Turks over the centuries, those practiced by the Romans, Carthaginians, and other less-than-kindly peoples. She went over those inherited from her own progenitors. None seemed adequate—until finally she recalled her latest interview with Meister Gansfleisch. She halted. Instantly, her inner turmoil subsided. Coldly and practically, she reviewed every aspect of the situation, for after all there was much more than vengeance to be considered. She summoned Niobe, who entered fearfully, aware that something drastic had occurred. She permitted her hair to be rearranged. She donned a black and gold peignoir.

"And now," she ordered, "bring Meister Gansfleisch to me."

She went into her salon, reclined once more on the

chaise longue, and closed her eyes, imagining the fate she had in store for Papa Schimmelhorn.

Meanwhile Niobe—reluctantly, because she feared the alchemist—made her way to his turret quarters. She knocked timidly on his dark door.

"Go away!" his hoarse voice replied. "Whoever you may be, *begone!*"

Niobe knocked again, even more nervously. "B-but Meister Gansfleisch," she called out, "I—I come from the Princess. She's sent for you. You must come right away!"

There was silence, interrupted by muttering and an indignant squeaking. "Very well," Meister Gansfleisch called back, "if *she* has ordered it, then I will come. But it will take me a few minutes to make ready. Wait for me."

Niobe waited, listening to more squeaking and scurrying from within. As a matter of fact, she had arrived at a critical juncture. After his latest interview with his employer, the alchemist, overcome by despair and despondency, had finally succumbed to Twitchgibbet's sales pitch and had agreed, if his familiar could put him in touch with the appropriate authorities, to follow Faustus's example. Twitchgibbet had been delighted, for he knew that the transaction would mean promotion for him, at least to a rank where he would no longer be required to possess any creature as lowly as a rat, and possibly even to the recruiting staff. He had scampered around excitedly while his master rummaged around for the necessary tomes, for black tapers and other oddments, for words of power and protective spells. He had chafed at his rattish inability to assist with the drawing of the complex pentacle the ceremony called for—and then, at the very last moment, with the preparations virtually complete, Niobe's knock had come.

He kept on arguing while Meister Gansfleisch tidied up, washed his hands, and put away an assortment of dried lizards' eyes, pieces of hanged criminals, and other minor tools of wizardry. He even dared to disobey him to the extent of keeping up his protests after he had been ordered to keep quiet.

As the alchemist joined Niobe in the corridor, he squeaked out, *"You'll* be sorry, stupid! You just wait and see!" Then he crouched down by the jar holding the poor homunculus, gnashing his teeth at him through the glass, and promising to make life really miserable for him the next time Meister Gansfleisch's prolonged absence could be counted on.

Meister Gansfleisch himself couldn't help feeling that he had been accorded at least a temporary stay of execution. He had no real desire to convey title to his immortal soul, and only Twitchgibbet's promise that, were he to do so, the devil would deliver the Princess over to him as certainly as he had delivered Helen of Troy to Faustus had induced him to agree. He followed Niobe agitatedly, wondering what the Fräulein had in mind, hoping—yet scarcely daring to hope.

She was waiting for him on the chaise longue. She nodded to him coldly as he entered. With a gesture, she dismissed her handmaiden. She motioned him to a chair.

Obediently, he sat.

"Gaspar," she said, piercing him with her eyes, "your opinion has often been given me when it was not asked for. Often it has been absolutely insubordinate. And often it has been completely worthless. Therefore you should be especially grateful for what I am about to say to you."

She leaned forward intently, and his long, gray fingers fought each other in his lap.

"Gaspar, where this wretch Schimmelhorn is concerned, you were completely right."

Gaspar Gansfleisch's heart skipped a beat.

"I have studied the situation very carefully," she went on, and he noticed that as she spoke her lips drew tightly back from her sharp teeth. "Schimmelhorn's sexual appetites and proclivities are thoroughly undisciplined. I have— well, I have had other, and very reliable, reports. They are interfering, as you pointed out and as my great collateral ancestor has said, with the alchemical researches and processes in which you are engaged. Therefore I have decided that we must take certain measures. . . ." She paused. "Do you recall mentioning what the Arabs did to Ismail?"

Meister Gansfleisch jerked. His jagged smile appeared. He licked his lips. "Yes, yes, Princess!" he replied. "Oh, *indeed* yes. Indeed I do. And I have a *wonderfully* sharp knife, Your Highness—it would be over in a moment, indeed it would!" He licked his lips again. "Or perhaps we could just let Twitchgibbet bite—"

She silenced him peremptorily. "Don't be a bigger fool than you already are," she snapped. "I can allow no violence to him. We shall accomplish the same end, but quite legally and much more subtly. Among the Golden Doctor's most secret formulas, those which I have shown to no one, there is one which will serve our purpose admirably. I have certain necessary arrangements to make first, but I want you to have everything ready in your laboratory. Return here in exactly half an hour, and I will give you full instructions. Even if you have to work till dawn, I want it ready for me when I wake tomorrow. Do you understand?"

Meister Gansfleisch rubbed his hands together excitedly. He told her he understood perfectly—that she could count on him—that it would be a pleasure.

He backed out bowing, and almost skipped down the corridor, chuckling and cackling to himself.

Fräulein von Hohenheim waited until he was safely out of earshot. Then she picked up her phone and called Herr Doktor Rumpler. It went against her grain to do so, but Swiss good sense told her that, after all, they were in the thing together, and the stakes were high enough so that no chances should be taken.

"Gottfried—" she said, in a voice as warm and soft and feminine as possible. "You—you do not mind if I call you Gottfried?"

She had never used his first name before, and now she

could practically feel him quiver over the telephone as he assured her ardently that he didn't mind at all.

"Gottfried, my friend, I fear that I have bad news for you, about—about this man Schimmelhorn."

"Has something *happened* to him?" asked Dr. Rumpler anxiously, suddenly seeing mountains of gold vanish into nothingness.

The Fräulein told him that Papa Schimmelhorn was quite undamaged, but that his extra-professional activities had taken an alarming turn. He was no longer satisfied with Emmy and Niki; he had been pestering all the pretty pussycats on Little Palaeon; the local lads were beginning to look at him with murder in their hearts.

Warmly, Gottfried Rumpler averred that he had every confidence in her ability to handle Papa Schimmelhorn, and to protect him from the fury of the natives.

"Ah, Gottfried!" she replied. "You do not understand. Paracelsus himself stated most emphatically that sexual excesses made alchemical research impossible."

"But, my dear Fräulein"—his tone suggested that after all boys would be boys—"Schimmelhorn's, er, excesses have never interfered with his past accomplishments. Indeed, his grandnephew Anton Fledermaus—a most engaging and reliable young man—states that they are absolutely essential to his success."

She lowered her voice. Things were different now on Little Palaeon, she stated tensely and impressively. Papa Schimmelhorn was neglecting alchemy almost completely. Even Meister Gansfleisch, that good and patient man, was in despair. Strong measures were required immediately.

"Well, well!" Dr. Rumpler was disturbed. "It if is indeed so, what measures do you propose to take, dear lady? I suppose I could send—well, reinforcements. That is to say, more—"

The Fräulein permitted herself a fraudulent but quite convincing sob. "I—I was hoping, Gottfried, that you, because you are a *man*, could think of something *practi-*

cal. Sending more young women would only make matters worse."

"Then what the devil can we do?"

"Gottfried, dear friend," she answered, "I am afraid that there is one way only. We must deprive him, if not of the desire, at least of the ability."

She heard her associate's gasp of horror.

"But—but we could not do *that!* It—it would not be legal! And such a cruelty! My dear Fräulein—"

"Oh, Gottfried, Gottfried!" she interrupted him. "You, of all people, need not call me Fräulein—to you, I am Philippa." She sobbed again. She promised him they would not injure Papa Schimmelhorn. She told him about Paracelsus's formula—perfectly harmless and quite temporary since there was an infallible instant antidote. "You, dear Gottfried, must phone Frau Schimmelhorn; she will understand; she will give us her permission."

The change in her demeanor, her obvious wish to take refuge behind his own strong masculinity—these were potent arguments, but still he hesitated.

She sobbed into the telephone. "Oh, *please*," she begged, "only *try* to understand. *Gottfried, he has even been molesting me!*"

Abruptly, Dr. Rumpler saw Papa Schimmelhorn in a new light. "It is an outrage!" he cried out. "It is beyond belief! The man is nothing but a beast! My Philippa! My *dear* Philippa! I shall telephone Frau Schimmelhorn immediately! Then I shall call you back."

He broke the connection, and the Fräulein replaced her own phone on its cradle. *Dummkopf!* she thought at the no longer listening Doktor. *It is fortunate you are such a male chauvinist! If you had not been, my little play would not have been so beautifully successful.* She laughed unkindly. *Well, after the formula has worked on Schimmelhorn, probably I shall have to use it on you too. Dear, dear Gottfried, I can hardly wait.*

Smiling to herself at this pleasant prospect, she sat back to await the Rumpler call.

It came sooner than she had expected. Mama Schimmelhorn had been at home, knitting a comforter for Pastor Hundhammer. She was surprised, she told the Herr Doktor, not at the news of Papa Schimmelhorn's transgressions, but that he had managed to misbehave under the very eyes of eminent Swiss bankers, and that they had been unable to prevent it. Und now he vas shpoiling eferything so maybe der church vould nodt get der shteeple after all?

Dr. Rumpler told her somberly that he sincerely hoped the church would not lose out, but that he was much concerned—and besides, surely the Rumpler Bank and its associates were entitled to a modest profit on their investment? To this, she wholeheartedly agreed—and did the Herr Doktor want her to fly at once to Zürich to take disciplinary measures?

Hastily, he assured her that this would not be necessary, that there was a simpler way to reform her husband than by twisting his ear and applying an umbrella-point to his brisket. Then he outlined the Fräulein's proposal: the subtle substance to be used had been invented by one of the greatest of all Swiss physicians; it had been thoroughly tested and was guaranteed to be instantly reversible.

"So it does nodt hurt Papa?" she replied. "It only, for a vhile, takes der lead oudt of der pencil, so he iss like old Heinrich Luedesing und cannodt chase die naked vomen any more? Vell, maybe it teaches der old goat a lesson!"

Then, congratulating the Herr Doktor on his perspicacity, she gave her formal permission for Papa Schimmelhorn's deactivation; and he said good night with her chuckles still echoing gruesomely in his ear.

"And did you record the conversation, Gottfried?"

"*Natürlich*, dear lady!"

"Ah, Gottfried," she whispered, "you are so resourceful! I do not know what I would do without you. . . ."

Master Gaspar Gansfleisch returned to his turret in fine fettle. He entered briskly, whirled around two or three times in glee, ignored Twitchgibbet, and, humming an unmelodious but triumphant tune, set to work erasing the almost-completed pentacle in which the sale of his soul was to have been consummated.

Twitchgibbet realized that, as he had feared, his hopes for a quick promotion had evaporated. Trying not to grind his yellow teeth, he pleaded with the alchemist to reconsider.

"Master," he whined, doing his best to sound truly humble, "how come you're doin' this to me? Okay, I'm just a petty fiend and not a VIP like Mephistopheles and all those higher-ups, but I got some rights, ain't I? Ain't I always done everything you said, like the contract called for? Ain't I, huh?"

Meister Gansfleisch paid no attention. He finished rubbing out the pentacle, and started putting away the black tapers and the other clutter he had brought out for the ceremony.

"You just listen to me, Master—me, who's been your faithful servant," squeaked Twitchgibbet, keeping the whine in his voice. "Don't say I didn't warn you. And now you've let this what's-her-name Princess catch you by the balls—"

"*Silence, vermin!*" roared Meister Gansfleisch.

Instantly, Twitchgibbet subsided, but to himself he muttered, *You just wait, old Meister Smartass, you think you got me the way that gal's got you, but there ain't been a contract yet ain't got no loopholes in it. Just wait and see. . . .*

The alchemist finished tidying up. He changed into his more formal robes. He locked the door behind him.

Promptly on the half-hour, he knocked on the Princess's door.

Niobe admitted him.

He advanced, bowing his servility, and the Princess nodded to him coldly, condescendingly. Again, she was reclining on the chaise longue, holding on her lap an ancient book in tooled white pigskin and closed with brazen clasps.

She opened it. She beckoned to him to advance. "Here,"

she told him, "is the formula of which I spoke, written in Paracelsus's own hand. You will sit at my table here and copy only it. Then I will check your copy against the original. After that, we will do the same with the following formula, which reverses the effect. You will not sit with your back to me, and you will not attempt to look at any other pages of the manuscript. Is that completely clear?"

Meister Gansfleisch, who would gladly have mortgaged away his narrowly saved soul for a chance to read the book from start to finish, indicated that it was.

"Very well," she said. "Begin."

With a trembling hand, while the Fräulein watched him like a hawk, he copied the crabbed Latin of the manuscript. Scarcely concealing his excitement, he read it back to her. He did the same with the successive formula.

She closed the book. "Now," she commanded, "you will return to your laboratory, and you will set to work at once to make an adequate quantity of each of these. As you are aware, I know enough of the arcane sciences to know that you have all the necessary substances, and that the entire operation should not take you more than two or perhaps three hours. Therefore, when you have finished, you will bring them to me instantly, no matter what the time of night."

"Of course, Your Highness, of course!" crowed the alchemist. "Oh, I can hardly wait to see the expression on that old lecher's face when—when—"

"I am sure," she told him, with a momentary smile, "that it will be adequately rewarding. But"—her expression hardened—"you will do your gloating very quietly, and only to yourself. You will not indicate to Schimmelhorn in any way that you are gloating. You will treat him with special courtesy, and you will obey any and all of his requests pertaining to his work. I have business appointments I must keep in Zürich and I shall remain here only long enough to make sure our treatment is effective. I shall be gone for at least a week. During that time, if Schimmelhorn gives you what you call his shopping lists, you will go to Athens and faithfully purchase everything he requires.''

Meister Gansfleisch started to protest, but she cut him off peremptorily. "Be still!" she ordered. "For the time being, you must be content with what you will be doing to the man. Later—well, we shall see.''

She made a gesture of dismissal. Wisely, bowing, he started to back away from her.

"I shall compound this—this medicine, *he-he!*—oh yes, Princess! I shall compound it speedily, and with all my art." In his mind's eye, he again saw Papa Schimmelhorn's countenance as it would appear in the first dreadful moment of realization. "Yes, yes, Your Highness! And I shall have it ready this very night, I promise you! And—''

Decisively, she pointed at the door; and, clutching his copies of the formulas, he backed into the corridor.

Niobe shut the door.

"What a revolting creature!" remarked the Princess. "Niobe, go and bring Mavronides to me. It will be refreshing to talk to a man so simple and honest and devoted.''

While she waited, she leafed through Paracelsus's comments and instructions, as she often had, taking mental notes of those that might be useful to her either in her capacity of princess-priestess or as a power in the Swiss banking world. When Niobe appeared with Mavronides, she laid the book aside almost reluctantly.

"Sarpedon," she said, smiling at him regally, "be seated and listen closely to what I have to say.''

Then, mincing no words, she told him exactly what had happened, of Papa Schimmelhorn's immense effrontery and what was being done about it.

"Meister Gansfleisch," she informed him, "will bring the prepared formulas to me tonight. I want you to wait up until I send Niobe down with the one for Schimmelhorn. This must be served to him in his breakfast, and there must be no mistake. Therefore I entrust the task to you. You are to put it in a dish only he will eat, and you must serve it to him personally. Is that clear?''

While she was speaking, Mavronides's face had mirrored first his shock and incredulity at Papa Schimmelhorn's unbelievable impertinence, then the acquiescence born of a lifetime's loyalty.

"It is clear," he answered. "My lady, Schimmelhorn shall have it in the morning."

VI.

Der Lead in der Pencil

Next morning, when the serving maids arrived with breakfast for Papa Schimmelhorn and his pussycats, they were ceremoniously accompanied by a thoroughly cheerless Mavronides, who supervised the setting of the table and personally uncovered the steaming dishes. The largest serving of scrambled eggs, small sausages, ham, and hashbrown potatoes—a Schimmelhorn favorite—he placed before his victim.

"You are unhappy, Herr Zorba?" roared Papa Schimmelhorn, digging in heartily. "Something iss maybe wrong? Sit down und haff some coffee, und I vill tell you shtories aboudt how I haff shtayed so full with vinegar!"

Reluctantly, Mavronides sat; reluctantly, he sipped at the cup of coffee Niki poured for him. He informed Papa Schimmelhorn that, no, there was nothing wrong; it was just that he had soon to get about his duties; there were so many things to do, so many problems. He sighed, and Papa Schimmelhorn, who by this time was beginning to suspect that he himself might possibly have caused a problem by his ill-considered overture to the Fräulein, decided to question him more closely when they were alone. When Mavronides finally left, he made no effort to detain him.

"Poor Zorba!" he remarked as he cleaned his plate and stole an extra sausage from Miss Emmy. "Alvays respon-

79

sibilities! Vot he needs iss a vacation. I vill tell him he must go to Schvitzerland und maybe climb die Alps.'' He removed his napkin and stood up. ''Vell, I see you later. Now I must go to vork vith Meister Gassi.''

He had been surprised, not just by Mavronides's attendance at his morning meal, but also by his dark solemnity. Now another surprise awaited him. Meister Gansfleisch, in his laboratory, was no longer his usual rude and sour self; instead, he smiled, patted his coworker on the back, asked him many a solicitous question about his health, told him how well he looked, how strong and hearty, and appeared to be doing everything in his power to assist instead of hinder him.

Vot iss? thought Papa Schimmelhorn. *All at vunce, Meister Gassi becomes maybe der bluebeard of happiness? Vell, it more easy, so okay.*

All day they worked together in harmony. Papa Schimmelhorn set up the coathanger trellis on which to grow his crystal in a huge glass vessel which previously the alchemist would not even let him touch; he filled it with noxious fluids of his own brewing, compounded by substances that Meister Gansfleisch provided without a murmur; he added item after item to his shopping list without evoking even a single protest—batteries, a generator, and a great many outlandish electronic components. Each one was cheerfully noted down, and the few questions the alchemist came up with were obviously asked only to make everything quite clear. Twitchgibbet was conspicuous by his absence.

He worked away until late in the afternoon, when he announced that the day's tasks had been accomplished, and that he would have to hurry so that before supper he could do his setting-up exercises—ho-ho-ho!—which kept him young and virile despite his years.

To his astonishment again, Meister Gansfleisch actually seemed pleased. Almost literally dancing from one foot to the other, he accompanied his enemy to the door, cackling about how much he envied him, and wishing him all the pleasures promised by the company of such pretty pussycats. Only when he had locked and barred his door did his expression change. His face became a mask of gloating malice. He whirled around three times, widdershins. He clapped his hands. Unlimbering his favorite flagon, he drank down a tremendous toast to the defusing of Papa Schimmelhorn. Then, as quickly as he could, he hurried back to his own turret to see if, during the next hour or two, his telescope might show him some dramatic evidence of his accomplishment.

As for Papa Schimmelhorn, all unsuspecting, he too returned to his apartment, imagining as he strode the warmth with which his pussycats would welcome him. He found them, appropriately garbed for the sport in which they expected to indulge, hiding coyly behind the bedroom door. As he entered, they both kissed him. Then Niki, giggling, led him to the bed, pushed him down on it playfully, and started working on his shirt-buttons, while Emmy applied herself more intimately to his zipper. After a few minutes of fun and games, they had him wearing nothing but the hair on his great chest.

And nothing happened.

The pretty pussycats played a little harder, and Papa Schimmelhorn started getting worried. "How stranche!" he muttered. "Nefer since I am maybe eight years old—"

For the next half-hour, Emmy and Niki, who were very talented, applied all their cunning, all their tricks and artifices, to the problem of arousing him—to no avail. For the first time, he would not arouse. For the first time, his vinegar had failed him.

Finally, in shock, he sat up on the edge of the bed, and a tear flowed down his cheek into the forest of his beard. "*Ach*, it iss no use!" he moaned. "Now I am chust a poor old man like Heinrich Luedesing. I am like Ismail, only vithoudt der shnipping."

"Maybe you're just *tired?*" murmured Emmy consolingly.

"You haven't been out laying those island girls?" suggested Niki more practically.

"*Nein*," he mourned. "I haff been goot all day, efer since this morning before breakfast. All I do iss vork vith Meister Gassi, like I tell you." He shook his head slowly, like the tolling of a doomsday bell. "*Nein*, it iss because now I am an old man and no goot anymore." Suddenly he pictured himself relegated to some New Haven rest home, hobbling around with a cane or perhaps even in a wheelchair, cackling with other impotent old men, and visited pityingly by the ladies of Pastor Hundhammer's church bearing small comforts and uplifting literature. He groaned tragically.

Niki and Emmy, wounded in their professional pride, renewed their efforts, but again without effect. His gloom deepened. His pronouncements regarding his condition became even more dismal. Finally, they gave it up, but they kept on trying to cheer him: probably he'd be back to normal by next morning; perhaps he'd simply been overexercising his subconscious; probably all he needed was a tonic—

"*Nein, nein*," he told them. "I feel it in die bones. Vun oder two more years, und—*poof!*—no more Schimmelhorn. All I am goot for now is to do der vork vith Meister Gassi und maybe make vun or two more cuckoo clocks vhen I go home. But you are predty pussycats, young und full vith vinegar. You must nodt vaste your time vith a poor old man vhen on der island iss so many fine young shqvirts." He sobbed heartrendingly, and Gustav-Adolf jumped up on his lap, making feline noises of concern. "Now I must be brafe, und pet mein Gustav-Adolf inshtead of lidtle pussycats, und be alone to forget maybe dot I haff no lead anymore in der pencil, und—und chust be a chenius. So, Niki und Emmy, you take a nice long valk on der seashore like ve used to, und listen to die vafes, und schvim vith porpoises, und vhen you come back for supper I am perhaps more cheerful."

They kissed him; they caressed him; they helped him dress. Then, obediently, they did as they were bidden—and Meister Gansfleisch, seeing them through his brass telescope, crowed triumphantly and set off instantly to tell the Princess that her formula had been successful.

The next few days were anguished ones for Papa Schimmelhorn. Not only did he have to endure the awful burden of his infirmity, but suddenly the population of Little Palaeon, until now so friendly, had become remote and almost fearful; on several occasions, he was sure that children, seeing him shamble by with drooping shoulders and dismal countenance, made surreptitious signs against the evil eye. Only Ismail, convertly and from a safe distance, occasionally gave him the sympathetic glance of a fellow sufferer. Despairingly, he composed a radiogram to Mama Schimmelhorn, not very subtly imploring her to send him a small quantity of his mutated catnip immediately "for a friend," and bribed a Cretan fisherman to fetch it from the main island. He received no answer, Mama Schimmelhorn having read it with many a snort and chuckle.

However, his work progressed; the curious crystal, immersed in its strange, bubbling, stirring fluids, began to grow even without the electric currents to which he was going to subject it. Still, nothing seemed to go exactly right. Meister Gansfleisch's exaggerated solicitude for his health, always expressed at precisely the wrong moment, invariably agitated him into the most vivid daydreams of pretty pussycats and of the magnificent performances of which he always had been capable.

Niki and Emmy, doing their duty by the Rumpler Bank, tried their utmost to console and encourage him. During his free daylight hours, they tried to get him to play with them along the beach or in the water, or at least to take some interest in the island's ancient ruins, its domestic fauna, or the many legends they had heard from its inhabitants. At night, they cuddled closely to him in the enormous bed, trying to soothe his restlessness and quiet his tragic sighs. It was all in vain. Innocent play reminded him only too bitterly of more exciting pastimes; the ruins recalled his own decrepitude; the fauna inconsiderately seemed to think of nothing but reproducing their own kind; and the legends, cruelly, dealt invariably with Olympian seductions. More and more frequently, he sent the girls to wander by themselves while in his solitude he either worked away or, almost as frequently, apathetically surrendered to despair. Gustav-Adolf his only company.

Finally, reaching for a straw, he buttonholed Sarpedon Mavronides, who had been avoiding him, and confided all his troubles.

Mavronides listened, frowning ominously.

"*Ach, Gott!*" Papa Schimmelhorn finished his recital. "I do nodt undershtand, Herr Zorba! All of a sudden— chust like dot! Nefer before in all mein life it happens, nefer! Vot iss *wrong?*"

For a moment, Mavronides's black eyes stared at him piercingly. Then, with a glance over his shoulder and in a very low and apprehensive voice, he said, "*The Gods have punished you.* You had been told—the Fräulein von Hohenheim is a Princess and a Priestess! She is the guardian of our Sacred Mysteries. She—she *herself* is sacred. And you—*you* have dared to make unclean advances to her! Do you wonder that the Gods are vengeful, that they have deprived you of your manhood? You are fortunate that they did not destroy you—that *she* did not order you dragged away to—to the Labyrinth!"

Without another word, he turned and left, leaving Papa Schimmelhorn even more disheartened than before.

Miserably, the hours and days dragged by; more and more often he found himself thinking sentimentally of home and Mama, of his own deep bass voice dominating the choir at Pastor Hundhammer's services, of working at Heinrich Luedesing's and at his basement bench, but even these nostalgic maunderings invariably evoked other memories—of pretty Misses Kittikool and MacTavish in bed with him en route to Hong Kong, of Dora Grossapfel's tight stretch-pants and how easily they could be removed, of . . . It was almost too much for him to bear.

Yet the work went on, and on the fifth day after the Fräulein's departure, the time arrived for Meister Gansfleisch to go to Athens on his shopping tour.

The alchemist had been enjoying himself hugely. Frequently, as he watched Papa Schimmelhorn shuffling around the laboratory, he had restrained his laughter only with the greatest difficulty. Indeed, he now felt so secure in his victory that he scarcely resented the errand the Fräulein had commanded him to carry out.

Every day, in the privacy of his turret, he gloated to poor Twitchgibbet, praising his own cunning and perspicacity, and making it quite clear that really competent thaumaturgists had no need for the Powers of Darkness, and especially for fiends as low in the Hellish pecking order as his familiar.

Twitchgibbet, his plans for his and Meister Gansfleisch's futures ruined, watched him angrily with his glowing-ember eyes, confined his comments to an occasional rattish squeak, and in his mind reviewed the contract that bound him to the alchemist, the orders he had been enjoined to obey, and all the ways to circumvent them and get at least the satisfaction of revenge. *I gotta be nice to that stupid homunculus when I let him out to feed him*, he muttered to himself, *like I gotta be perlite to that damn cat—but ain't nobody said I can't pertect myself if that cat attacks me, if he comes in that there window and goes after—hey, that's better!—I'll say he busted in and went right after Humphrey! That's what I'll tell the old fart when he gets back home. Thinks he can get by without us, huh? Well, I'll learn him better. And won't they be pleased down below when I explain it!*

Meister Gansfleisch arrayed himself in his ill-fitting suit; he brushed at his scuffed yellow shoes; he made sure that everything too secret was safely stowed away, that every window was secured. "I shall be gone two days at least," he informed Twitchgibbet, "depending on how long it takes me to find the trash that fool Schimmelhorn has

ordered. Be sure you nourish Humphrey once a day, you
hear me? And don't let him get more than a foot or so
away from his bottle. You'll be responsible, and just
remember"—he cackled merrily—"if you slip up I'll
complain to the management."

Picking up an old-fashioned straw suitcase, and putting
on an ancient, shapeless hat, he left, double-locking the
door behind him.

As soon as he was sure that he now definitely would be
alone, Twitchgibbet, who had been crouching all the while
beside the bottle containing Humphrey, went over to the
window to which he had referred in his soliloquy. In the
corner of the turret nearest the parapet, it was tall and
narrow, formed of three hinged-and-leaded sections that
opened separately; and he knew, having experimented previously, that he could twist the catch with his agile rat's
paws and pull it open. He also knew that under it, much
less than a good cat's-leap distant, ran a leaden rain-gutter,
which could be reached also from the battlements, where,
though barred from the rest of the chateau, Gustav-Adolf
sunned himself, took his exercise, and sniffed the breezes.
He knew, too, that Gustav-Adolf was aware of exactly
where he was, for many a time he had heard him jump
from parapet to gutter to windowsill, sniffing at the smell
of rat, growling softly in his throat, and then departing
angrily when he found that he could go no farther.

Meister Gansfleisch had always been extremely careful
to let no unhealthy fresh air into his living quarters, but he
never had issued orders on the subject, so Twitchgibbet
felt perfectly free to open up the window. *I gotta watch till
I see that cat coming my way*, he told himself. *I gotta
watch real careful. Chances are he won't do nothin' till
late afternoon, but I can't take no chances*. He scuttled to
the window directly overlooking the parapet, from which
his master had watched Papa Schimmelhorn's turret for
incriminating evidence, and waited patiently.

Gustav-Adolf emerged two or three times during the
day, once to use his catbox, which he preferred out-of-

doors, and once to take a two-hour nap in the warm afternoon sunlight. Finally he came out again, stretched luxuriously, and said a few consolatory words in Cat to Papa Schimmelhorn who, crushed by despondency, was staring bleakly out over the sea. Then he swaggered along the parapet's very edge toward the trap awaiting him.

As a fiend in rat's clothing, Twitchgibbet—as he had bragged to Meister Gansfleisch—had never had any trouble killing any cat. He squeaked, trying to sound as much like a badly frightened rat as possible, and gleefully saw Gustav-Adolf look up, lay back his ears, and bush his long, striped tail. He hurried back to the homunculus. "Okay, Hump," he snapped, "let's get you outa there."

As well as he could, he helped Humphrey climb out of his bottle, which he did with difficulty, and then seated him in the small chair next to it. "You stay there, you little turd," he said. "I'm goin' to put on a show for you, a real good show!"

His plan was simple. He was going to leave the window open, crouch behind it, let Gustav-Adolf enter, then bang it shut again and have it latched before his victim, finding out that he was up against a rat-fiend rather than a rat, could panic and escape. He scurried to the window and made ready.

Gustav-Adolf, knowing none of this, advanced against him as, in his young cathood aboard a Scandinavian merchant vessel, he had advanced against the dock rats of Port Said and Marseilles, the godown rats of Singapore, and all their kin from Rio to New Orleans. Cats are patient creatures, and it was fun to stalk a rat even if you were sure there'd be no way to get at it. He launched himself down to the rain-gutter, looked up—and to his delight and astonishment, saw that the window was open wide. "Hey, wouldja look at *that?*" he growled—and leaped.

He landed squarely on the sill, half in, half out. He paused for an instant, his eyes adjusting to the gloom of Meister Gansfleisch's residence. The opened window barred him to the left, so he turned right to reconnoiter, crouching, lashing his tail.

And Twitchgibbet swiftly banged the window shut. Gustav-Adolf whirled—but he was not quick enough. The latch, which his own paws could never have manipulated, had snapped to. They faced each other. He looked into Twitchgibbet's red eyes, at his long teeth. He was an astoundingly big rat.

"Cat," hissed Twitchgibbet, tensing himself to spring, "yer gonna be dead, dead, *dead!*" He licked his lips, already tasting cat's blood.

Gustav-Adolf looked at him quite undismayed. "Yuh gotta be kiddin', punk!" he growled. "I could beat hell outa two lousy rats like you with three paws tied behind m'back!"

Twitchgibbet snickered evily. "You think I'm just a rat, huh? *I'm a fiend from Hell!* Get it, dimwit? You ain't got a—"

And it was at this instant that, for the first time, Twitchgibbet saw the devices Mrs. Laubenschneider had woven into Gustav-Adolf's flea collar—and realized that they were very potent ones indeed, guaranteed to keep much bigger and more powerful fiends at bay.

"To me a goddam rat's a goddam rat!" shouted Gustav-Adolf, lashing his tail even more ferociously.

Twitchgibbet uttered one completely rattish squeak and bolted. He did not even hit the floor before Gustav-Adolf had him. His powerful teeth bit into his neck; they reached his spine; they crunched down inexorably. Gustav-Adolf shook him savagely until the rat body he had infested was quite limp and dead. The fiend who was the real Twitchgibbet remained only for a second; then he felt himself suddenly sucked back, by forces against which he was quite powerless, to face what he knew would be, if not a general court, at least severe company punishment. He vanished utterly, leaving behind a strong sulphurous stink, at which Gustav-Adolf wrinkled his sensitive nostrils.

Well, another day, another dollar! thought Gustav-Adolf. *Don't tell me there's a rat anywhere I can't clobber!*

"I have killed a rat! A great, big, dirty rat!" he boasted

loudly, as cats will when they wish to proclaim such successes. "Said he was a fiend from Hell, he did—"

At this point, he became aware that he was not alone. Across the room, from a tabletop, a thin, tiny voice was calling out, "Oh, bravely done, Grimalkin! Indeed bravely done! Thou hast slain the magician's filthy rat, his foul fiend! Oh, God will bless you for it, I do promise you!"

Gustav-Adolf stared. He had never in his life beheld so small a person. He crossed the room, jumped up on the table, and sniffed at him. He smelled quite human and seemed extremely friendly. With a tiny hand, he scratched Gustav-Adolf behind the ears.

Gustav-Adolf purred. Then he decided that, even if he could not bring his prey to Papa Schimmelhorn, he would at least have to apprise him of the victory, so, alternately at the door and at the window, he began singing again his loud song. His voice was quite as robust as his master's, and his production even more determined.

"I have killed a rat! The grandfather of all dirty, nasty rats! I have—"

He carried the rat's remains to the door, and started in again.

So abstracted was Papa Schimmelhorn that many minutes passed before he began to get the message. He knew that Gustav-Adolf had gone out on the parapet, and that normally there was nowhere he could go from there. But his voice sounded strangely far away and muffled.

Papa Schimmelhorn went out on the parapet himself, and found that he could hear more clearly and that now the sounds appeared to be coming from the Gansfleisch turret. He frowned. *He has caught a maus*, he told himself, *oder a rat, but how—?* He broke off abruptly. He knew of only one rat in the vicinity, and that was the alchemist's rat-in-residence—and Twitchgibbet wasn't any ordinary rat. "*Mein Gott!*" he cried aloud. "*Vot happens?* Maybe Gustav-Adolf has been hurt! Maybe inside Meister Gassi's haus he iss getrapped!"

He hurried across to the other turret, and found every window tightly shut. But now it was quite clear that Gustav-Adolf was inside.

Forgetting his own sorrows, he at once made up his mind. "*Ach*," he muttered, "efen if I get more trouble, I must safe him! It iss lucky mein old Uncle Georg vas a lockschmidt und taught me how to open up." Hastening in again, he rummaged in his carpetbag, found a small, neat package of old tools, dashed down the stairs to the corridor beneath the battlements and up the stairs at its other end.

"You chust vait, Gustav-Adolf!" he called out. "Don'dt let der rat bite! In a few minutes I haff you oudt!"

He set to work on the enormous ancient locks, hoping no one would hear either him or Gustav-Adolf, and telling himself that the servants always stayed as far from Meister Gansfleisch and his familiar as possible. The first lock gave him little trouble; he had it open in three minutes. The second took a little longer. He worked to the accompaniment of vociferous feline boasting from behind the door, and occasionally he asked Gustav-Adolf please to be a goot boy und patient. Once or twice, he thought he heard a tiny, tiny voice added to the chorus, but he was too busy to pay it any heed.

Finally the second lock yielded to his expertise. He pushed the door open.

He looked around. "Bah, such a shtink!" he exclaimed. "I think Meister Gassi und his rat maybe are nodt housebroken." His eyes searched the room for where Twitchgibbet might be lurking.

Gustav-Adolf was doing a victory march back and forth against his legs, purring and trying to call attention to his victim.

"*Donnerwetter!*" gasped Papa Schimmelhorn, looking down and seeing the corpse. "You have *killed* der rat!"

"Yer goddam right!" replied Gustav-Adolf in Cat. "Deader'n a doornail!"

"Vell, you are a clefer cat"—somberly he shook his head—"but I think Meister Gassi vill be very angry vith

us, und maybe die Prinzessin too. Iss bedter ve get rid of
right avay, und then lock up again, so no vun knows." He
picked up Twitchgibbet by his naked tail. "Ve must hurry!"

Suddenly, just behind him, a very small voice spoke.
"Pray, good and kindly sir," it said, "do not berate your
gib-cat. He is a noble creature. Alone he slew the foul
fiend who served the wicked Gaspar Gansfleisch and who
has tormented me these many years."

Papa Schimmelhorn dropped the rat. He turned. On a
little chair on a tabletop, he beheld a being ten or eleven
inches tall garbed in worn and faded Elizabethan clothing:
miniature doublet and hose, a tiny ruff. It wore an infinitesimal moustache and beard very like William Shakespeare's, and its white hair and pallid, sunken cheeks
showed every evidence of extreme old age.

"Aber—aber nefer haff I seen anybody so *shmall!*"

"No doubt, no doubt!" answered the little man. "In my
present form, my name is Humphrey, and I am what
thaumaturges and necromancers call a homunculus. I was
a free spirit, trapped by arts magical into this small body
artificially created by the famous Dr. Dee, who lived four
hundred of your years ago. Pray seat yourself if you would
hear my tale. . . ."

Papa Schimmelhorn, dismayed, pulled up a chair, and
Gustav-Adolf jumped into his lap. He listened while his
small new acquaintance explained how he had been brought
into existence, interrupting only twice, once to remark that
it did nodt sound like much fun, nodt like making babies,
and again to ask incredulously whether for four hundred
years Humphrey had actually lived inside that bottle?

"Und all *alone?*" he said. "Vithoudt efen vunce in a
vhile a predty lidtle girl hum-uncle-us?"

Humphrey nodded sadly. He described his months and
years within the fluid the bottle held, without which he
could survive for only a few hours. He explained that
fortunately it usually kept him in a somnolent condition,
from which he could rouse himself only with great effort,
except when he was taken out to receive nourishment or to

serve the arcane purposes of those into whose possession he had come over the centuries. He spoke of Dr. Dee, who had used him courteously and, withal, kindly enough; he spoke of the rapacity and greed of alchemists and princes, of treacheries meditated and contrived by men and women of high station, of the cruelties practiced upon his small person by any number of vicious charlatans and even more vicious practitioners of the darker arts. "But the worst of all, by far the most accomplished in his cruelty," he declared, "has been this Gansfleisch. Were I, sir, to recite to you one jot, one tittle, of what he and his fiend have done to me, it would, I do aver, bring tears to your gentle eyes. But now your rare, heroic cat has saved me from the rat-fiend—much to my astonishment, for I have seen that creature more cruelly kill any number of ordinary cats! And I do implore you, sir, that you, when you depart, will take me with you and save me also from his master."

Papa Schimmelhorn's heart went out to him. Suddenly he remembered the secret compartment installed by the Fräulein's ancestor behind the carved marble surrounding the fireplace, which he hadn't mentioned to Niki or to Emmy: and he realized that it was quite big enough for Humphrey in his jar. *Und vhy nodt?* he asked himself. *Ve get rid of der dead rat, und here I lock up eferything chust like it vas, und lidtle Herr Humphrey iss qvite safe in der bottle put avay. Vhen Meister Gassi gets back from der trip, perhaps he thinks der Defil has—how do you say vith used cars?—repossessed Tvitchgibbet, maybe because he does nodt make die payments, und also shtolen lidtle Herr Humphrey.*

"Gustav-Adolf iss a goot cat," he explained to Humphrey, "but I think vhy he can kill der rat iss because of Mrs. Laubenschneider's collar for die fleas. Okay, ve take you vith us vhen ve go, und sometimes you can tell me shtories aboudt machicians, und I vill tell you aboudt predty pussycats und how I am a chenius."

While Humphrey stared and listened in amazement, he consulted his cuckoo watch to see how much time remained before the girls returned for dinner, found that he had two hours at least, and set to work removing all evidence of Gustav-Adolf's battle, wrapping the rat's remains in a discarded plastic bag. At Humphrey's suggestion, he lifted him, chair and all, and lowered him gently back into the jar. The fluid in it was vaguely fragrant, and he was surprised to find that, though it undoubtedly was a fluid, it actually wet neither Humphrey nor his own hands. After Gustav-Adolf jumped up on his shoulder, he carried the jar out to the corridor, put it down, and with his locksmith's tools, locked the door again. Then he picked up the jar and the packaged rat, and in a matter of minutes, observed by no one, they were all back in his own quarters.

He lifted Humphrey out again, set him on a table by the fireplace, and sat down next to him. "You are indeed a good and very great magician!" piped Humphrey, his tiny eyes fastened on the cuckoo watch. "And I am grateful beyond measure for the refuge you are providing me. But now, tell me, sir, what it is that *you* want from *me?* We homunculi are but feeble creatures, even in our youth, and I, as you know, am very old and tired. Were it not for the nutrient fluid which I dare not leave for more than an hour or so a day, I would not be long for this world. So I do pray you, do not ask of me that which would exhaust me utterly."

"But Herr Hum-uncle-us," replied Papa Schimmelhorn in puzzlement, "I do nodt vant *anything* from you."

"What?" Humphrey touched him with a minuscule hand. "Your goodness is beyond belief! All magicians want *something* from us."

"I am *nodt* a machician," said Papa Schimmelhorn. "I am chust a chenius who makes cuckoo clocks und vatches and sometimes antigrafity und time machines."

"Then I must reward you without your asking. Benevolent Genius, if that is what you declare you are, having listened to Gansfleisch and his fiend, I have learned what they have done to you. Be not deceived! Your sudden impotence was not the work of Fate. Indeed not! It was a

work of malice. Gansfleisch himself suggested it to the
Princess in her wrath, and it was he that very night who
compounded the prescription she gave him, which next
morning was administered to you. Oh, I have heard him
gloating about it with his fiend, telling how he also made
up the antidote, now in her possession, which she has
sworn to withhold from you!"

Papa Schimmelhorn groaned sepulchrally. The knowledge that there was an antidote, a substance that would
restore his full functioning, but that it was permanently
and probably irrevocably denied to him, suddenly made
his sad state even sadder.

"But—but Herr Humphrey, *you* do not have this antidote vhich puts der lead back inside der pencil?" he asked
hopelessly.

The homunculus touched his hand again. "No, Master
Schimmelhorn, I do not have it. But I believe I can do
even better for you. I can convey to you the secret of the
world's most powerful love potion, one confected by Count
Cagliostro for Augustus the Strong, Elector of Saxony and
King of Poland—the very same potion which enabled him
to prevail over the mothers of his three hundred and fifty-
two acknowledged bastard children. It is most simple to
compound, and I doubt not all its ingredients can be found
among Meister Gansfleisch's substances. Aye, simple as it
is, it is most subtle and efficacious. It need not be swallowed, nor administered in food or drink. It hath no odor.
A gentle spray under the nose of the intended lover or
intended mistress—that is enough. It is instantly volatile.
I shall whisper it in your ear. A single breath, and the
Princess shall at once be your slave. In all the world, you
alone shall exist for her! Stricken by conscience, begging
for forgiveness, she'll bring the antidote to you. Oh, she
will play a pretty Titania to your Bottom, I warrant you!"

"*Ach*, die Greek customs I do nodt know about," said
Papa Schimmelhorn suspiciously.

"It is but a figure of speech," Humphrey told him,
"from a play of Master Will's. But now I weary. Lean
forward to me so I may whisper it. . . ."

Papa Schimmelhorn leaned forward obediently, and Humphrey stood on tiptoe to reach his ear. He whispered the formula. Three times he repeated it. "Remember," he said urgently, "its power is incalculable. The last ingredient especially must *only* be added just before you tightly seal the bottle. And you yourself must never breathe a bit of it. Use it when you and the Princess are quite alone, or at least when she looks directly at you, for she will be affected even as a new-hatched gosling is upon emerging from the egg!"

Papa Schimmelhorn promised him that he'd exercise the utmost care, thanked him from the bottom of his heart, restored him tenderly to his jar, and secreted it safely in the compartment.

Then he hastened down to the laboratory and set immediately to work.

Hope welled within his breast, but he controlled himself. He first made sure that the former Twitchgibbet had been completely incinerated in the hottest of Meister Gansfleisch's several furnaces and the ashes flushed tidily down the john. Then, eagerly, he searched the alchemist's shelves and cupboards for the substances Humphrey had specified. In a few minutes he found every one of them. Excitedly, he poured and weighed, mixed and measured. Some of the substances clearly were organic and of dubious origin; others were mineral; one or two of them fumed and sizzled when they were brought together. Finally, his vial held about a jiggerful, looking disappointingly thick and grayish-green, to which Humphrey had warned him he was not to add more than one drop of the final ingredient, a thin, purplish fluid in a pipette.

For a few moments, he contemplated it, holding the pipette over the vial with his right hand, the vial's special cork in his left. *So Herr Humphrey said vun drop only*, he thought, *und maybe he iss right. But he iss so shmall, maybe he thinks vun drop iss bedter for hum-uncle-usses. Die Prinzessin iss maybe nodt as tall as Mama, but she iss a big girl. . . .*

Deciding to take no chances, he held his breath, added three drops as quickly as he could, and clapped the cork in. To his amazement, he saw that the fluid in the vial was no longer murky; instead, it was crystal-clear. He stared at it, and his infallible subconscious spoke to him. "Papa," it declared, "dot shtuff vill vork! Predty soon—ho-ho-ho! —der lead iss back inside der pencil chust like old times."

He was so inspired by the thought that he stayed in the laboratory until dinnertime, working at various parts and pieces of his gold-making machine and letting his fancy wander once again among the pretty pussycats he had known in years gone by and the many more he now could hope to know in the years to come, and every once in a while he even thought about the Princess.

At dinner, Niki and Emmy found him so much like his old self that at first they thought he had already been miraculously restored and tried to tempt him into bed. But he was forced to make it known that nothing of the sort had happened, and to urge them to take a walk down to the village as they had planned, so that some of the local youths—he made a great show of sighing—could show them the more picturesque of Little Palaeon's ruins by moonlight.

He returned their parting kisses; he gave each of them a grandfatherly embrace; he told them nodt to do anything he vouldn't do. Then, as soon as he was sure of their departure, he took Humphrey's jar out of the compartment, and lifted him out again.

"Ah, Master Schimmelhorn," said the homunculus when he had awakened fully, "were you able to decoct the potion?"

Papa Schimmelhorn took the vial out of his pocket and showed it to him.

"And it is well and truly sealed?"

"*Ja gewiss.*"

"And you were careful not to add more than the small portion of the last ingredient, as I did warn you?"

Untruthfully, Papa Schimmelhorn informed him that he

had added one drop only. "But now I haff der problem," he went on. "Die Prinzessin hates me. How can I fix so she und I are all alone? Oder so ve are close togeder und she looks only at me vhen she shniffs der potion?"

Humphrey's tiny brow wrinkled in thought. "Have you no friends within this castle?" he asked. "I have heard Gansfleisch speak of a Grecian named Mavronides, whom he dislikes and who is reputed to have great influence with the Princess."

"*Ja*, dot iss Herr Sarpedon Mavronides, der major-domo, only I call him Zorba. He vas mein friend until I chase her. Since then, he iss angry vith me, und does nodt shpeak. Also iss Ismail, whom die Arabs shnip vhen he iss a lidtle boy so he vorks in der harem."

Humphrey nodded. "And how are your enquiries now progressing? Have you reached the point where you can turn even a flake of sullen lead into bright gold? In my experience, such a successful issue could plead more forcefully for you than any appeal to mercy or sweet reason, for gold can swiftly change the minds of princes and princesses. Were I you, Master Schimmelhorn, I would repair directly to this Sarpedon, inform him that you're on the very verge of the result she wishes, then tell him that you yourself are deeply conscience-stricken, and full of sincere shame for your despicable assault upon her royal person"—he looked up with the tiniest of winks—"and that your whole desire is to most humbly beg her august pardon."

"Goot, goot! Herr Humphrey, you are a shmart hum-uncle-us. I try it. Nodt tonight, but tomorrow after vork vhen Herr Zorba goes around making die inspections. Somehow ve make it vork."

After that, they conversed for an hour or so. Papa Schimmelhorn learned that, aside from the nutrient fluid in the jar, which needed replacement only once every hundred years, Humphrey required no more than a thimbleful of fine brandy and honey every day, which Papa assured him he would provide as soon as possible. He learned, too, that the homunculus was thoroughly tired of his long existence, and that he yearned to revert once more to his proper state as a free spirit, but that the artificially grown body in which he had been trapped held him fast by means magical—so much so that even if it were to die, he would still remain bound to it until it was utterly destroyed. This had given necromancers and thaumaturgists almost unlimited power over him. Only one other way could he be set free, and that was to escape the pull of Earth and reach deep space, which had been his erstwhile habitat.

Papa Schimmelhorn listened to him with intense interest, murmuring sympathetically. "*Ach*," he muttered, "iss too bad die big vomen from Beetlegoose are nodt around, because they haff shpace ships und vould maybe giff you a free ride. But do nodt vorry. Chust leafe it up to Papa Schimmelhorn. I am shtupid in der IQ, but in der subconscience I am a chenius. Somehow I fix."

Then until Humphrey, tiring, had to be lifted back into his jar, he told him stories about how he and Mama and Gustav-Adolf had been kidnapped by huge spacefaring female chauvinists from the ninth planet of a star Mama had christened Beetlegoose. He told of their adventures getting there and back, and described a few of the extraordinary inhabitants of other planetary systems the big women had encountered in their travels. Indulging in no false modesty, he of course related how he himself had saved the Beetlegoosers from being an endangered species.

And Humphrey, as he said good night, cried out in wonderment, and remarked that surely Master Schimmelhorn's voyagings had been more remarkable by far than even those of Sir John Mandeville.

VII.

Love Story

All next day, Papa Schimmelhorn labored happily and hopefully in the laboratory, rejoicing in the turn of events and in Meister Gansfleisch's continued absence. His first order of business—while holding his breath very, very carefully—was to prepare a tiny plastic ampule of the love potion, one that could be snapped instantly and inconspicuously between two fingers when the time came. Then, with renewed enthusiasm, he finished constructing the complex base on which his crystal would be mounted, and began preparing the curious assortment of gadgets he had accumulated. By now he knew exactly where the stuff that Meister Gansfleisch was off purchasing would go, from whence it would draw its power, and—in a vague and general way—how the enormous forces he was going to generate would function.

He worked almost without pausing, chuckling occasionally to himself when his subconscious showed him mental pictures of the phenomena that would occur and of the alchemist's reaction to them. "Ho-ho-ho!" he chuckled. "Chust vait till Meister Gassi sees der purple ray und hears der moaning—" He amused himself by providing appropriate sound effects. "Und all die gears shcraping, und in der air die electricities. Maybe he thinks der Defil has come for him because iss no more Tvitchgibbet!"

99

He knocked off at midafternoon, having done everything that could be done prior to the arrival of his new equipment, and went back to his own quarters. There he found that Niki and Emmy, faithfully, had brought him a small brandy bottle and a jar of honey from the village, and had left them for him, together with two ham-and-cheese sandwiches. So he fetched Humphrey out again, and they enjoyed a light lunch together, conversing pleasantly and optimistically, Humphrey assuring him that never since the eighteenth century, when he had stayed for a few months with the celebrated Count de St. Germain, the inventor of the potion, had he enjoyed such pleasant and learned company.

"Und now, Herr Humphrey," Papa Schimmelhorn declared, lifting him carefully back into his jar, "I do vot you haff said, und find Herr Zorba, und tell him how I am sorry I vas such a *schwein*, and maybe I can kiss der foot of die Prinzessin und make apologies und promise I vill nefer be so bad again." He exhibited the little ampule. "Und maybe vhen she gets here I also haff der gold I make from lead to show her."

"And at that point," Humphrey chirped, "you will break your little glass under her pretty nose, and—and— Oh, how I do wish I could be there to see it! Aye, forsooth, and to see the look on that vile Gansfleisch's ugly face when he finds out that she's in love with you!"

Papa Schimmelhorn promised to report everything to him promptly and in detail, and wandered off to seek out Mavronides, whom he found superintending gardeners in the castle courtyard.

Mavronides regarded him sadly and disapprovingly, and at first, when Papa Schimmelhorn asked him in all humility if he could speak with him in private, he made no answer. However, when the request was repeated most politely, he nodded curtly, and gestured to his onetime friend to follow him. Under a shaded portico, he halted. "Herr Schimmelhorn," he said, "you have been my friend, and to you I still am in debt for saving my dear grandson's life. But you have offended greatly. Believe me, I would sooner fight the Mino—'' He broke off in midword. ''Never mind. It is enough to say that I would sacrifice my life before I would even contemplate a deed like yours.''

Papa Schimmelhorn hung his head in shame; he shuffled his feet in what was obviously deep embarrassment; he stated fervently that his conscience had given him no peace, that his tormented nights had been haunted by dark dreams of his unworthiness and of divine punishment. He swore passionately that he realized the depths of his iniquity and that there was no real way to make amends—that even all the gold he now knew he would be able to produce could not atone for the offense he had committed. His sole desire was to see the Princess, bend his knee to her, and make his crude but sincerely heartfelt apology.

Sarpedon Mavronides frowned. ''You are *certain* now that you can make lead into gold?'' he asked.

Papa Schimmelhorn vowed that it was indeed so, that probably on the morrow he would be able to finish the machine, that after that it would simply be a matter of hours before the first gold was produced.

For a moment, Mavronides was silent, sunk in thought. Then, ''Perhaps that may have some influence,'' he said. ''I know the Princess never wil! forgive you, but she is gracious—possibly she will condescend to let you make apology. At any rate, when she returns I shall intercede for you.''

Saying no more, he turned back to his gardeners, and Papa Schimmelhorn returned to his apartment to tell Humphrey all about it.

It was nearly midnight a day later when Meister Gansfleisch returned home. Followed by Ismail and another servant carrying Papa Schimmelhorn's packages and boxes, he went directly to his laboratory, ordered them to put everything down outside the door, and waited until they'd gone before he dragged the stuff inside. He glanced hastily around, observed that Papa Schimmelhorn had indeed been working hard, cackled at the very satisfying thought that this was because he now was incapable of other, less arcane pursuits, then hurried as fast as his legs would carry him up to his turret.

He unlocked the door. He entered, turning on the light. Everything seemed in order, yet instantly he sensed that everything was not. Something definitely was missing. He frowned nervously. He looked around again, apprehensively—and suddenly it came to him.

Twitchgibbet, the ever-present, was nowhere in sight.

He stamped his foot. "Show thyself, rat-fiend!" he commanded.

There was no answering squeak, no responsive scurrying. There was only silence.

"*Show thyself!*" he cried out shrilly. "Appear! By all the Powers of Darkness"—he named several of the more prestigious ones—"I conjure you! Appear at once!"

And, in the dead stillness that answered him, he looked around and saw that not only Twitchgibbet had disappeared—so had Humphrey the homunculus. And so had Humphrey's jar.

The alchemist was frantic. He scuttled round his rooms, examining each window, every door. Everything was exactly as he'd left it. He searched every nook and cranny, every cabinet and closet. He moved books out of their cases and tore his bed apart. For half an hour, he turned everything upside-down before he realized that nothing had been hidden, nothing disturbed. His treasures were intact: the ancient books, the bronze key to one of the seven forbidden doors to the Labyrinth. His mind tossed him vagrant thoughts, wild speculations: Papa Schimmelhorn and his tomcat had somehow broken in, stolen his familiar and his Humphrey, and evaporated. That notion was too ridiculous even to entertain—Twitchgibbet had made mincemeat out of too many cats. Or perhaps the Princess had ordered their removal to render him less powerful? Or could Twitchgibbet himself have defected to the enemy? No, no—for Twitchgibbet was bound to him by contract.

Then a new idea hit him right between the eyes, an idea that had already occurred to Papa Schimmelhorn.

He sat down, remembering how he had defied the Powers from whom he had secured his familiar, how he had announced that any thaumaturge as capable as he could do without their help, how contemptuously he had canceled out the deed of sale he had been about to consummate.

Obviously, that was it. Twitchgibbet had quite simply been repossessed, and Humphrey had been spirited away with him to punish the man who had dared to flout Hell itself. Come to think of it, there *was* a distinct scent of sulphur and brimstone in the air. It was a frightening and a curiously satisfying thought. Clearly, it meant that Twitch-gibbet's management did not undervalue Meister Gansfleisch. As for the loss of the homunculus, Humphrey had never been of any great assistance to him, having made it clear that he disapproved of almost all the Gansfleisch projects.

Still shaken, but with his self-esteem restored, he prepared to go to bed, first carefully drawing several potent diagrams and intoning any number of efficacious protective spells against any of Twitchgibbet's associates who might just possibly come visiting. He drifted off to sleep, making plans for what steps to take if Papa Schimmelhorn did indeed, against all probability, succeed in the quest he had undertaken—how he might claim credit for it, how he might get his unwelcome colleague out of the way completely. Dreaming, he smiled in his sleep. He was sitting on a toadstool, and a perfectly beautiful fairy godmother touched him with her wand, and instantly he turned into the handsomest of princes. And there was the Fräulein-Princess-Priestess opening her arms to him. . . .

Papa Schimmelhorn had spent the day largely in luxurious idleness. He had gone once to the laboratory to check on things and make a few last-minute adjustments, he had played hide-and-seek with Gustav-Adolf on the battlements, and after lunch he and Humphrey had had an informative and very pleasant chat during which he had been given a great deal of background material—all distinctly nasty—regarding Meister Gansfleisch. He had promised Humphrey on no account to trust the alchemist, to take suitable precautions against spells and poisons, and to be especially careful after he had administered the potion to the Princess. "For you see, good Master Schimmelhorn," declared Humphrey, "the foul creature is mad for her himself, and when he learns that she's in love with you—as, mark my words, she will be!—he'll stop at nothing to destroy you. Aye, and her too, and the very world itself if need be!"

The idea of Gaspar Gansfleisch harboring such a passion in his bony bosom seemed supremely ludicrous to Papa Schimmelhorn, and he said so, shaking his head in wonderment. He actually began to feel a little sorry for the alchemist—something Humphrey's quick eye detected instantly. Then, after being warned solemnly not to give in to so noble a sentiment, he played a game of chess with the homunculus, ending in a friendly stalemate. Finally, after supper, he had gone for a long swim with his pussycats, who were nice enough to say that, even in his present sorry state, they much preferred him to the young men of Little Palaeon. He retired early and slept soundly, waking only occasionally to worry over whether the potion would work or not, whether he'd be able to administer it successfully, and—most important—whether it would affect the Fräulein strongly enough to ensure her administration of the antidote. Then he would wonder whether he had indeed put in enough of the final and critical ingredient, fret about it for a moment, and go to sleep again.

Had he known that during the evening Sarpedon Mavronides had phoned the Fräulein, reported his alleged pangs of conscience, and announced that the long-sought transmutation was about to be achieved, he would have fretted even more, for she had declared unequivocally that, though she would return to witness the triumphant process and would consent to hear his servile apology, under no circumstances would she pardon his transgression. *He'll have the antidote*, she told herself, *but not until he's a long, long way from Little Palaeon, and then*—she smiled thinly—*I'll turn it over to that wife of his.*

Knowing nothing of all this, Papa Schimmelhorn hastened down to the laboratory right after breakfast, and found that Meister Gansfleisch, looking much the worse for wear, had preceded him. *Ho-ho! Meister Gassi!* he thought. *So during der night you haff come back und found oudt about Tvitchgibbet und der hum-uncle-us! Und maybe sometime ve find oudt if you think der Defil comes for them. Vell, so long you do nodt blame Gustav-Adolf, iss all right.*

He greeted his colleague boisterously, slapped him on the back, and made coarse jokes about the pretty pussycats in Athens. The alchemist was doing his very best to pretend that nothing had gone wrong. He squeezed out one or two sour smiles, tried to control the nervous twisting of his hands, and insisted on going over the Schimmelhorn shopping list and checking it against his purchases.

Everything, Papa Schimmelhorn informed him, was in order; and at once he set to work, installing batteries, generators, Tesla coils; starting appalling flows of current into the now-roiling fluids around the crystal; meshing gears which, to the untutored eye, appeared to serve no purpose whatsoever; and rapidly bringing into being a device that looked as though it had been dreamed up by Dali and Picasso in cahoots with Enrico Fermi, Eli Whitney, and Thomas Alva Edison. At two o'clock, he announced that the crystal had matured, and with Meister Gansfleisch's reluctant help, lifted it from its tank, dried it off, and nestled it into its gears and terminals. It was many-faceted, multi-particulate, and resembled a tesseract with delirium tremens. The fact that it continued to vibrate, moan gently, and give off a pulsating blue light did nothing to soothe the jangled Gansfleisch nerves.

Papa Schimmelhorn soldered-in the old shoe-shop X-ray machine, made any number of additional connections, some of wire and some of plumbing, and announced that they were all set to go. There was a large dial, calibrated from 0 to 100, and this he carefully set at 12.5. He pushed a dramatically red button. The motors screamed; the gears scraped threateningly; vicious lightnings slashed and thundered over the quivering Tesla coils—and suddenly the blue light from the crystal concentrated itself into a three-inch-square beam, turned darkly purple, and—moaning horrendously—focused on a slightly raised ceramic platform squarely beneath the crystal.

"*Ach!*" shouted Papa Schimmelhorn. "How beaudtiful! Maybe it iss a laser? I vish I undershtood!"

He pushed another button, and turned it off.

Filled with fear and excitement, the alchemist was squirming back and forth. "Herr Schimmelhorn! Herr Schimmelhorn!" he screeched. "Is it possible? Will it really work? Will this—this *thing* really turn lead into gold?"

"*Natürlich,*" replied Papa Schimmelhorn. "Meister Gassi, how many times I tell you? I am a chenius."

"Well, let's *try* it then!" Meister Gansfleisch croaked. "Immediately! At once! We must be sure before we show it to the Princess! Think how disappointed she would be—"

Under the on-off buttons, there was a keyhole from which a small key protruded. Papa Schimmelhorn turned this and withdrew it. "Ve do nodt need to try," he said. "Already I haff told you it vill vork." He filed the key away in a shirt pocket. "Und now I haff turned off der ignition so no vun can shtart und perhaps get hurt. Ve vait until comes back die Prinzessin."

The machine's pyrotechnics died down slowly; its noises dwindled; the solid purple ray dissipated, turning pale blue again. Only the crystal still seemed to be alive.

Meister Gansfleisch, who had fully intended to sneak back into the laboratory as soon as Papa Schimmelhorn was safely out of it, to try it out himself, felt that his mind had treacherously been read. Silently vowing vengeance, he pretended to restrain himself, letting his hands fight each other behind his back, gnashing his teeth very much as Twitchgibbet had done, and covering it all up with a tortured grin. He even answered Papa Schimmelhorn's *bye-bye*, and contented himself with glaring daggers at his broad retreating back. Then he hastened off to give Mavronides a horrifying description of the fiendish device that had been brought into being, stated that in his opinion— though he fervently hoped it would indeed make gold—as much care should be taken with it as with a nuclear power plant, and shivered verbally at the thought that it might endanger the ecology and pollute the pure air of Little Palaeon.

Mavronides, of course, immediately got on the phone to the Fräulein, gave her a rundown on the alchemist's report, agreed with her that without doubt it was biased, and was informed that she would arrive back on her island on the following day.

At suppertime, he himself conveyed the news to Papa Schimmelhorn, advising him to appear as abject as he could and to wear his best bib and tucker on the morrow, and rather gloomily wished him well.

"Pray to the Gods that your machine will really work," he said, "for then your chances of—well, of escaping without punishment may be much better. I also shall pray for you."

"Punishment? How? Efen if she iss die Prinzessin, shtill she iss a Shviss banker, und cifilized."

Mavronides laughed a hollow laugh. "In Switzerland, she is a banker, true. But I have told you—here on Little Palaeon, because she is the Princess and the Priestess, she has powers of life and death. Not even the authorities in Crète dare to interfere."

Later, at the first opportunity, Papa Schimmelhorn talked it over with Humphrey, who informed him that, though he had overheard few details of the island's secrets, what he had heard indicated that they were ancient, dark, cruel, and often bloody. He advised his friend to walk very carefully, to take no unnecessary risks, especially where good manners were concerned, and to be sure to use the love potion exactly as he had been instructed to. Papa Schimmelhorn, though he did not pray to the Gods as Mavronides had suggested, did thank his subconscious and his lucky stars that he had had the forethought to fortify the potion.

The Fräulein-Princess-Priestess Philippa Theophrastra Paleologus Bombast von Hohenheim reached her domain shortly after noon the following day, and was escorted to her apartments by Sarpedon Mavronides, a groveling Meister Gansfleisch, and a retinue of servants. Assisted by her handmaidens, she arrayed herself in court costume for her formal greeting to her subjects in the Throne Room, to which neither Papa Schimmelhorn nor his two pussycats were invited. When the ceremony was over, she stood up regally, her tresses shining under the great jewels of her tiara, her figure splendid under its pearls and cobalt blue.

"Have the man Schimmelhorn taken to the laboratory!" she commanded coldly. "We shall see what he has or has not accomplished."

She ignored Meister Gansfleisch's protest that the presence of the machine's inventor would be quite unnecessary, that he himself could operate it just as well if Schimmelhorn were forced to deliver up the key; and two footmen were despatched to fetch the genius from his turret.

The Fräulein did not hasten. She gave them ample time to complete the errand, and even more time for him to worry about the encounter. Finally, attended only by Mavronides and the alchemist, who was bowing and scraping at her side, she made her way to the laboratory. At the door, she stood aside so that the alchemist could open it. She dismissed the footmen. She entered.

Papa Schimmelhorn stood next to his machine. Seeing her, he dropped down on one knee, hung his head, and mumbled, "Serene Highness, Serene Highness!" sorrowfully.

"Tell the man to rise," she ordered.

"Stand up, Herr Schimmelhorn," commanded Mavronides.

Papa Schimmelhorn came to his feet, and Meister Gansfleisch bustled up from behind him, pushing him aside, and fishing in the pocket of his robe. "See, Your Highness! See what I have for you!" Eagerly, he held out a small, big-bosomed, big-bottomed, snake-entangled lead statuette. "It is ancient, Your Highness. It is your own Serpent Goddess! I have chosen it *especially*. It is *symbolical!*"

She brushed him off. "I suppose it will do as well as anything," she said, and indicated Papa Schimmelhorn. "Give it to him!"

Angrily, running his dry tongue around his twisting lips, Meister Gansfleisch did as he was ordered.

Papa Schimmelhorn received the tiny figure. He placed it squarely in the center of the ceramic plate.

She gestured to Mavronides. "Have the machine turned on," she said.

Papa Schimmelhorn pushed the big red button. The motors screamed; the gears screeched against each other; flashes and glowing balls of lightning rent the air; the blue ray darkened, turned a savage purple, and, moaning hideously, drowned the statuette in its dark light.

Mavronides took a quick step backward, making a protective sign. Meister Gansfleisch squirmed aside. Only Papa Schimmelhorn and the Princess held their ground.

For five full minutes, during which he stood with his eyes fixed on his cuckoo watch, the sound and fury maintained their crescendo. No one could hear the small voice of the cuckoo when the time came. He pushed the off-button. Gradually, the purple ray thinned and paled; the din subsided; the electrical discharges died away.

The statuette was still there on the plate. It had not moved. But it was no longer dull and leaden. It gleamed. There was no doubt, no doubt at all, that it was now of purest gold.

Papa Schimmelhorn picked it up. Holding it cupped

reverently in his two hands, a votive offering, he turned toward the Princess, scarcely a foot away. With an effort— for her astounding cleavage drew them like a magnet—he raised his eyes to hers.

"Serene Highness," he whispered, "der gold iss yours!"

And simultaneously, his sly right thumb crushed the tiny ampule. For a moment, he held his breath. . . .

Suddenly, the pupils of her great eyes widened; suddenly, her entire expression underwent a sea-change; suddenly, it no longer resembled any expression he had seen before.

But she was not staring at the statuette. Her gaze was fixed on Papa Schimmelhorn himself.

She accepted the golden object without even looking at it; and when she spoke her voice was slow, and very gentle, and wonderfully melodious. "You have done well," she murmured. "You have done *very* well. . . ."

"Yes, yes, indeed we have!" chattered Meister Gansfleisch. "You can't imagine how hard I've worked. You—"

She did not even look at him. "Sarpedon," she said, "tell this—this creature to go away. He can come back and make his usual stinks and messes some other time."

She waited while Mavronides, none too gently, hustled him to the door.

"And now," she added, "I shall repair to my own apartments. I have much to—to think about. In one hour, send Herr Schimmelhorn up to me."

What had happened to Fräulein von Hohenheim had been so abrupt, so overwhelmingly complete, that she could hardly remember or believe the state of mind that had preceded it. There before her stood Papa Schimmelhorn, whom suddenly she knew she had never really seen before; and gazing at him thus for the first time, she realized that previously she had never even known herself. How could she have believed throughout her adult life that she passionately hated men when, in actuality, she now knew, she had hated only the contemptible inadequacy of all those whom she had encountered. She, Swiss banker, Princess-Priestess, sacred guardian of even more sacred mysteries, temporal ruler of this ancient isle, spiritual shepherd of its populace! A woman of such powers and attainments—and almost terrifyingly beautiful, besides—needed no ordinary man. What her soul secretly demanded, what it had always secretly yearned for, was a hero—a hero in the classic mold. And there he stood before her, bearded like Zeus, tall as a Titan, thewed like Hercules, as old as Priam but still with all the vigor of his youth, all the noble simplicity of his Homeric passions!

Gods! she thought. *What have I done? What have I done to him?* Turning to Mavronides, she gave him her instructions, and doing her best to hide her inner turmoil swept out of the laboratory and hastened to her chambers, where swiftly she called Niobe to her, divested herself of her Borgian panoply, donned a chaste peignoir of gold lamé, let free her glorious hair. Parting its canopies, she knelt beside her great four-poster bed and kissed its pillows, its coverlets.

She ran into the salon again, found Niobe staring at her open-mouthed. "Don't just gape, child!" she exclaimed. "Fetch me a fine white wine, the very finest, properly chilled! Fetch two stemmed glasses—the best crystal—to drink it from. Then get Ismail for me. I shall prepare the menu for a banquet—ah, how we'll feast tonight!—and Ismail shall serve it to us here; he knows the proper etiquette. Be sure the table's set for two. Oh, but *of course*—I haven't told you! Today, Niobe, my eyes were opened. The Gods have spoken. For the first time, today, I recognized Herr Schimmelhorn for what he is. He's an Olympian! Such men have not existed since heroic times. Now hurry, hurry, hurry!"

She busied herself excitedly, setting a small table next to the chaise longue: two crystal goblets, two small damask napkins, and finally—with trembling hands—a little vial containing the antidote prepared by Meister Gansfleisch. Ismail came, all bows and smiles, having heard from

Niobe about her transformation, and he received her banquet menu for transmission to the chef.

When all was ready, she tried to settle down and wait with all the dignity befitting a Princess. She could not. She paced around the room, into the bedroom to the mirror; she smoothed the bedclothes with a smile.

Finally, precisely on the hour, she heard Mavronides's discreet knock on her door.

As Niobe opened it, Mavronides whispered, "Soon you will know your fate!" in Papa Schimmelhorn's ear. "I do not think the Princess is now *very* angry, but still you must remember to be truly abject, truly penitent."

"The Princess wishes you to come to her alone, Herr Schimmelhorn," Niobe said; and she accompanied Mavronides as, bowing, he turned away, waiting only long enough to give Papa Schimmelhorn a gentle shove and close the door behind him.

Papa Schimmelhorn advanced hesitantly into the room, eyes down, a properly penitent expression on his face. So preoccupied was he with being appropriately abject that he did not even see the Fräulein's features. Slowly, he advanced toward her. At her feet, rather clumsily, he knelt. "*Küss die hand*, er, Serene Highness," he began. "*Ach*, I vant to make der apology—dot iss—"

He broke off. Standing there, she had extended her two hands to him.

"It is not you who should apologize, mein Herr!" she murmured passionately. "It is *I*! To think what I have *done* to you! But come, take my hands! Stand here a moment with me. I shall make amends. . . ."

He took her hands, a little apprehensively.

"It was just that I did not recognize you for what you truly are. All my life I, the Priestess of the Minotaur, have waited for a hero—an Achilles, an Odysseus, a Theseus! You came—and I did not know you. I have done you a grave injustice. It was unforgivable. But fortunately—ah, how fortunately!—it is reversible. We shall drink wine together, and in minutes you shall be restored!"

Papa Schimmelhorn came to his feet. He looked down into her eyes. They were no longer icy wells that could swallow sacrificial virgins; instead they were deep, warm glowing pools in which a lover happily could drown himself.

She seated him. With her own hands she poured the wine, and—as she added the antidote to his—she kissed him on the lips. She sat down next to him, and raised her glass.

"My Prince!" she whispered. "My love! I have waited much too long for you."

They drank, and looked into each other's eyes, and drank again; and Papa Schimmelhorn, having experienced one astonishment after another, and only now realizing just how effective Humphrey's love potion had really been, found himself almost tongue-tied. He felt familiar electric currents surging through him. He stared admiringly at the Princess. "*Ach Gott!*" he cried. "*How beaudtiful!*" Then, "Down der hatch!" he shouted, and drained his glass.

She laughed a girlish laugh at his simplicity. She took him by the hand. She led him to the bedroom; seated him on the edge of the great bed.

Very slowly, she turned around before him. She came toward him.

"And now, my Prince," she ordered. "Undress me!"

Just as he always had, Papa Schimmelhorn rose to the occasion.

It is not surprising, considering the dreadful shock of his sudden deprivation, the stark misery of having to endure it, and the overwhelming rapture of an instant and complete recovery, that the afternoon passed joyously and tumultuously for Papa Schimmelhorn. Nor, considering that in all her life she had never before plumbed the wellsprings of her own passion nor found an object worthy of it, is it at all astonishing that the Fräulein revelled quite as enthusiastically in him and in her newfound self.

In his time, he had made love to any number of pretty pussycats, of all sizes and complexions, temperaments and aptitudes, some simpering and bashful and inexperienced, others bold as brass and as experienced as motel mattresses. Philippa Theophrastra Paleologus Bombast von Hohenheim was something else again, and had he been in any condition to think clearly he might, even then, have realized that he was in bed, symbolically, not with a pretty pussycat at all, but with a very much larger and thoroughly untamed member of the same general species. The Princess was, to put it mildly, a tigress—a lovely tigress, a sweet tigress, an ardently loving tigress, but a tigress nonetheless—and one who had been given a mighty overdose of what was beyond doubt the most effective love potion in all history. However, in his innocence, Papa Schimmelhorn simply assumed that she was a superpussycat, congratulated himself on his good fortune, and made the very best of his opportunity.

Their conversation, throughout the afternoon, was fragmentary—brief expressions of mutual desire, mutual surrender, mutual conquest, unimportant grace notes to the unvoiced but stormier music they were making.

Finally, as the afternoon waned and suppertime approached, at her suggestion they bathed luxuriously together, and she, radiant now, reassumed her gold peignoir and brought him a splendid brocade dressing gown, made a century and a half before for a world-renowned ancestor, which she declared only enhanced his royal bearing and heroic stature. Niobe, summoned, brought them another bottle of cool white wine, and over it they conversed lightly, the conversation of new and eager lovers, in which words seem almost meaningless and sentiment governs absolutely.

Papa Schimmelhorn, thoroughly bedazzled, paid little heed to what she said. She spoke of secrets underneath the earth, secrets she would eventually reveal to him. She told of ancient mysteries and ceremonies in which no one shared but her loyal subjects on Little Palaeon, of snake goddesses and priestesses, of youths and maidens bull-dancing laughingly, dangerously, of how little the foolish

archeologists who had excavated Knossos on the main
island really knew about the history and the myths of
Crete. But also she sang love songs to him, pausing occasionally to offer him her wine glass and to kiss him
caressingly.

Suddenly she sighed. "My love, my love!" she cried.
"I have been enraptured, ensorcelled! But I must not forget—
you yourself must not allow me to forget—that I have
duties! Before we banquet, I must see Sarpedon and give
him his instructions for the household. He is the most
faithful of my servants, and would be injured were I to fail
him. Besides"—she kissed him once again—"I must tell
him about *us*, so that he too can rejoice and begin planning
proper celebrations. So dress yourself, my adored, for you
have duties too."

"*Ja*," replied Papa Schimmelhorn regretfully. "I must
go back und feed mein Gustav-Adolf. He iss a brafe cat.
No oder cat could haff killed dot Tvitchgibbet."

For a second, doubt assailed him—should he have
mentioned it? But she only laughed delightedly. "Killed
Twitchgibbet?" she exclaimed. "No wonder Gaspar
Gansfleisch looked so sour today when you made gold for
me. Go! Feed your cat quickly, then hurry back and tell
me all about it, how we're rid of that disgusting rat at
last!"

"I vill hurry, Serene Highness—"

Immediately, she shushed him, touching a finger to his
lips. "How can *you* call me that? I told you—you are
my Prince. To you I must always be Philippa, or your
love, your darling—oh, call me what you will, as long as I
am yours!"

"Okay, shveetheart," said Papa Schimmelhorn, pulling
on his pants. "I vill hurry und feed Gustav-Adolf, und
maybe chanche der catbox, und tell my pussycats tonight I
don'dt come back."

For just an instant, her eyes narrowed. Then she laughed,
the sort of laugh Hera might have uttered on hearing of
Zeus's extra-Olympian escapades; and she made a mental

note to add one more instruction to those she was preparing for Sarpedon Mavronides.

Once more they kissed, and he hurried back to his apartment, finding to his relief that Niki and Emmy were away. Only Gustav-Adolf greeted him, and with no enthusiasm. "Where ya been, chum?" he growled in Cat. "No, ya don't hafta tell me." He sniffed. "As if I didn't know! And me up here alone without even a pretty little tortoise-shell to play with. Huh! If that's all the thanks I get, you can bite yer own goddam rats from now on!"

Papa Schimmelhorn did his best to soothe him, told him again what a splendidly heroic cat he was, and explained that the Princess herself would eventually come and pet him and tell him so. Then he fed him an enormous helping of raw liver, freshened his catbox, and brought Humphrey out of the compartment.

The homunculus was all agog to hear about the working of the potion. He leaned forward eagerly in his small chair as his huge friend gave him an only slightly expurgated, almost blow-by-blow account of what had happened, clapping his little hands at the news of the making of the gold and Meister Gansfleisch's discomfiture, and literally jumping up and down when Papa Schimmelhorn described how he had snapped the ampule under the Princess's nose. However, as the narrative progressed from laboratory to salon, and from salon to bedroom and to bed, he began exhibiting signs of distinct disquiet. Finally, when the raconteur reached a momentary lull between bouts of love-making, he interjected a worried query.

"Forgive me, good Master Schimmelhorn," said he, "but just how *many* drops of the last ingredient did you put into the potion?"

"Vhy, three," replied Papa Schimmelhorn cheerfully. "Because die Prinzessin iss nodt lidtle like a girl hum-uncle-us, I giff her more."

" '*Od's blood!*" cried Humphrey. "Fair sir, 'tis a wonder she survived it! 'Twas enough—aye, and more—to bring poor dead Cleopatra back to life! Pray do take care, for now there's no telling *what* she'll do, of that I do most fervently assure you! I tremble at the very thought. And, for the love of God, tell no one about me—not even her—oh, most especially not *her!* Never forget—she is a pagan priestess!''

"Don'dt vorry!" chuckled Papa Schimmelhorn. "I haff promised nodt to tell, so no vun knows. But die Prinzessin iss a nice girl, vith maybe too much vinegar, vhich iss all right in bed. Anyvay, noding happens—you can trust Papa Schimmelhorn. I am a chenius."

"So, I dare say, was that Dr. Faustus about whom Kit Marlowe wrote," answered Humphrey lugubriously.

Papa Schimmelhorn gave him a thimbleful of honeyed brandy to cheer him up, promised him again that he had no need to worry, returned him to his jar, and hastened back to his Princess.

When he arrived, Sarpedon Mavronides was on the point of leaving. He stepped respectfully aside so that Papa Schimmelhorn could enter. He swept them both a deep, low bow. "Highness," he said, "I shall telephone Herr Doktor Rumpler as you have ordered, and inform him that the gold-making machine is a success. Otherwise, as you have instructed me, I shall tell him nothing except that he is not to try to call you for three days. Your other orders I shall carry out immediately." Then, as he bowed again and backed out, he murmured, "May you sleep well, Your Highnesses," and softly closed the door behind him.

Instantly, the Princess threw her arms around her lover, drew his lips down to hers, and some time passed before he was able to come up again for air.

"Mein gootness! Philli, shveetheart, haff you heard vot Herr Zorba calls me? Chust like you, a Highness. Vot iss? *Königliche Hoheit* Schimmelhorn der First?" He roared with laughter. "Imachine! A Highness who makes cuckoo clocks und cuckoo vatches!"

Her laughter echoed his as she led him to the table where the first course of the banquet, laid on by Ismail, awaited them. She seated him. Once more, she herself poured their wine.

"My love!" she breathed. "My dearest dear love! Of course Sarpedon called you Highness, for you are now my Prince. But no, you never can be Schimmelhorn the First— that would not be correct. Just as I am the Princess Philippa, so you too must be known by your first name. Come, tell me what it is." She laughed again. "Certainly you cannot be Prince Papa, nor can I call you Papa in our bed."

Papa Schimmelhorn blushed. Under the table, he shifted his feet in much embarrassment. "I—I nefer use it since I am a boy," he told her. "Vhen I am a young man, all die pussycats say it does nodt sound like me. I—I do nodt like efen to shpeak it."

She leaned a little forward, displaying the cleavage he now knew so well. "Even for *me?*" she whispered.

He blushed even more vividly than before. "For you, shveetheart—for you, I—I write it down."

Nearby there was a notepad on which she had written down her orders for Mavronides. She passed it to him.

Hesitantly, he scribbled. Reluctantly, he passed the paper to her.

She looked at it.

"It iss pronounced Owgoost," muttered its owner, unnecessarily.

"August!" she said admiringly. "It befits you, love. It has a truly royal sound to it. Prince August the First! It's perfect! But if you truly do not like it, if it pains you to hear it spoken, then we shall reserve it only for the most solemn ceremonies, when its use is, of course, *de rigueur.*"

It came to Papa Schimmelhorn that Mama, were she to learn about it, would take a decidedly dim view of his sudden ennoblement and, more especially, of the reasons for it, but something told him that it might be imprudent to mention it. In the past, he had always managed to squirm across similar bridges when he came to them, and at the moment it was far easier just to relax and enjoy the pleasant perquisites of princehood.

They feasted sumptuously. They sipped superb wines. Attended by an enormously cheerful Ismail and a Niobe happy as a lark, they made love subtly with their eyes, their fingertips, their whispered words. Papa Schimmelhorn described, very dramatically, how Twitchgibbet must deliberately have left the window open hoping to trap Gustav-Adolf, and how Mrs. Laubenschneider's hex signs had enabled Gustav-Adolf to turn the tables on him. He described his picking of the locks, his removal of the evidence, and told her—to her infinite amusement—how, in his opinion, Meister Gassi must have blamed the whole thing on a visitation from der Defil. However, remembering his promise, he made no mention of the homunculus.

"Well, we have no further need for Gaspar Gansfleisch now," she said. "With the gold you'll make us, we can buy the world! I have long been disgusted with the man, and now we can be rid of him. Well, we'll leave that for later." She touched his cheek. "Let us devote ourselves to sweeter matters, those which—oh, so unkindly!—duty forced us to interrupt earlier today."

They lingered over a liqueur while Niobe cleared the table and Ismail bore everything away. Then, with a glad shout, the Prinz lifted his Prinzessin bodily and, to the accompaniment of her enchanting laughter, carried her back to bed.

Next morning, after enduring breakfast as another unkind interruption, they shut themselves away again until almost noon. They bathed; they dressed; they lunched in privacy, Niobe and Ismail quietly flitting in and out. Then came the day's first audience, with Sarpedon Mavronides, who told them joyfully that everyone in the castle and on the island was ecstatic at the news of the Princess having found her hero, that one and all looked forward eagerly to being received by him, that even now they were preparing their humble presents and, for when the time came, their sacrifices.

The last remark puzzled Papa Schimmelhorn, but as the

Princess seemed rather pleased, he decided that it referred simply to some quaint, harmless local custom, and asked no questions.

Mavronides also reported on his phone call to Dr. Rumpler who, he declared, had first been tremendously excited at the tidings, then had offered to fly to Little Palaeon immediately, and finally had accepted the Fräulein's dictum with obvious reluctance.

"As for your other orders, Highness," he went on, "I have carried them out faithfully. I have informed Meister Gansfleisch that, because of his bad manners during the transmutation, you have barred him from the laboratory until further notice, and though I could see by his eyes that he hated me, I knew that he would not dare to disobey. Finally, as you requested, I paid the two young ladies the sums due them, together with a generous bonus, and they are now on their way back to, I believe, Amsterdam."

Papa Schimmelhorn's jaw dropped. "Die young ladies?" he gasped. "You mean my predty pussycats?"

"Yes, my true love," murmured the Princess. "I think you will agree that you no longer need them." She ran a consolatory hand along his thigh. "And now," she said, "let us make gold together."

VIII.

Prinz Owgoost

The two burly footmen who once had fetched Meister Gansfleisch to a painful audience with the Fräulein now stood guard against him at the laboratory door, fortified by a variety of signs and sigils rather similar to those used by Mrs. Laubenschneider to protect Gustav-Adolf against spooks and goblins. They bowed respectfully as the Prince and Princess unlocked the door and went in, and assured them that no intruders had even sought to gain entrance. All was secure, they declared, and promised fervently that it would remain so.

For the next three hours, pausing only occasionally for light dalliance, Papa Schimmelhorn and the Fräulein made gold. She, not at all dismayed by the horrendous moanings, uncanny writhings, and apocalyptic light displays of the device, clapped her hands in glee whenever she saw it operate and an object, made of dull lead scant minutes earlier, emerged as pure gold.

"But why," said she, "do you set the dial so low? If you turned it up to fifty or perhaps a hundred, surely we could make much more gold?"

"*Ach*, if I do dot," he answered, "der beam vill shpread, und—und . . ." But describing complex asymptotic curves was too much for him. "Maybe it shpreads a mile, maybe two. Also vot it does vill chanche, und maybe it iss dancherous. Later I make adchustments. Now ve must shtart vith chust a lidtle.''

He began with a small sack of birdshot he had found in his own turret and four pieces of lead pipe borrowed from Sarpedon Mavronides; then he converted three leaden mortars dating back to the sixteenth century and with mysterious lettering on them, which had long been the property of Meister Gansfleisch and to which magical properties had been attributed; he followed these with a lead spoon and a variety of small lead vessels, with whose purpose he was unacquainted, but which the alchemist had cherished. Not till the Princess was quite sure that the laboratory was fresh out of lead did she consent to terminate the proceedings. She embraced her lover ecstatically. ''My Prince, my *King!*'' she cried. ''You have entranced the woman in me with your strength, your passion! Now, by the magic of your genius, you have captured the rest of me—the Princess, the Minoan Priestess, yes, and the Swiss Banker! Truly, love and gold are universal solvents, and together we shall make more of each—much more! But tell me, do the flying hours escape? Does not the day grow late and duty call?''

''*Ja*,'' replied Papa Schimmelhorn; and the cuckoo watch, at his behest, sang out its hours, minutes, seconds.

The Princess kissed it. ''Oh, let it speak for us!'' she said, ''as long as it remains silent in the night and does not interrupt our endless hours of love! But now—now Sarpedon again awaits instructions. Will you attend with me?''

''*Ach*, such an honor!'' He shook his head regretfully. ''Aber, lidtle Philli, I must go up und feed mein Gustav-Adolf, und use der bathroom, und see vhere I can find some more lead for tomorrow.'' It occurred to him to quip that at least there was again plenty of it in der pencil, but he decided that this would be indelicate.

She told him not to worry about the next day's supply, that Mavronides would get them all they might require. Then, with one of the footmen carrying the newly manufactured gold in one of Meister Gansfleisch's wooden boxes, he escorted her back to her own apartments. There, at the door, she flowed into his arms. They kissed. And he made his way to his now-pussycatless turret, where he found that every evidence of Emmy and Niki ever having been there had been removed. He thought of the good times they had had together. With a mournful sigh, he reached for Gustav-Adolf, who was glaring at him.

"So they haff left you all alone, poor Gustav-Adolf?" he said sympathetically. "Vell, don'dt you vorry. Now I am a Prinz, predty soon eferything vorks oudt, und you can leafe und fight die oder cats und chase die predty tortoiseshells. But you must shtay here until ve are qvite sure from Meister Gassi you are safe."

Gustav-Adolf shrank back from him. He growled and hissed. "Goddam ol' hippercrite!" he grumbled. "How'd *you* like t' be stuck up here all day, huh, supposin' it was the other way around, with me doin' the tomcattin' like I oughta be? Just take a gander at that there door, too." He glared at the door to the battlements, which someone had inadvertently left shut. "How'd *you* like it if you couldn't even get out to the john?"

Papa Schimmelhorn, of course, could not speak Cat, but he still managed to get the drift. He apologized to his friend, and quickly let him out onto the battlements, where—after he himself had retired into the bathroom—Gustav-Adolf used his catbox furiously, kicking out enough of its contents to make certain that there'd have to be a clean-up job. Then he stalked back with a massive feline dignity, and grunted, "Well, chum, what's to eat?"

Half a pound of steak later, he decided that he was partly mollified, and jumped to his favorite perch on the Schimmelhorn shoulder. *But I'll be durned if I purr fer the old bastard,* he thought, *not fer a while I won't! That'll learn him!*

By this time, Papa Schimmelhorn had taken Humphrey out for his afternoon tot of honeyed brandy, and the homunculus was questioning him anxiously about how matters were proceeding.

"Now look you, Master Schimmelhorn," he said worriedly, "for the moment you and—if you do not resent my so calling her—your inamorata, the Princess, seem to have held this vile Gansfleisch off successfully. But have a care! Why, 'tis scarce a fortnight since he was trying to sell his immortal soul to Satan for some devil's promise of her in his bed, and it was only when she became angry with you and seemed to favor him that he rubbed out the pentacle he had prepared, imagining that he could gain his ends by other means—as you learned much to your sorrow. Be warned, my good kind friend!"

Papa Schimmelhorn promised him that Meister Gassi wasn't going to get away with anything. He explained, with many a chuckle, that he was now a Prinz, und maybe soon he vould be able to shnap his fingers und say, "Off vith der head!"

"Oh Lord, deliver us!" cried Humphrey. "Sir, do you not know what being the Prince of such a pagan isle may mean? Have you no notion of what their evil customs may demand of you?"

"Vell, I haff heard shtories aboudt how sometimes ein Prinz had vot-you-call 'right of der first night' vith all die predty lidtle pussycats." Again he chuckled. "But maybe meine Prinzessin does nodt like dot, *nein?*"

"*Jus primae noctis*—ah, if that were all!" Little Humphrey actually started to get down on his knees. "I do beg and pray you—for never an instant relax your vigilance! I trust you have not yet married her?"

"Married?" laughed Papa Schimmelhorn. "I could nodt do. Iss Mama. Ve are now married more than sixty years. She vould nodt approfe."

At the moment, he had no desire at all to wiggle out of his very pleasant situation, but the idea had occurred to him that the fact of Mama might very well, in an emergency, enable him to do just that, as he had wiggled out of other situations in the past. He did his best to assuage Humphrey's fears and to convince him they were groundless; he gave him an extra thimbleful to cheer him up; he played a game of chess with him which he let him win. Finally, when Humphrey expressed concern regarding what remained of the love potion, he promised that after he had sealed it in another ampule it would rest securely in the secret compartment, where Humphrey himself could keep an eye on it. Somewhat reassured, Humphrey bade him farewell till the morrow, and said that he would pray for his continued safety and protection. Then Papa Schimmelhorn retired him for the night, insulted Gustav-Adolf by telling him to be a good cat, and went off to rejoin his Princess.

Halfway there, to his astonishment, he was intercepted by Ismail. "Noble Effendi! Most High and Potent Prince!" Ismail began, whispering and darting cautious glances over his shoulder, with many profound Oriental bows and apologies. "You have spoken of a substance which you believe could restore my manhood. Effendi, could you send for it without delay, before—that is, though Allah is compassionate, all men are mortal, and who knows what the future holds? If anything should happen so you could not send for it. . . . You understand, Effendi?"

Papa Schimmelhorn, recalling that his first radiogram to Mama requesting a shipment of the mutated catnip had not even been acknowledged, decided that he would have to try a different tack. He requested pen and paper, which the eunuch produced out of his garments. "I write anoder radiogram," he told him, "to mein grandnephew, Lidtle Anton, in Hong Kong. Iss bedter *he* asks Mama for der catnip." He wrote the message out, instructing Little Anton to procure the catnip subtly and have it delivered directly to Ismail, whom he told not to worry about customs laws because of Little Anton's extensive experience as a smuggler.

Having given the eunuch enough money to pay for the radiogram, and having cautioned him against sending it from Little Palaeon, he went his way, an obscure worry nagging at his mind. Why, he wondered, had poor Ismail been so concerned that something might prevent him from getting the catnip? And why, for that matter, had Meister Gansfleisch and Mavronides been so upset just because he had mentioned bulls? And what did his little Philli mean when she spoke of sacrifices? But the worry lasted for moments only, succumbing to the euphoria induced by his enjoyment of his princely privileges.

So, for the next several days, the Prinz and the Prinzessin made love and gold exuberantly. They paid no attention to Meister Gansfleisch whom, looking even more haggard and hag-ridden than before, they occasionally encountered in the corridors, the Fräulein having given him permission to use the laboratory, under the close supervision of the footmen, in the mornings; and Papa Schimmelhorn, riding high, did his best to allay Humphrey's growing concern, pacified Gustav-Adolf's restlessness by sneaking in a pretty little calico Mavronides found for him, and gave little or no thought to what the other actors in the drama might be doing.

The other actors, as a matter of fact, were doing all sorts of things. The news of the Princess's liaison had of course spread through the castle in minutes, through Little Palaeon in hours. Meister Gansfleisch, however—and this was a measure of his unpopularity—did not learn about it for two solid days, during which he paced up and down inside his turret, drank too many of his own incredible mixed drinks, gnawed his fingernails to the quick, and wondered what on earth he could have done to turn the Princess against him so completely and so suddenly. Then, early on the third day, on his way downstairs to complain to Mavronides about his breakfast, he had overheard two giggling serving maids discussing, not the liaison itself, but the new Prince's astounding prowess. He had halted in his tracks, astonishment and rage surging in his thin frame. Heart beating like a triphammer, he had cried out, "*Wretched women, do you tell the truth?*" in an absolutely awful voice.

The little serving maids, who swore afterward that he had threatened them not just with curses but with living serpents, nodded mutely, screamed, and fled; and the alchemist, now like one possessed, had almost run to find Mavronides and demand of him also whether it was true.

Sarpedon Mavronides, gazing at him in cold disgust, told him flatly that it was not his business, and advised him that he would be prudent to stick to his rats and stinks and stenches. "Get back to your moldy turret!" he commanded. "And do not dare to meddle in the affairs of your betters. The Princess is right. Herr Schimmelhorn is a man like those who made Crete's greatness in the ancient days. Begone!"

Gaspar Gansfleisch whirled and fled. Once more in his turret, it took him only moments to decide what he must do. He needed allies—and he knew exactly where to find them. Now, he told himself, was the time to consummate the sale he previously had canceled. He sat down at his desk; he made the calculations for an auspicious hour. Then he fetched out all the equipment he had prepared before: the black tapers; the inverted cross; the skulls and other relics from executed criminals, from suicides; the special parts of toads; the drowned cats' eyes; the vile and septic substances reputed to have so strong an influence in the ceremony he was preparing. He brought out his grimoire, an ancient manuscript so vibrant with its evil that he himself kept it under lock and key at night. He drew his pentacle with special care. Boldly and clearly, he wrote the Words of Power, the dreadful Names that surrounded it. Then, disciplining himself, he sat down to wait. His dinner came. The servant knocked and left it just outside the door. He brought it in, dabbled at it. Night fell. He lit one tall black candle, and by its light sat very carefully rehearsing the procedure he would have to follow. It was almost midnight when he felt that at last all was ready. He lit the tapers. Wild-eyed, fully robed now in vestments bearing the correct signs and symbols, he began invoking the Powers of Darkness, calling Names that should have been unutterable, uttering Words of Power of which even he was frightened. His voice ever more strident, ever more commanding, he strode around the pentacle. He persisted for five minutes, ten, twenty, twenty-five. . . .

And nothing happened.

No fiends howled. No damned souls shrieked or whined. No terrible Presence appeared within the pentacle. Not so much as a mephitic whiff of smoke indicated that the Powers he sought to contact were responding. Even the black tapers burned warmly, steadily, instead of guttering as they should have done.

Getting increasingly frightened, angry, and hysterical, he kept it up for another quarter-hour. The only response— and he wasn't even sure of that—was an occasional steady, intermittent humming, very much like a telephone's busy signal.

Obviously, nobody down below wanted to talk to him.

For a time, he raved aloud, blaming it all on Twitchgibbet, blaming his own rash hastiness in canceling a half-negotiated contract. Then he took thought of other ways to injure Papa Schimmelhorn and take revenge on the woman who, Princess or no Princess, had dared betray the greatest alchemist in Europe. Magic, he knew, would almost certainly prove futile against Philippa Theophrastra Paleologus Bombast von Hohenheim, considering her heritage, her learning, and her redoubtable intelligence. So would such expedients as poison—even if directed against a personage as inconsiderable as Gustav-Adolf—for her power on Little Palaeon was very real, and without massive assistance he wanted to run afoul neither of it nor of the quaint ancient practices it controlled.

He wrestled with the question until dawn—and came up with two inspirations. The first was simple. On the pretext of buying necessary supplies for a new and very profitable project—he told himself that he could always think one up if anybody questioned him—he would go over to Crete next day and, from a safe telephone, call Herr Doktor Rumpler and tell him of the Fräulein's cataclysmic love affair and the imminent danger it posed to the Rumpler

Bank's financial interests. Then he would let nature—Swiss banking nature—take its course.

The second inspiration involved much more complex and subtle measures. Meister Gansfleisch hugged himself when he thought of it, and almost pranced up and down as he planned it. So Satan didn't want to buy his soul, or else was playing hard to get? Well, there were other powers to go to who would reward him generously without even exacting the same sort of contract. Meticulously, going back over the associations of a lifetime, he began planning all the other calls he would have to make from Crete.

Gottfried Rumpler, in the meantime, had been having his own troubles. When the Fräulein, so much to his astonishment, had appealed to him for help in arranging the deactivation of Papa Schimmelhorn, when she herself had placed their association on a first-name, man-to-woman rather than banker-to-banker basis, while he knew that he was not yet in Seventh Heaven, he did feel that he had at least been allowed to peer through its portals. From that time on, until Mavronides had called—Mavronides and *not* the Fräulein—with the glad tidings that Papa Schimmelhorn had succeeded, and the shocking message that he was not to call her for at least three days, he had given his imagination free rein. At night, when he went to bed, he was unable to keep his mind on his *petite amie*, for his glands kept reminding him of the Hohenheim eyes, the Hohenheim breasts, and all the other wonders of the Hohenheim anatomy. He would fall asleep only to dream, as he had before, that he was chasing her through endless golden labyrinths—with the difference, now, that he was catching her. It reached a point where his Brigitte, sulking and mortally offended, told him flatly that he should see a psychiatrist. But then Mavronides, with a few cold words, had shattered all his hopes.

While Meister Gansfleisch was suffering and raging in his turret, still ignorant of what had transpired, Herr Rumpler, equally ignorant, was undergoing torments which, while perhaps less dramatic, were no less painful. Clearly, something was very wrong. He tried to tell himself that possibly she was simply waiting for the original success to be confirmed, that when it was she herself would phone him as warmly as she had before, and summon him to Little Palaeon so that they could share their joy. But he did not believe it. Thoroughly distraught, he even made an error in a simple business transaction, something he had never done before, and he began to worry that perhaps the Fräulein, now that the goldmaker and his device were in her grasp, was planning somehow to seize everything herself. It was almost more than human flesh could bear.

Then, on the third day, before he had even had a chance to put in his phone call to Little Palaeon, Gaspar Gansfleisch phoned him.

Miss Ekstrom, who had been getting more and more worried about her employer's state of mind, took the call. No, she was not sure the Herr Doktor was available. She would enquire. Who should she say was calling?

She listened for a moment. "It's somebody named Gaspar something," she told Dr. Rumpler. "He sounds really weird, and awfully upset about something. He says he's calling from some place on Crete." She grimaced, and looked down at the phone which, smothered by her palm, was still making noises at her. "Do you want me to tell him you've gone off to Stockholm or somewhere?"

"No, no!" the banker cried. "I will take the call. Only give me a moment to—to compose myself!"

Miss Ekstrom picked up her phone again, interrupted Meister Gansfleisch's assertions that he was the greatest alchemist in Europe, that he was being cruelly and unjustly misused, and told him firmly that though the Herr Doktor was extremely busy, he would be with him shortly.

Dr. Rumpler, now convinced that something really dreadful had happened on Little Palaeon, forced himself to sit back in his chair and assume his normal magisterial dignity. He signed to Miss Ekstrom to transfer the call.

"Yes," he said, "I am Herr Doktor Rumpler. You wished to speak with me?"

At his end of the line, Meister Gansfleisch uttered a strange sound, half glad shriek, half strangled sob. "Herr Doktor, Herr Doktor!" he cried out. "You have no idea what has happened. I shall tell you—*I*, who am the greatest alchemist in Europe, in the world! It is your thrice-accursed creature Schimmelhorn, he who has dared to make gold in ways unorthodox!"

"But if he has indeed made gold," interrupted the banker, "does it make any difference—?"

"*Difference?*" Gansfleisch screamed. "Does it make any *difference?* I shall tell you what difference it has already made. He has already seduced our Princess, our Priestess, your associate, Fräulein von Hohenheim, the descendant of the Golden Doctor, Paracelsus. He and she have been wallowing in her bed for three days together. Now she is proclaiming him her Prince, her hero! Suppose he has—probably fraudulently—produced a little gold? What do you think will become of *your* financial interest in it now, Herr Doktor Banker Rumpler?" He uttered an uncanny cackle. "Where will you be when she enthrones *him* here on Little Palaeon? When she marries him according to her foul pagan rites?"

Dr. Rumpler clutched the telephone as though it were about to writhe and strike at him. "No, no!" he croaked. "*Marry him?* That is impossible! It—it would not be legal! Schimmelhorn is already married! I have met his wife! She never would permit it—*never!*"

"Illegal?" Gansfleisch's uncanny laughter answered him. "And she would not permit it? Herr Doktor, such things mean nothing on Little Palaeon, where our Princess rules as absolutely as any Caesar, as any Czar!"

"But—but how *could* he have seduced her? Surely, Meister Gansfleisch, you remember that we have rendered him completely impotent? That you yourself compounded the concoction?"

"Yes," replied the alchemist bitterly, "yes, I did

indeed—but at her request I also compounded the instant antidote, which she took into her charge. Then—then—" His voice broke. "She has gone mad, Herr Doktor—stark, raving mad! That is the only explanation. It must have happened when she first saw the gold the monster made. She is insane! She thinks him an Olympian, a demigod! Especially since she's given him the antidote. Even now Mavronides is busy preparing all sorts of ceremonies at which he will be formally introduced to all her subjects! What can you do about it, Herr Doktor? Heh, answer me *that!*"

Dr. Rumpler could not answer. He was gasping. His eyes were bulging quite appallingly. His mind was flashing him alternate pictures of Papa Schimmelhorn and his Philippa, joyously practicing all the wrestling holds of love, and of the two of them, having somehow diddled the Rumpler Bank out of its just share, happily cornering the world's entire gold market. It was a toss-up to which hurt the more.

"*What shall I do?*" he roared, leaping to his feet. "*I* shall tell you, Gansfleisch! I, Gottfried Rumpler, am not just a banker! I am a colonel also in our Swiss Army! It will take me a few days to make my plans—three or four perhaps—then I shall take immediate action. I myself will come to Little Palaeon. I shall bring my aide, Herr Grundtli. I shall also bring the greatest of our Swiss psychiatrists, for—as you say—it is obvious that the Fräulein has lost her mind, that she has contracted some grave mental illness. Never fear, Meister Gansfleisch, everything will be—ah—adjusted. Yes, indeed. You can take my word for it!"

Meister Gansfleisch laughed a hollow laugh, and hung up without so much as a good-bye, leaving Dr. Rumpler once again shaken and deflated. He began to pace up and down his office. Something told him that Gaspar Gansfleisch, mad as he seemed to be, had told him nothing but the truth—and yet he hesitated to accept it. He asked Miss Ekstrom to bring him a generous glass of cognac, and then to leave the room. He sat down at his desk and telephoned the Fräulein's private number. Niobe answered it, very coolly. Yes, she would see if the Princess cared to speak with him. He waited. He could hear booming masculine laughter in the background, disturbingly. It was a long wait, and when she finally came to the phone, he found himself perspiring freely.

"Good afternoon, dear Philippa," he cooed, as much in the tone of their previous call as possible. "You asked me not to phone you for three days, so I have not done so. By this time, I suppose you have confirmed the validity of Herr Schimmelhorn's great discovery?"

"Oh, Herr Doktor!" she replied. "So it's *you*. No, we found no need to confirm anything, but we have been enjoying ourselves tremendously. Every day we have been making gold, of which I shall send you a few samples shortly, but also, my good financial friend, ah!—also we have been making love!"

"Making—er, *love?*" he gulped, as though unforewarned.

"Yes, mein Herr, it has been idyllic. Day and night! Never since Homeric times, never since the great days of ancient Crete, has there been such stupendous lovemaking!" Her lovely laughter followed this remark; merry male laughter echoed it.

"*But, my Philippa!*" he cried out in anguish.

"I am not *your* Philippa," she answered scornfully. "Our association is purely a commercial one, mein Herr. I am *his* Philippa, just as he is my Prince, just as he will be my consort as I rule over Little Palaeon, and my co-priest in the sacred ancient rites I have inherited, and which we guard. Stick to your bookkeeping, Herr Rumpler, and do not poke your nose into my private affairs, hear me? There will be plenty of gold to keep you happy, I promise you!"

"B-b-but you yourself are a Swiss banker!"

"Yes," she told him. "Yes, I am. But first I am a woman, then a Princess and a Priestess, as you know. Once I believed the Swiss banker in me to be uppermost, but now"—her laughter trilled, and there was the distinct sound of an exuberant kiss—"no more! I have learned better, my fellow banker!"

The phone went dead, and for an entire minute Doktor Rumpler stood staring at it as though hypnotized. Then, once again, he began to pace his office. Obviously, the alchemist was right. The Fräulein had indeed lost her mind. Keeping (discreetly) a *petite amie*, or even playing (even more discreetly) with an occasional pretty pussycat— that was one thing. But *marriage!* Marriage was as sacrosanct—or at least *almost* as sacrosanct—as a num- bered account at the Rumpler Bank. Besides, she had fallen in love, not just with a man of low intelligence (however much of a genius he might be subconsciously), not just with an aged relic (regardless of his alleged vine- gar), but with a man who, to any unbiased intellect, was in every way inferior to Gottfried Rumpler. She needed the best psychiatric treatment money could buy. But of course—at that point he paused to call Miss Ekstrom for the brandy bottle—the matter of getting her to hold still for that treatment was something else again. Besides, the fact that there was a genuine and efficient gold-making ma- chine involved made several of the more conventional procedures decidedly inadvisable.

For two hours, Dr. Rumpler's mind battled the threats and shadows of the situation, dreamed up one reckless scenario after another only to discard it, considered the persons he might call in or hire as allies, and inevitably came up with only one approach that seemed to offer even the slightest hope of being successful. Finally, as the afternoon drew to a close, he gave up the struggle and phoned Mama Schimmelhorn.

When her telephone rang, Mama Schimmelhorn was just sitting down to a carefully prepared luncheon of consommé, a light seafood salad, puréed spinach, and game hens stuffed with artichoke hearts, mushrooms, and walnuts. She had just seated her two guests, Mrs. Hundhammer and Mrs. Laubenschneider, and was looking forward to catching up with the local gossip, even though it had seemed a bit watered down since her husband's departure.

"*Verdammte* telephone!" she grumbled. "Alvays vhen you sit down, und no madter vhere! Und probably iss only somevun to sell der vacuum cleaner oder der life insurance—imachine, at my aiche!"

She reached the instrument and lifted it, determined to give it a piece of her mind.

"*Ja*," she snapped. "I am Mrs. Schimmelhorn, und I do nodt vant to buy—" She broke off abruptly; she listened; then in a very different tone she said, "*Ach*, Herr Doktor! It iss so nice you phone, und maybe giff me news of mein old goat, und how he iss behafing"—she chuckled wickedly—"vith no lead in der pencil."

At the luncheon table, Mrs. Hundhammer and Mrs. Laubenschneider pricked up their ears and strained to hear; and Mama Schimmelhorn, divining that they would, delicately kicked the hall door closed. She was astounded to hear Herr Doktor Rumpler groan.

"Vot iss?" she asked. "You haff maybe der indichestion?"

Dr. Rumpler groaned again, striving to find the proper words. "Dear lady," he said, "my *dear* Mrs. Schimmelhorn. Oh, if it were only that! I must tell you that we have—well, we have run into grave difficulties. Your husband has succeeded. He has made gold—"

"*Es ist ganz gut!*" put in Mama Schimmelhorn. "Now ve can haff der shteeple for der church, higher efen than die Methodisms."

"Yes, yes, you shall have it!" he hastened to assure her. "But the problem with your husband—ah, it is not just a problem with your *husband*. It involves also—"

"More naked vomen?" she hissed. "Dot iss impossible! Vith no lead in der pencil, how can he—?"

Very painfully, Gottfried Rumpler's mind had flashed him a vivid picture, in full color, of one very special naked woman. He groaned again, even more profoundly. "Dear lady!" he exclaimed. "This involvement is, I must warn you, most serious. You see, it does not concern the, well, the island girls—it is an involvement with my associate, my associate in banking, my associate in this present enterprise."

Mama Schimmelhorn was outraged. "*Such nonsense!*" she cried out. "All his life, Papa chases naked vomen, but *boys?*—I tell you, *nefer!* Und a Schviss banker! No vun vould beliefe!"

"*Dear* Frau Schimmelhorn," moaned Dr. Rumpler, "still you do not *understand*—my associate is a *woman!*"

"*A voman Schviss banker?*" She gasped incredulously. "Schviss bankers alvays are all *men.*"

"Not anymore, alas! Since Women's Liberation, things have changed. She is a very competent and most successful Swiss banker."

"Und now mein old goat iss chasing her, *nicht wahr?* But *how*, vith no lead inside der pencil?"

"Dear lady, it is not so much that he is chasing *her*. It is *she* who has fallen madly in love with *him*. It is she who gave him the antidote. You cannot begin to imagine the terrible situation we must face and solve. Somehow we must save both him and her!"

"*Safe* him?" snorted Mama Schimmelhorn. "Chust vait until I catch up vith der bumbershoot!"

"Then you can come and help us? You can leave for Switzerland right away? Dear lady, my aircraft will pick you up tomorrow—"

"Right *avay?*" she barked. "I cannodt leafe right avay. I cannodt leafe until Lidtle Anton gets here. Two days from now he shtarts from Hong Kong, und I haff promised him to be here. But maybe he can come vith me to Schvitzerland. Because Papa likes him, maybe he iss a help."

Gottfried Rumpler remembered Little Anton well. He almost sighed with relief. Surely he could trust him—

especially now that Pêng-Plantagenet were clients of the Rumpler Bank—and he realized that it would probably be easier to explain the true state of affairs to him than to Mama Schimmelhorn. "Thank you, dear lady," he said fervently, consulting his very complicated wristwatch for Hong Kong time. "That is an *excellent* suggestion. I was much impressed by the young man, and I shall phone him tonight and tell him everything; then you and he can discuss it thoroughly as you're flying over."

He thanked her once or twice more, promised faithfully to deliver a threatening message from her to Papa Schimmelhorn, and said good-bye. For the next several hours—until after eleven, which he judged would be a good time to put in his Hong Kong call—he worried and fretted, and imagined all sorts of painful scenes involving the Fräulein and her lover. Then, fortunately, he had no trouble reaching Little Anton, and much less than he had expected in explaining matters. However, though Little Anton chortled over the lead-in-the-pencil story, whoooed admiringly at the Rumpler description of the Fräulein, and displayed an active interest in the history, antiquities, and customs of Little Palaeon, he could promise nothing except that he'd *try* to come if Pêng-Plantagenet's business did not interfere. When he said good-bye to Dr. Rumpler and hung up, it was on a rather wistful note. "*Prince Papa!*" he said over and over again. "Who ever would've thought it? Talk about smelling like a rose!"

As for Mama Schimmelhorn, she had replaced her phone with the iron determination she always showed in such contingencies; and, by the expression on her face, her two friends judged it might be better not to question her. She pulled back her chair. She sat. Daintily, she spread her napkin. "Vell," she finally said, "iss more of der same. Anoder naked voman. Und now Lidtle Anton und I must go all der vay to Schvitzerland. *Ach*, Papa—you chust vait!" She smiled grimly to herself. "Und now, Mrs. Laubenschneider, you vere going to tell me all aboudt Dora Grossapfel und die red bikini. . . ."

* * *

Meister Gansfleisch, meanwhile, had followed through with the plans he had prepared so carefully the night before. Immediately after his call to Gottfried Rumpler, he made another, to an erstwhile colleague of his, a Transylvanian who while still a boy before the war had been strongly suspected of vampirism, who during the war had been a known and feared collaborator, and who—after his country had·been swallowed behind the Iron Curtain—had connived his way into a position of great power as head of a State-operated psychiatric institution. This call took much longer to put through, and the conversation it entailed had to be couched in terms so carefully veiled that the various Secret Police monitors listening in could not possibly fathom its real meaning. Luckily, to ingratiate himself with his new masters, the Transylvanian had written a dissertation thoroughly disproving and denouncing alchemy in terms of orthodox Dialectical Materialism, and by subtle references to this, Meister Gansfleisch was able to inform him—without going into any detail—that great discoveries were in the wind, and that he himself (out of his well-known love for Socialism and the Dictatorship of the Proletariat, and of course for an appropriate reward) could make certain that they would in no way profit Capitalist Imperialism.

At that point, things became rather more involved. The Transylvanian broke off to make a call on another line while Meister Gansfleisch waited nervously. Then he informed the alchemist that, as they both agreed, it was all superstitious nonsense, and that he should disabuse himself of the insane notion that anything could be accomplished by such means. Perhaps, he suggested, his old friend Gaspar had been working himself too hard, breathing the venomous effluvia of his furnaces and flagons? And might it not be an excellent idea for him to take a short vacation, just a day or two, perhaps in Athens, where a tourist guide of his acquaintance—a charming girl!—would be delighted to show him the wonders of the Acropolis, the Parthenon?

Meister Gansfleisch asked how he might find her.

The Transylvanian chuckled. "Don't worry, my dear fellow. Just be aboard the morning plane tomorrow. She'll meet you at the airport. I suppose you're still wearing that same suit, aren't you? . . . Good, good. I'll describe you to her. She'll have no trouble recognizing you. And don't you worry. Your little holiday will be worthwhile. It'll do you worlds of good, I promise you."

Hoping that he had read the omens rightly, Meister Gansfleisch went back to Little Palaeon and its chateau, sought out Sarpedon Mavronides, explained that he was truly anxious to get back into the Princess's good graces by making a discovery to delight and honor her, and said it would be necessary for him to visit Athens for two days to procure the rare and precious substances he needed.

Mavronides, showing no curiosity, replied loftily that neither his presence nor his absence would be noticed, warned him against spending money recklessly, and told him not to hurry back.

Seething at the snub, but delighted at the way matters were progressing, the alchemist made his simple preparations. Working late into the night, he carefully wrote down as accurate a description of Papa Schimmelhorn's gold-making machine as possible, listing all its parts as he remembered them and from copies he had made of the shopping lists, and giving as clear a word-picture as he could of the phenomena that accompanied its functioning. He also fetched out of hiding a small once-leaden fishing sinker of Mavronides's that Papa Schimmelhorn had absent-mindedly left lying on the floor after its transmutation. He then made up his own shopping list, for appearances' sake, packed his disreputable valise, dusted off his yellow shoes, and went to bed to dream of his revenge. In his dream, Satan himself was offering him the Princess, stripped to the buff and displayed against the tanned hide of Papa Schimmelhorn.

He awakened early, hitched a ride with Ismail down to the jetty, and persuaded a grumbling boatman to ferry him over to the main island just in time to catch the first flight to Athens. There he looked around. No one answering the description of his Transylvanian colleague's charming girl was anywhere in evidence. However, he saw that he was being closely observed by a very large woman of uncertain years, with very hairy legs and definite secondary male characteristics, who looked more like the less-pleasant sort of prison matron than like a tourist guide. Presently, her eyes narrowed and, with an almost imperceptible gesture to a pair of blocky, expressionless off-duty secret police-man types, approached him. She smiled with a mouthful of threatening teeth, and said, "You are nice tourist, sir? Yes? Perhaps you would like to see the Parthenon, the Acropolis, also those places where the Greek gentlemen maybe took their boys?"

Then, out of the corner of her mouth, she whispered, "Meister Gaspar Gansfleisch, yes?"

"Yes," replied the alchemist, and mentioned his Transylvanian friend by name.

"Then you will want refreshment, is it not?" stated the matron. "My name it does not matter. You may call me Hulda. We go to a fine restaurant, in a private home. You do not even pay. It is—ha-ha!—on the house." She crooked a finger at her male counterparts; she grasped Meister Gansfleisch's arm. "Now you come with me, yes. Eat, eat."

The alchemist wasn't hungry, but he decided that it all was probably part of the protocol of plotting, and besides, there wasn't anything he could do about it. He went along. Outside the terminal, a cab awaited them. They climbed in. Behind them, another cab picked up their followers. Hulda familiarly squeezed his knee. "Pretty soon," she promised him, "you have a good full stomach, yes, like me."

The driver needed no directions. He threaded his way through narrow streets, sped down wide boulevards, entered a section of the city that looked as though, in its day, it must have harbored Spartan spies and Trojan terrorists. The cab halted in front of an especially sinister establishment with flies in the window and a cracked sign saying food was served within.

"We have private room, very nice," proclaimed Hulda, dragging him from the cab.

They entered smells and shadows; they were ushered through a feeding throng into a curtained room; they sat. Then waiters came, plying Meister Gansfleisch with mutton and pilaf, with grape leaves and sour wine, with comestibles he didn't even recognize. Hulda, to encourage him, devoured great gobbets of the stuff and insisted that he do the same, until finally he could eat no more. He belched unhappily.

At that point, as though on cue, two more men entered. One was tall and cadaverous, with corded muscles and pale, blank eyes. The other, with his shaven head, looked like a B-movie android. They sat down at the table. They stared at Meister Gansfleisch.

The taller man leaned forward. "Tell," he said. "*All*."

And Meister Gansfleisch, stuffed like a Strasbourg goose and thoroughly traumatized, did as he was bidden. He did not speak of alchemy, except to refer to it slightingly and as a hobby of the Fräulein's. He emphasized falsely that his own background was definitely modern and scientific, and he conveyed the notion that, while Papa Schimmelhorn's subconscious genius was genuine enough, it would never have gotten off first base had it not been for the solid Gansfleisch knowhow. As for the curious customs of Little Palaeon and the Fräulein's sacerdotal role, he passed them over contemptuously as rank superstition—which, however, might very well serve a useful purpose.

Occasionally, as he talked, the tall man interrupted with a pointed question, while his androidal companion took it all down on a minicorder, but it was when Meister Gansfleisch produced the golden sinker and passed it to him for examination that he became really interested. He asked for a complete list of the components of Papa Schimmelhorn's device; he asked intimate questions regarding the growing of its essential crystal, the electrical values involved, the meters and mechanical devices governing its operation, and the phenomena that occurred when it was turned on.

Gaspar Gansfleisch stuttered out the explanation that, while his role in its construction had been crucial, Papa Schimmelhorn had been so secretive that many details remained hidden even from him.

The tall man fixed him with his eyes. "Well, it is not important," he declared. "What is important is how big it is, *and can you operate it*?"

The alchemist replied that the entire device was mounted on an insulated plastic base perhaps four feet by seven, that at no point was it more than five feet high, and that he was an expert in its operation, Papa Schimmelhorn having instructed him and permitted him to watch the entire procedure. He also added, untruthfully, that he himself had used it during its inventor's absence.

They went over all these points several times, until finally the tall man appeared satisfied. He gestured to his companion, who gave Meister Gansfleisch a small alarm clock. "It is not a clock," he stated. "It is a very secret, most efficient instrument for communicating with us. You must wait until almost everybody in the castle is away. It must be at night, at a time when you are sure they will be away for at least three hours. Then you must set the time and alarm just as you would if you wanted it to wake you. We will know instantly that all is ready. Do you understand?"

Meister Gansfleisch rubbed his hands together gloatingly. "I understand, Comrade!" he declared. "I do understand— and I know just the time. It has something to do with the phases of the moon, when they're going to hold the most important of their horrid pagan festivals. And there'll be times when everybody at the castle will be away. Sometimes they'll be at the island's other end, where the great mound is, over the—the Labyrinth, where all the ruins are. Sometimes they make pilgrimages there, and go there with their sacrifices. Oh, we'll have opportunities, Comrade, indeed we will! And when the time comes, I will pretend that I am very ill, and I'll await you." He showed his teeth like Twitchgibbet. "Oh, I can hardly wait!"

"You will wait *very* patiently," declared the tall man, "and I would advise you to let no one know that you are waiting. Try to worm your way back into the favor of this man Schimmelhorn and of the Swiss woman capitalist. That is all. And now Hulda will show you the famous sights of Athens, and you will make a great deal of fuss about your shopping, so no one can suspect."

The two men left by a back door, and Hulda escorted Meister Gansfleisch to the street again. All that day, she hustled him from one famous ruin to another, from one shop to another, and at suppertime to another restaurant worse, if anything, than the first one. Finally, they went to a hotel, where the alchemist rejected her comradely offer to share his bed.

Next morning, when he awakened, she was gone; and he spent a few more hours shopping ostentatiously before catching the afternoon plane back to Crete.

Ah, ah! he kept telling himself during the flight. *How lucky I have been that I wasn't able to sell my soul as I started out to! Oh, I shall have a fine revenge indeed. The comrades will reward me richly. They will load me with their medals, and make me an Academician. I shall be world-famous! Certainly, I shall be director of my own laboratory. Probably . . .*

A cheerful Ismail was waiting for him at the airport. Mr. Mavronides, he said, had sent him specially, for the Princess had issued orders that, after supper, everyone on the island was to attend in the great courtyard of the castle, where His Highness, the Prinz Owgoost, would be formally presented to them, and they would be allowed to give him gifts and do obeisance.

"His Highness *who*?" grunted Meister Gansfleisch foolishly.

Ismail gave him an enormous smile. "His Highness the Effendi," he replied, "the great Effendi Schimmelhorn, who has promised to restore my manhood. Come, I have a cab waiting. We must hurry!"

The ceremony at which Prinz Owgoost was to be presented to his enthusiastic subjects had been carefully and lovingly prepared by the castle's staff under the supervision of Sarpedon Mavronides. Before the great doors, on a dais, stood the Princess's Throne; next to it, on only a slightly lower level, stood another, equally ornate and somewhat larger, brought out of storage for the great occasion. Tapestries and banners hung down at either side, and a purple carpet stretched from the thrones themselves into the courtyard where the commonalty were to assemble.

The Prince and Princess banqueted together, sipping their wine from golden vessels newly manufactured by the Prince that morning. They kissed. They murmured endearments. Night fell.

"And now, my hero," said the Fräulein, "for a short while we must part, for my people will expect us to be attired in the antique style, and Ismail is waiting in your turret to help you dress." She touched a finger to her lover's lips to silence the enquiry he was about to make. "No, do not worry—you will be a splendid sight, for you will wear the costume that last belonged to my great-great-grandfather, and it will fit you perfectly, I promise you. Now go!" And with a final kiss, she sent him on his way.

Back in his turret, Ismail was indeed awaiting him. So was the costume. To Papa Schimmelhorn's astonishment, he saw that it consisted of (a) a magnificently carved and gilded bronze helmet with a nose-piece, (b) a ditto bronze cuirass and greaves, (c) a heavy, straight bronze sword in a silver scabbard, complete with sword belt, (d) a pair of silver-studded sandals made of goatskin, and (e) a curious little skirt fashioned apparently of the same material. All, though obviously of antique design, appeared to be of Renaissance manufacture.

He regarded the whole assembly dubiously. "Vhere iss der undervear?" he demanded.

Ismail bowed. "Highness," he replied respectfully, "in Minoan times, in ancient Crete, they did not have underwear. When you are seated on your throne beside Her Highness, your subjects must be able to look up at you and see you truly are a man!"

Though he grumbled when Ismail insisted politely that he remove even his polka-dotted shorts, the argument that the Princess would be upset if he did not follow local custom prevailed; and presently he stood before the mirror splendidly arrayed, and surveyed himself. He remembered Grecian amphorae he had seen, decorated with the glorious warriors of the heroic past, and he was forced to admit, in all modesty, that they really couldn't hold a candle to him, an opinion in which Ismail obviously concurred. Only Gustav-Adolf refused to be impressed. "I'll be a goddam mouse's uncle!" he growled to his little calico. "Didja ever see anything to beat *that?*" Then he turned his striped back, and absolutely refused to be coaxed onto the Schimmelhorn shoulder.

Ismail threw the door open. He lifted a huge brazen gong, a vast padded hammer. He handed Papa Schimmelhorn a tall spear with a long bronze point. Down the turret stairs he went. He struck the gong a thunderous blow. "*Make way! Make way!*" he shouted. "Make way for His High Mightiness, our Princess's royal lover, our beloved Princess's consort!" He struck the gong thrice more. "*Make way! Make way!*"

And Papa Schimmelhorn, getting into the spirit of the thing, followed him with martial tread, striking the bronze haft of his spear against the flagstones of the corridor at every *bong* and glaring ferociously at the ancestral portraits on the walls as he strode past them.

Presently, having somehow acquired an entourage of open-mouthed small boys, they emerged into the castle courtyard, now thronged with several hundred islanders, and lighted by myriad torches. Ismail advanced enthu-

siastically, making his gong resound and his "*Make ways!*"
boom out thrice as dramatically as before, and Papa
Schimmelhorn followed him majestically. There was a
gasp of awe and wonder from the multitude.

The Princess, already on her throne, stood up and came
toward him, and he saw—a little apprehensively when he
recalled that he was wearing only a small goatskin skirt—
that she too was in Minoan costume, her richly glowing
hair coiled upon her proud head, her open bodice leaving
her breasts arrogantly bare. As Mavronides came forward
to take his spear, she held her hands out to him. She led
him to the second throne, seated him on it with a kiss,
resumed her own. Instantly there was music: silver cymbals sang, and harps; pipes trilled; rams' horns and conchs
brayed; strong young voices soared in a paean of rejoicing.

Then the Princess raised a hand, and abruptly all was
still.

"Now," she cried out triumphantly, "my people, I give
you your true Prince, he who will rule here with me—I
give you my love, my hero, Prince August the First, who
shall be the father of my sons!"

As she spoke in Greek, Papa Schimmelhorn did not get
the full meaning of what she said until Mavronides whispered a translation in his ear. He gulped. Fathering sons
was something he most decidedly had not contemplated.
But he looked again at the Princess's open bodice and
quelled the touch of panic that had assailed him. Surely the
remark was just part of the ritualistic mumbo jumbo of
being a Prince, and nothing to be taken seriously.

The crowd was cheering now, and Sarpedon Mavronides
and his assistants were starting to marshal it toward the
dais and the thrones. There were village dignitaries and
their wives; there were husbandmen and fishermen, their
wives and children, grandfathers and grandmothers; and all
of them bore gifts: baskets of lush grapes, huge flagons of
sweet wine, sheep and goats, calves, prize specimens of
the local handicrafts, intricate mosaics of the Princess and
her Prince especially done for the occasion.

Solemnly they advanced. The men and women knelt before the Princess. They knelt before the Prince, kissing his extended hand in fealty, the younger girls peeking under his little skirt and giggling and nudging each other at what they saw or thought they saw, the young men standing straight and tall and flexing their muscles to impress royalty with their strength and eagerness.

Papa Schimmelhorn conducted himself with a truly regal dignity and benevolence, murmuring words of praise and bestowing gracious looks of acknowledgment and gratitude. Meanwhile, Mavronides's staff took charge of all the presents, and the Princess, leaning forward, whispered that almost all of them—all but the portraits and the handicrafts—were to be sacrifices during the festivities of the next few days.

Slowly, the line passed by, while Prince and Princess did their royal duty. Then, at its very end, to Papa Schimmelhorn's astonishment, Meister Gaspar Gansfleisch put in his appearance, looking very contrite and woebegone. He dropped to his knees before the thrones; he dabbed at his red eyes with a messy handkerchief. "Great Prince," he said, "I have a confession, and if you permit it, amends to make. I have served your Princess now for several years, most faithfully, but I am weak and fallible. When it appeared certain that you would accomplish, with your wonderful machine, what we alchemists have so long striven for, I was poisoned with jealousy. I denounced you to Her Highness. While my familiar was still with me, I even conspired against you with the Powers of Darkness, never suspecting that you yourself are the greatest alchemist of all. Now I pray only that you and your noble Princess will forgive me, and that I may be allowed to serve you humbly."

Papa Schimmelhorn quickly drew back his right hand, which Meister Gansfleisch was doing his best to seize and kiss, and patted him benignly on the head. "Okay, I forgiff you, Meister Gassi," he said. "Und because you say you now do nodt haff Tvitchgibbet, if you are goot und vork hard maybe I get Gustav-Adolf sometime to catch for you anoder rat."

The Princess, not quite so magnanimous, muttered something threatening about the Labyrinth, and dismissed him with a curt gesture. Bowing and scraping, he backed away, and was immediately replaced by an ancient Greek Orthodox priest who appeared from behind the Throne, blessed the royal couple, then blessed the crowd. Again the Princess whispered in her consort's ear, "Pay no attention to him, my love! He's simply here for appearances' sake— he's really one of us."

Sarpedon Mavronides raised his hand. Once more, music filled the courtyard. Decorously, the joyous crowd dispersed. The Princess waited until all had gone. Then she stood, Papa Schimmelhorn following her example. Mavronides handed him his spear.

"And now," she said, "I shall return to our apartments, where Niobe will ready me for bed—and for you, my heart, my love! So go to your turret, divest yourself of your habiliments, and hasten back to me. Tonight there is much that I must teach you, much that you must learn, secrets I can share with you alone!"

"I vill hurry," promised Papa Schimmelhorn. "It does nodt take me long to chanche, but shtill I haff to feed mein Gustav-Adolf, und also die lidtle calico—so cute togeder!— und vash my hands vhere I touch Meister Gassi."

The Princess wrinkled her delightful nose. "Do wash them carefully, then," she laughed. "We'll want no taint of him about our bed."

Ismail appeared, complete with gong and mallet. "*Make way! Make way!*" he shouted.

Back they paraded through the passageways, but at the turret door Papa Schimmelhorn dismissed him. As quickly as he could, he removed his armor, his goatskin skirt. He took a good hot shower, and donned his denims. Gustav-Adolf still wasn't speaking to him, but the little calico purred and rubbed against his ankles, and both of them accepted the roast lamb they were offered. Then Papa

Schimmelhorn took Humphrey out of his retreat, revived him with his honeyed brandy, and gave him a complete report of the evening's happenings.

Sadly, Humphrey shook his head. "I like it not, good Master Schimmelhorn," said he. "There's dire peril in these pagan doings—peril you wot not of, not merely to your mortal body, for even though now you be a Prince, there's peril too to your immortal soul! Oh, and place no dependence on the sweet promises of Gaspar Gansfleisch, nor in his repentance. That toad, ugly and venomous, bears no precious jewel in *his* head, I assure you." He looked at Papa Schimmelhorn lugubriously. "I shall say nothing more, not now. But hark you! If you feel endangered, if by foul plotting or mischance you on a sudden find you know not where to turn, before you act, I implore you, consult with me. Though I be small, still have I lived, even in this poor shape, a good four hundred years and more." He sighed. "I have learned much about this unkind world, this vale of tears."

Papa Schimmelhorn, thinking vividly about the Princess's open bodice and how even it, by this time, had quite certainly been taken off, shook off his own vague apprehensions, promised Humphrey that he would indeed consult him before doing anything at all rash, returned him to his jar, and hastened back to the waiting Fräulein.

Without a word, she kissed him. Without a word, she removed his denims, his polka-dotted shorts. Without a word, she drew him to their bed. There they made love wordlessly, and there Prinz Owgoost forgot all his timorous doubts. Now he felt strong, virile, unconquerable, as a true Prince should feel.

She stroked him gently. "My love," she said, "the time has come for me to share our greatest, our most sacred secret. Have you heard of the Minotaur?"

"*Ja!*" boomed Papa Schimmelhorn. "I know all aboudt— in der Cifil Var, in der big fight vith der *Merrimac*."

Her laughter rippled. "Darling," she exclaimed, "it is brave of you to jest—but our Minotaur is no jesting matter. Our Minotaur is no myth, no ancient fresco on a crumbling wall, as he is at Knossos. Here on Little Palaeon, in his Labyrinth, our Minotaur—the *only* Minotaur—still lives! And we, on Little Palaeon, live in terror of him!''

IX.

Minotauromachy

Papa Schimmelhorn had only the vaguest idea of what a Minotaur might be, and, to tell the truth, at the moment any such creature, alive or not, was quite outside his range of active interest, which extended no further than the bed and its enticing occupant. He decided, however, that it would be unprincely not to answer. "Shveetheart," he asked, "if he iss alvays inside der vot-you-call-it, der Labyrinth, vhy is eferybody so shcared of him?"

She drew him close. As though she feared she might be overheard, she lowered her voice. "Because he is terrible in his power. He is a demigod. His mother was a queen, and her own father was a god. She mated with a magnificent white bull, brought miraculously out of the sea—"

"*Ach*, so!" said Papa Schimmelhorn. "Chust like die sheepherders in Nefada, only der oder vay around?"

"It was a dark and dreadful thing she did. And *he* was born, with a man's enormous body and a great bull's head—yes, and in other ways also, which you can best imagine, he is like a bull. But he has great horny fingers instead of hooves, and like any man he walks erect; and he is more than ten feet tall. The kings at Knossos pretended they kept him there in their false labyrinth. They did it so the Athenians would send an annual tribute of youths and maidens to be sacrificed to him, but in truth he never took

151

them; the kings kept them for their own pleasure. But *he* was always here on Little Palaeon, in the true Labyrinth, and he exercised his awful power much more subtly, for those who dared venture into it he invariably made mad, and those who thought of conquering Little Palaeon he drove away in fear and trembling. Even the Nazis, when they were on Crete during the war, never set foot here. And so we reverence him, and seek to appease his anger with our sacrifices, and hold our great bull-dances and solemn festivals to honor him, just as we have for four thousand and more years. As our Prince, you will also be our Priest, so these are things that you must know. Tomorrow we begin the four days of our most awesome and most joyous rites. They will start in the afternoon with the bull-dancing here in our courtyard, and that, my love, will be followed by a splendid feast, dancing and drinking and making merry. On the second day, our women will make their pilgrimage to the place of the Labyrinth—that great mound at the island's end, where outsiders think there's nothing left but ruins and rubble—to pray that *he* will make them fertile. On the third, our men will go there, so that he may grant them virility and rich harvests. Each evening, too, there will be feasts again. And you, my Hero-Prince, will lead us in all these exercises and devotions, splendid in your armor, and I will show you how."

"You mean," said Papa Schimmelhorn, aghast, "I haff to dance vith *bulls?*"

She laughed softly. She kissed him here and there, ardently. "Of course you won't, my love," said she. "Nor will you have to dandle serpents when the snake-goddess is being worshipped. All that's for the common folk. They enjoy themselves tremendously, and they're really very good at it—they have to be, or they don't last very long, because it really is quite dangerous. Then, on the fourth day— But no, I'll not tell you now, because that's the most important. It is the day when we try to soothe him with song and music, and placate him with our sacrifices. It is the day, too, when you will be at your most glorious. But enough! We've more interesting things to do tonight than talk. Let us turn out the light. . . ."

They were awakened by soft music; then serving maids brought breakfast to their bed. They made love. They took an hour or two off to make a little gold, transmuting a leaden statuette of the Minotaur himself a local craftsman had fashioned for them. Then, after lunch, Papa Schimmelhorn returned once more to his turret to don his martial finery and be ignored again by Gustav-Adolf. When he rejoined his Princess, he was delighted to see that she was wearing her Minoan decolletage, and with great ceremony they descended to the crowded courtyard. The thrones now stood on a platform high above the ground, and during the night a grandstand had been erected, very much like those easily disassembled ones used by traveling circuses. A round, well-sanded area in the very center of the courtyard had been fenced in, its gate facing the great gates of the court itself.

Cymbals clashed; conchs and rams' horns roared; gongs boomed. An exultant shout came from the eager crowd. Sarpedon Mavronides raised his baton of office. And from a passage underneath the grandstand ran ten maidens and ten youths, all lithe as panthers, all beautiful, all completely naked.

The Princess's eyes burned with excitement. "There they are!" she cried, squeezing her Prince's knee. "The bull-dancers! Oh, how I wish that I were with them—that you and I together could confront the bulls!" She sighed regretfully. "But pleasures such as these are not for us—that is the price we pay for our powers and privileges."

Papa Schimmelhorn thought it a very small and welcome price to pay, but he was wise enough not to say so.

The bull-dancers came leaping forward, smiling, holding each other's hands. Below the Thrones, they stopped, raised their arms in salutation, made obeisance. Then they arrayed themselves on either side of the arena's open gate.

"*Look! Look!*" Leaping to her feet, the Princess pointed

at the great courtyard gates, now swiftly opening. *"Here come the bulls!"*

There were six of them, and they were by far the biggest and most ferocious-looking bulls Papa Schimmelhorn had ever seen, black, mighty-shouldered, red eyed, cruelly horned. They charged in, chivvied on by men with prods. The bull-dancers skipped and danced, leaped and pirouetted, drawing them on, urging them into the arena. The arena gate was closed.

Then, for the next two hours, except for brief breaks for music and refreshments, he was treated to an absolutely unparalleled exhibition of sacerdotal athleticism. The bull-dancers waited for the bulls to charge them; they vaulted to their backs, they somersaulted from the viciously hooking horns; they decked their bulls with flowers; they formed human pyramids as targets, only to dissolve them in the twinkling of an eye. Only two of them were gored, one not very seriously.

When it was over, the gates were again opened, and the bulls, now looking just as irritable but much less aggressive, were chased out again.

The bull-dancers once more came forward to the Thrones. "They are coming to us to be rewarded," the Princess whispered. "The lads will come to me, the girls to you. Watch me, and do exactly what I do. But"—smiling, she looked down significantly at the front of his small goatskin skirt—"be sure you do not praise any of them too obviously."

She stood. Prinz Owgoost stood up with her. The first youth came to her. She placed a hand on either of his cheeks, and kissed his lips. "You have done well," she said. "You have danced beautifully and bravely."

The boy blushed, bowed deeply, turned away.

In the meantime, Papa Schimmelhorn had followed the very same procedure with the first of the dancing maidens, parroting his Princess's words as closely as he could.

By the time all the dancers had been given their accolades, he had come to the conclusion that old Minoan customs had much to recommend them, and he told the Princess as much when, after the ceremony was over and the crowd had helped to dismantle the grandstand and replace it with benches and long tables, he and she repaired to her apartments for cooling wine and dalliance.

He presided with gusto at the feast that followed, served at the tables in the courtyard. Huge tuns of wine were broached; flesh, fish, and fowl of every kind, roasted or more delicately prepared, were brought in from the castle's steaming kitchens. Music and merriment prevailed, and the Prince made a great hit with the populace when, at the banquet's end, he stood and, in a great bass voice, yodeled for them and demonstrated his cuckoo watch to tumultuous applause.

That night he spent as little time as possible with Humphrey who, he was beginning to suspect, took an unnecessarily pessimistic view of things.

Next day, he and his Princess led the women's pilgrimage to the mound of the Labyrinth. They rode in a gold-and-ivory chariot drawn by six milk-white oxen, undoubtedly in honor of the Minotaur's male parent, each of which was ridden by one of the more comely bull-dancers. As all the younger women in the procession were attired, like their Princess, in Minoan bodices, the Prince found the proceedings by no means as boring as he had anticipated, and at that night's banquet he outdid himself.

On the third day, the royal couple's chariot once more led a procession to the mound. However, as this time it was the men's pilgrimage, Papa Schimmelhorn found it much less interesting. Still, he watched the athletic contests with enjoyment, challenged some of the sturdier young men to Indian-wrestle, complimented them generously whenever he overcame them, and accepted his Princess's praise with a princely dignity. After the feast that followed, he sang songs in German, French, English, and bad Italian. His subjects were entranced, and Sarpedon Mavronides especially was impressed. "Her Highness spoke the truth," he told Mrs. Mavronides. "He is a veritable demigod.

Surely the Gods themselves sent him here to Little Palaeon, to govern us and guide us." He shook his head as ominously as Humphrey ever had. "Let us pray for his survival."

Papa Schimmelhorn did visit Gustav-Adolf and Humphrey for a few brief moments, annoying the former by rumpling his back fur, and worrying the latter by telling him vot a goot time he vas hafing, and that all his fears were unfounded. Then he hurried back to his Princess without even bothering to take off his armor.

She removed it for him. She told him of her love for him, of her pride in his magnificence and his accomplishments. As they lay in bed, Niobe brought them wine.

"This, dear heart, has been the most splendid of our festivals, and you have made it so. And tomorrow you will see its culmination, for tomorrow is the day of sacrifice."

"You mean die animals? Die sheep und goats und lidtle chickens?"

She stroked him soothingly. "Ah, love, I can read your mind. Do you fear that you shall have to slaughter them? I know that you are far too kind and gentle, too truly brave, for that. Besides, we stopped slaying them publicly ever so long ago, when we gave up human sacrifices, so everything's already been attended to; the cooks have taken care of it. Tomorrow, late in the afternoon, we'll take them to a certain door that leads into the Labyrinth and leave them in the chamber there with proper ceremony. In the morning, they will be gone. The Minotaur will have accepted them. And then—then will come the climax." Her clever hands distracted his attention. "I'll tell you all about it at suppertime tomorrow."

"*Ach*, I can vait!" chuckled Prinz Owgoost, drawing her to him.

The days had not passed as pleasantly for Gottfried Rumpler as they had for Papa Schimmelhorn. To compound his worries, he began receiving anxious calls from the Schweizerische Frauenbank's junior officers, enquiring as to the whereabouts of their president. Was she actually on her Mediterranean island? And if she was, why was she refusing all calls from them—calls on business matters of great urgency? The idea of any Swiss banker, male or female, deliberately ignoring such transactions was unthinkable, and normally love could have had nothing to do with it. No, he told himself, there could be no doubt that Fräulein von Hohenheim was no longer sane, and that in her madness she might not only bring their venture to utter ruin, but also do irreparable damage to the Rumpler Bank itself and to the Rumpler reputation. The question now was whether he and his allies could assemble, make effective plans, and reach Little Palaeon in time to save the situation—and the poor, demented Fräulein from herself.

He paced interminably up and down, in his office, in his home; he snapped rudely at Miss Ekstrom and treated his *petite amie* so churlishly that she burst into tears and took a cab back to her own apartment. He made unnecessary phone calls to Mama Schimmelhorn, begging her to assure him once more that Little Anton was really on his way from Hong Kong. He had his private jet held in instant readiness, and went over the flight plans with his pilots and Herr Grundtli time and again. Accompanied by the most expensive psychiatrist in Zürich, who had been sworn to utter secrecy, they were to fly directly to New Haven, where they would pick up their two passengers. They would then fly to Lisbon, staying there the night. From Lisbon, they would fly to Crete directly, where a specially chartered helicopter would be waiting for them. He and Herr Grundtli would be discreetly armed with Sig-Neuhausen automatic pistols; he had no clear idea of how these weapons would be used, but was determined to take no chances.

There are times that try men's souls, and the souls of Swiss bankers are not immune to them. Delays plagued Herr Doktor Rumpler. Little Anton, after arriving a day late in New Haven, phoned him to explain that he would be unable to accompany his great-aunt after all, because of urgent business for Pêng-Plantagenet, but that he would go over the situation very carefully with her so that she wouldn't (as he put it) go off the deep end the minute she caught sight of Papa and the Princess. "Softly, softly catchee monkey, as we say in the Far East," Little Anton told him; and Dr. Rumpler, disappointed in this loss of a reinforcement, agreed unhappily that any softening-up that could be done on Mama Schimmelhorn would probably be worthwhile. Then one of his pilots reported that something on the plane had to be worked on for a few more hours. Then the psychiatrist was called away to attend the spectacular nervous breakdown of a notorious international figure traveling through Switzerland. None of the delays were too long, but by the time he finally was able to take off, Gottfried Rumpler was by no means his usual resourceful, redoubtable self. He even, at the last moment, allowed Herr Grundtli to persuade him that it would be wiser to go unarmed.

They picked up Mama Schimmelhorn not long after Prinz Owgoost and his Prinzessin, in their chariot, led the men of Little Palaeon on their pilgrimage to the mound of the Labyrinth; and Mama Schimmelhorn immediately set out to put everything in its proper order. She questioned Herr Rumpler closely about the Fräulein's background, ancestry, and commercial qualifications, about his own involvement with her, about why it had been necessary for Papa Schimmelhorn to work on a little island in the Mediterranean, and about the strange impulse that might have led such an unusual woman to fall in love with a dirty old man who could not keep his hands off pretty pussycats.

Dr. Rumpler did his best to answer her, perspiring freely and helping himself liberally to brandy and soda despite her warnings that it vas nodt goot for him. Sometimes he would point out that he already had gone over the whole business with Little Anton, who was supposed to have told her all about it, and she would say to nefer mind, chust tell it all again; and sometimes, to complicate matters, the psychiatrist, Dr. Nymphenbourg, would confuse the issues very learnedly. She continued the inquisition almost without interruption across most of the Atlantic, and by the time they reached Lisbon she knew almost as much about Little Palaeon and its Princess as Dr. Rumpler did. She knew that some strange pagan religion was practiced there, that visitors were unwelcome, and that until Papa Schimmelhorn had shown up the Fräulein had had the reputation of being a confirmed man-hater. It was all very curious. It did not fit in at all with her ideas about Swiss banking practice, and she said so.

Gottfried Rumpler agreed with her. He told her that he admired her astuteness, but pointed out politely that the transmutation of lead into gold didn't really fit in with those practices either, and that extraordinary ventures required extraordinary measures.

Mama Schimmelhorn snorted. She smelled a rat, she told him, and it was indeed fortunate that he had begged her to come along, because whenever she had smelled a rat she never yet had failed to get things quickly under control. She indicated the vicious tip of her umbrella. "Don'dt vorry!" she declared. "I get him shtraightened oudt—in der short-ribs vith der bumbershoot!"

Next day, at Lisbon, they were delayed again—the landing gear had shown signs of stickiness, and the pilots did not want to risk taking off until all had been set in order.

They were delayed again on Crete, where the chartered helicopter was unendurably delayed. Gottfried Rumpler, who had hoped to set down in the Fräulein's courtyard early in the afternoon of what was—though of course he did not know it—the Day of Sacrifices, did not reach the castle until long after nine P.M. In the clear bright light of the full moon, the edifice was fully visible from some distance away, though everything seemed very still and only two lights showed.

The helicopter pilot asked whether he should set her down, and Dr. Rumpler snapped, "Of course! Of course!"

They settled gently. The pilot shut the engines off. They disembarked, Mama Schimmelhorn disdaining their helping hands.

No one was there to greet them. They waited. After a few minutes, they saw a tall, solitary figure striding across the court toward them. It halted, glared at them reprovingly, and informed them in Greek that they were trespassing.

The helicopter pilot translated.

"*Trespassing?*" shouted Gottfried Rumpler, using his colonel's voice. "*I* am Fräulein von Hohenheim's associate in business. I am the co-employer of this man Schimmelhorn, and this lady who accompanies me is *Frau* Schimmelhorn. Do you understand, Herr Mavronides—for I assume you *are* Herr Mavronides? We are here to find out what is wrong. We demand to see the Fräulein immediately!"

"The *Princess* is not here. She is occupied with matters of grave import elsewhere. You cannot see her."

"Then we demand to see Herr Schimmelhorn!"

"You cannot see him either." Sarpedon Mavronides's voice, mournfully and ominously, dropped a full octave. "His Serene Highness, Prince August, has disappeared. He has been missing since suppertime, three hours after we had finished with the sacrifices. Her Highness is frantic. She is searching for him, and so is everybody else on Little Palaeon—and so far we have found no trace of him. We tremble to consider what may have happened!"

"Maybe he got avay again und iss chasing naked vomen!" Mama Schimmelhorn muttered scornfully; and Sarpedon Mavronides, though he looked at her as though she had just committed *lèse majesté*, estimated her potential very accurately and refrained from answering.

None of them saw another figure, smaller and slighter than Mavronides, who had started to dash out of a castle door toward the helicopter, then hastily checked himself and slithered back out of sight.

Meister Gaspar Gansfleisch had not been searching for his missing Prince. Nor had he expected a helicopter to arrive with Dr. Rumpler, Mama Schimmelhorn, and their companions. As soon as the Princess had ordered everybody on the island to comb the island for Papa Schimmelhorn, he had activated his alarm-clock communicator.

He had been waiting eagerly for someone else.

The Day of Sacrifices had gone very well for Papa
Schimmelhorn. He and his Princess made love and played
at making gold. Throughout the morning and early afternoon, there were no ceremonies to distract them; and when
he finally had to resume his armor so that they could lead
the sacrificial procession in their chariot, he felt that he
hadn't a care in the world. Ahead of them, the six white
oxen—now ridden symbolically by members of the kitchen
staff—walked slowly and with great dignity, tinkling silver
bells as they tossed their patient heads. Behind them came
Ismail, driving the station wagon and pulling an enormous
flatbed trailer piled high with sacrifices. Behind him followed a pickup truck and another trailer, and several wag-
ons drawn by assorted beasts of burden, all similarly laden.
Papa Schimmelhorn, who had expected at least slaughtered
animals and bloody carcasses, was tremendously relieved
to see that everything had been very neatly wrapped, much
as Mama Schimmelhorn wrapped her butcher-shop purchases for the freezer.

"You are surprised, my love?" laughed the Princess.
"Do not be. Legend tells us that in the early days, we used
to slay the creatures at his very door, and then drag them
into the chamber where these are going to be put. He
would accept them, but always it made him terribly angry.
After a time, he would throw out the skins and all the
other parts he didn't want, and then for hours the hideous
noises he so often makes would torture us, and all Little
Palaeon would quiver with his wrath. But he would keep
no part at all of the human sacrifices, so finally we decided
that he didn't like their taste, and we stopped offering
them. We also started wrapping all the parts he wanted. It
seemed the sensible thing to do."

The procession moved very slowly, enlivening its progress with song and merrymaking, but finally it reached a
limestone portal projecting from the mound, where there

was a bronze door, green with age. There Gaspar Gansfleisch awaited them with several of the castle servants. He knelt abjectly as their chariot rolled to a halt before him. He offered his back to the Princess as a carriage step, and cried out in admiration when Papa Schimmelhorn picked her up bodily and leaped out carrying her.

Graciously, she nodded to him. She stepped up to the door, opened it with a huge bronze key, flung it wide. A gasp from the assembled islanders acclaimed her action. She spoke, addressing the Minotaur in a high, clear voice. She praised him in archaic Greek, his power and majesty; she implored him to grant them fertility for their cattle, their crops, their families, to protect them from storm and strife, vermin and disease; she begged him to accept their poor and humble sacrifices. Sarpedon Mavronides whispered a running translation into his Prince's ear.

The Prince looked in. The chamber was enormous, paved and lined with cold limestone; and dark passages could be seen leading out of it. Under Mavronides's direction, the islanders started unloading the sacrifices, carrying them in, stacking them very neatly along the walls.

When they had finished, the Princess spoke again, echoing everything she had said before. Then she closed and locked the door again and, bowing repeatedly as she backed away, returned to the chariot. A glad cry went up as Papa Schimmelhorn lifted her into it, and the procession started back as it had come.

It was almost evening, and a gentle, warm breeze was blowing. The Princess moved closer to her Prince. Her hand played with the edge of his narrow goatskin skirt. "Now, my own hero," she said softly, "now we shall return. Once more we shall make love. Then we shall sup, and I shall tell you the one more role that you must play, the greatest, noblest, mightiest role of all—tonight at midnight, when the moon is full, when it has risen."

"*Ach!*" cried Papa Schimmelhorn, his vinegar bubbling up within him at the thought of the roles he had already played. "It iss hard to vait!"

They went back to the castle. They made love, and it seemed to him that this time the Fräulein loved him with what was, even for her, an unprecedented passion, her eyes burning with her ardor, her lips on fire.

Afterwards, she insisted that he once again put on his armor, except of course his helmet, before they dined; and while they ate and drank she was strangely silent. Finally, after a long time, she looked at him intently and said, "Oh, love, the time has nearly come! At midnight, the Fourth Day starts, and all the omens have been favorable. Now I can tell you that which you must do, how you shall do the greatest deed in Little Palaeon's long history!"

Puzzled, he looked at her enquiringly.

She seized his hands. Leaping up, she pulled him to his feet. "This very night," she cried, "we shall return to the Portal of the Sacrifices at midnight, just you and I and Sarpedon Mavronides, and once again I shall unlock the door and fling it open. And then, my Prince, my Hero-Prince! Then you shall stride forth in all your strength, like the demigod we know you are, and challenge the foul Minotaur to mortal combat!"

Papa Schimmelhorn's jaw dropped. He gulped, uttering a bullfrog croak.

She embraced him. "Not in four thousand years," she declared triumphantly, "has any man ever dared to face him thus! But *you* will face him—aye, and fight him to the death, and slay him! I'm certain of it! And if, by some remote mischance, the gods do decree otherwise, we will make rich sacrifices to your shade, and you will never be forgotten on Little Palaeon."

"Shveetheart," gasped Papa Schimmelhorn, "you—you made der choke? *Nicht wahr?*"

She looked a little puzzled, a little hurt. "Now surely *you* are joking, are you not?" said she. "Were you not to confront the Minotaur and destroy him, how could I allow you to sire my sons?"

He shuffled his feet uncomfortably. "*Ja, ja,*" he stammered, "I—I haff forgotten aboudt that. So—und it must be tonight?'' He half-tried to smile. "B-before ve make luff any more?''

"Tonight!" she told him. "This night of the full moon! We start within the hour!" She handed him his helmet. "Here, place this on your noble head and take your spear.''

The idea was seeping through to Papa Schimmelhorn that the lady meant exactly what she said, that within the hour she wanted him to face a terrible being more than ten feet tall, wily with the cunning of more than four millennia, with great sharp horns, clawed fingers, and—

He was no coward. On the time machine he had built for his old friend General Pollard, he had observed the dreadful Mongol invasion of the West and visited the bloody field of Waterloo. With Mama, he had survived his kidnapping by the overbearing women star-travelers of the planet she had christened Beetlegoose Nine, when he had been made aware of the strange inhabitants of other worlds— but none of these adventures had really been by choice. Papa Schimmelhorn was definitely a lover, not a warrior. He had no desire at all to tangle with the Minotaur.

He gulped again, and said the first thing his subconscious prompted him to say. "But shveetheart, mein Lidtle Philli, first I must go up to der turret und look after mein Gustav-Adolf. He iss a goot cat, *ja*. Remember how he has killed dot Tvitchgibbet? Und—und—'' He reached out to wipe away a tear. "If die Gods, like you haff said, let der Minotaur vin, I vant him to know I haff nodt forgotten him!''

She gazed at him in admiration. "Even now!" she exclaimed. "Even as you go forth to risk your life for me and for our sons, your thoughts are with your poor cat. How noble! How exalted! It befits you, love. Well, then, go—while I array myself appropriately. But hasten back, for as I said, we start within the hour!"

Papa Schimmelhorn kissed her with all the passion he could muster, now very much below its normal level, ducked out into the corridor, and quickened his pace to get as far away from there as fast as possible. He had no idea at all of where to run. Driven by one imperative, his mind started offering him alternatives. Should he dash to the sea, plunge in, and swim to Crete where, as a foreign prince, perhaps he could find political asylum? Or should he simply try to find a castle hidey-hole, where not even the Princess would think to look for him? Or hide out in the woods? Or creep into some peasant's humble stable? None of these seemed very practical, and as he scuttled first down one corridor, then another, he suddenly remembered Humphrey's plea. *Und vhy nodt?* he thought. *Der hum-uncle-us iss very old und shmart. Maybe he giffs der goot advice!*

He hurried to the topmost story, dashed down a corridor, skidded at its corner—and ran directly into Meister Gansfleisch, who had just closed the door to his own turret stairs behind him.

As he put on the brakes, the alchemist backed up, bowing profoundly. "Great Prince!" he whined, his voice dripping sincere concern. "What brings you here? Bless me, you look perturbed! Oh, distinctly so! Is there anything I, your devoted servant, your poor disciple, can do to aid you?"

Papa Schimmelhorn looked at him. Since his public repentance, Meister Gansfleisch had been extremely servile and obliging, going out of his way to perform the most menial tasks, anticipating every little royal wish. Suddenly now, he saw him not as a onetime deadly enemy, but at least as a possible temporary ally. He forgot all about seeking Humphrey's counsel. Trying to catch his breath, he poured out his tale.

Meister Gansfleisch listened unbelievingly, scarcely able to keep his hands and features from revealing his delight and his excitement.

"Und so," finished Papa Schimmelhorn, "I try to get avay! I do nodt vant to kill der poor Minotaur, und I do nodt vant der Minotaur to kill me! But how—*vhere* do I go? Iss novhere on der island. My lidtle Philli finds me eferyvhere!"

"Please, please, Your Highness, Your *Serene* Highness!" Meister Gansfleisch reached out to touch his arm, and Papa Schimmelhorn didn't even shrink away. "I know *just* how you feel. The Minotaur would tear you to *shreds.*" He narrowed his eyes shrewdly. "But, Highness, you have been kind to me. You have forgiven my envy and my animosity. *I* can show you where to hide. After all, it would only have to be for a few hours."

"Und then?" Papa Schimmelhorn asked dismally. "Vot aboudt vhen die Prinzessin finds oudt?"

"Why, then it will not matter. She may be annoyed, of course—I'm sure she will be. But don't forget that she's in love with you, madly in love! She will forgive you. Then it won't be till the next full moon before she can offer you to the Minotaur again, and in the meantime perhaps you can persuade her that the Gods don't want you to confront him. Yes, that's a splendid notion, indeed it is! You'll disappear, and come out again when all's clear, and tell her that the Gods themselves snatched you up—perhaps up to Olympus—and who'll be the wiser?"

"But *vhere?*" pleaded Papa Schimmelhorn.

"Shh!" Meister Gansfleisch touched a gray finger to his lips. He made a great show of darting precautionary glances one way and another. "I know just the place—a place no one will ever think of looking for you." He lowered his voice. "It is on the Mound of the Labyrinth itself, on the other side, not very far away. You can easily reach it without being seen if you go quickly along the beach under the cliffs, then climb the path that rises below the little copse. I alone have the key, and I will let you take it." He hesitated, putting a little extra whine in his voice. "But if I do this, Highness, will you promise never to tell anyone that I have done it? And will you intercede for me with *her* when you return and she is no longer angry? So that I can again use my laboratory without restriction? Will you do these small things for your servant, Highness?"

His Highness, who at that moment would have promised anything for a key to a secure hiding place, declared fervently that he would indeed.

"Then wait a second, just a tiny second!" Meister Gansfleisch, hardly able to contain his glee at the way things were developing, scuttled up his stairs, hurriedly took the bronze key from its strongbox, and—allowing himself only a moment to gloat luxuriously—brought it to Papa Schimmelhorn, who took it with a sigh of gratitude.

"Yes, yes! We will get you there without being seen! Though the moon has risen, there will be many shadows in which to hide. Highness, go directly to the beach—you do know how?"

Papa Schimmelhorn did indeed, having gone there more than once with Niki and Emmy. "*Ja, ja!*" he answered. "*Es ist gut!* At night iss nefer anybody there."

"And you know the path of which I spoke, rising to the copse?"

"*Ja, ja!*"

"Well, at its very top, take a sharp turn to your left, through the thicket, and you'll see the door immediately in front of you. Unlock it. Let it close behind you. It will be dark—it was once a hermit's chapel—but you won't mind that for only a few hours. In the morning, enough light will seep in so that you can see the door and open it again."

He handed the key to Papa Schimmelhorn, who took it with tears in his eyes, thinking that Humphrey had been wrong—that this toad did at least vear a precious chewel in der head—and that he would tell him so.

Two minutes later, slipping quietly out of a back door to the castle, he was on his way.

The walk took him three-quarters of an hour. Two or three times, he had to seek the shelter of the shadows, once from a pair of lovers too busy with each other to see him anyhow, and once or twice from drunken villagers noisily making their way home. As fast as possible, he climbed the path up to the copse. He pushed his way through the dark thicket. There, as Meister Gansfleisch had promised him, was the door, revealed clearly by the moon. It too was of metal, of brass or bronze, but it was

comfortingly smaller than the one for sacrifices. He slipped
the key into its hole. He turned it. The lock protested, but
it moved. He removed the key. He entered. He pushed the
door shut, heard the lock's heavy click behind him. He
took two slow steps forward into the darkness—

With no warning whatsoever, his feet flew out from
under him, and he was plunging down a stone slide,
smooth, slippery, and precipitous. Instinctively, he reached
out for a handhold, for anything to break his fall. His
hands touched nothing but polished limestone. Then, just
as abruptly, he hit bottom, slid a dozen feet, and was
harshly halted by a wall he could not see. His spear,
coming down behind him, hit him in the posterior beneath
his goatskin skirt, luckily with its blunt end.

For a minute or two, he just sat there, letting his eyes
get accustomed to the darkness, and gradually he saw that
the darkness was by no means absolute. There was a glow
ahead of him, faint, nebulous, emanating from the limestone ceiling of the tunnel in which he sat, and he could
see the open mouths of other tunnels gaping ahead of him,
dark and uninviting. Slowly he stood. In the distance,
resounding eerily from the stone walls, came a medley of
ungodly noises, moans and screeches, as though Twitchgibbet and all his big and little friends had combined with the
most revolting contemporary punk rock groups to strain
the limits of disharmony.

He listened. Still in shock, he looked at his environ-
ment. He walked apprehensively to the first gaping tunnel,
looked down it, saw that still other tunnels opened into it.

Suddenly he realized that he had been betrayed—and the
dreadful degree of his betrayal. "*Lieber Gott!*" he cried,
in a voice straight out of Greek tragedy. "I am *in* der
Labyrinth!"

His eyes darted hither and yon, searching for a possible
escape route. There was none.

And now, in the distance, over the cacophony, he heard
a sound far more ominous, infinitely more frightening: the
sound of massive footsteps, coming closer, closer, echoing

and re-echoing as heavily clawed toes struck the flagstones—
and with that sound came another, a terrible roaring, rather
like a cross between an enraged lion and a chain saw.

He turned. He ran a dozen steps. He recognized the
utter futility of running. The footsteps and the roaring
grew louder, louder, until they filled the entire passageway.

Papa Schimmelhorn froze. Eyes bugging out, he stared
down the limestone tunnel.

The Minotaur appeared. At first, he simply loomed, his
outlines indefinite. Then Papa Schimmelhorn saw that he
was indeed more than ten feet tall, that he was horned and
horribly fanged, that his enormous arms and hands were
raised to seize and clutch. He wore a massive crossbelt,
brightly jeweled, and nothing else, and his maleness was
appalling in its magnitude.

Papa Schimmelhorn, with a sob, bethought himself of
those Swiss pikemen who, in the old days, had held off the
vaunted knights of Austria and Spain. Preparing to sell his
life dearly, he tried to remember how they held their
spears.

Roaring, the Minotaur came on.

Papa Schimmelhorn stared at him again—and his spear
fell from his hand.

X.

Among the Missing

Knowing little or nothing of Labyrinths and Minotaurs, and knowing her own husband very well indeed, Mama Schimmelhorn was neither surprised nor frightened at the news of his vanishment; and Sarpedon Mavronides, his wits about him, at once took steps to see that, at least for the time being, she would be tucked away where she could neither lock horns with the Princess nor learn about the perils threatening him.

He turned to her with a profound bow. "Gracious lady," he said, "this isle is fraught with dangers. Its cliffs are high and steep, the waters that surround it treacherous. The Prince—that is, er, your esteemed husband has been fond of walking all alone in the moonlight—"

Mama Schimmelhorn sniffed.

"—and also of swimming out to sea, and even though he is a powerful man, we naturally have feared for his safety. But at this time there is nothing you yourself can do to help either him or those who seek him. May I escort you to his turret, to the rooms he occupied, where you can refresh yourself after your journey? If you wish, I shall send a servant girl up to you, perhaps with tea and cakes. You can rest there till we have something to report."

"I do nodt need to rest," stated Mama Schimmelhorn.

"But my dear Frau Schimmelhorn," put in Dr. Nymphenbourg, catching on, "wouldn't it really be a good idea? Then when they bring him back, they'll know just where to take him."

She regarded the psychiatrist with distaste, hating to admit that possibly he had a point. Hefting her umbrella, she hesitated.

"Yes," said Mavronides, "you will be there to comfort him, especially if he has been injured. One reason we have been so worried is because today he did not feed his cat, something he always does."

"You mean Gustav-Adolf iss up inside der turret?" she demanded.

"Yes, Madame."

She tapped the umbrella's ferrule on the stones decisively. "Dirty old man!" she snapped. "Imachine! Nodt efen feeding poor Gustav-Adolf. An oudraitch! Vell okay, I vill go up and vait for him, und I vould like a lidtle tea, perhaps vith some schnapps inside, und for Gustav-Adolf maybe some raw liffer."

"I shall escort you," said Mavronides. He turned to Dr. Rumpler, who had been fizzing angrily. "Herr Doktor, my apologies. I shall return immediately. Perhaps you and your assistants would do the Princess the favor of helping her to search for him in your fine helicopter?"

Dr. Rumpler frowned. He said that of course they would be glad to help. He ordered Mavronides to be quick about it.

"Perhaps also," Mavronides added, "we first will try to find the Princess herself so that you may speak with her."

Mama Schimmelhorn made a rude noise, but when he bowed to her and requested that she follow him, she went without demur.

Once in the turret, Mavronides phoned the kitchens, found one serving maid still on the job, and ordered tea, little cakes, schnapps, and raw liver. Mama Schimmelhorn, busy petting Gustav-Adolf and letting him tell her how he and his pretty calico had been abandoned, scarcely said good-bye to him; and she devoted the next few minutes partly to the cats and partly to a minute examination of the turret, looking for evidences of feminine occupancy. In the courtyard, the helicopter's rotors boomed again as it took off.

The tea came, and she had the girl put it on the little table where Papa Schimmelhorn had been in the habit of having his discussions with the homunculus. She sipped, ate her small cakes, fed Gustav-Adolf and his purring girl-friend, and discoursed at length on her husband's unnumbered misdeeds.

So preoccupied was she that some time passed before she noticed that a tiny, feeble voice was calling to her.

"Vot iss?" she asked, wrinkling her brows. "Papa has maybe somevhere left der radio on, oder der TV?"

She listened attentively. It was indeed a voice, a very little voice, and it was calling out quite clearly, "*Help! Help! Help!*"

"Vhere are you?" she demanded.

The voice had sounded as though it were coming from behind the fireplace, so from her black handbag she took her hearing aid, an instrument she needed only occasionally, to listen to her husband through a door or floor. She pressed it against the marble.

"Pray help me, gentle lady!" the tiny voice was pleading. "By God's grace, I do implore you! I thirst and hunger and grow faint. The Prince, who whilom always treated me with kindness, now has fled away and left me here!"

"*Ach, so!*" growled Mama Schimmelhorn. "Iss nodt bad enough he forgets to feed die katzen. Now ve find somevun else!"

"My name is Humphrey, gentle lady," said the tiny voice, "and I am trapped behind this fireplace, where he has left me."

"Okay," said Mama Schimmelhorn, "ve try to get you oudt. Maybe I can get somevun vith der hammer oder der crowbar und break it down."

"No breaking will be needed, praise God!" the voice informed her. "I am here in a secret orifice. If thou wilt press with thy two fingers two spots upon the marble to the right, it all will swing away and reveal my hiding place."

There were two spots, and two only, visible on the marble slab. She pressed each with an index finger, and abruptly the slab swung back.

Peering inside, she saw a large glass jar of obvious antiquity. Then, in it, she saw Humphrey. The poor homunculus, standing on his chair, was doing his best to cling to the jar's rim.

"Vell," she remarked, "a lidtle man! Shmaller efen than on Beetlegoose. Vot next?"

"Pray take me out!" the little man was saying. "This fluid I live in will not injure you, nor will it soil your hands. Oh, take me out and seat me on my chair, for I have much to tell you!"

"Okay," said Mama Schimmelhorn. "Keep die britches on." She wrestled out the jar. She placed it on the table. Reaching into the fluid, she lifted Humphrey out, fished out his chair, seated him.

Humphrey leaned forward. Ever so gently, he touched one of her fingers with his little hands. "Before we speak—oh, do not waste a moment, I implore you!—pray lock and bolt the door. No one here, in this pagan keep where the Black Arts are practiced and *she* rules, must know about me. I would be in mortal peril!"

"Already I haff locked und bolted," she replied. "Alvays in foreign countries I do first."

Humphrey emitted a small sigh. "It was your brave and generous husband who protected me," he told her, "just as your noble cat first saved me from that cursed rat-fiend, Twitchgibbet—"

"Vait a minute! Hold die horses!" she broke in. "Begin in der beginning. Nefer in all mein life I see a man so shmall. Vhere vere you born?"

He sighed again. "Alas!" he said. "Gentle lady, I came into existence without being born. This wretched body was

created by process magical four hundred years ago, as a
trap for me, and I shall not offend your tender sensibilities
by telling how 'twas done. I am what necromancers and
the like term a homunculus . . ."

And he went on to tell her his whole story, very much
as he had already told it to Papa Schimmelhorn.

She was enchanted by him, by his faded doublet, his
worn, patched hose and rumpled ruff, his miniature beard.
At first she listened to him incredulously, but his sincerity—
and indeed the very fact of his existence—convinced her.
When he informed her that honeyed brandy was his sole
sustenance, she hurried to find the brandy bottle and the
honey jar, and filled his thimble for him twice.

"*Gott in Himmel!*" she said. "Such a long life, und so
interesting! Vhen ve go home, maybe you come vith und
shpeak to die ladies of mein church? They vould luff to
hear all aboudt."

Humphrey replied that he was grateful for her good
opinion, but that his sole desire on earth was either to
return to England, where he had been brought to life, or
even better to find his way somehow to outer space, where
his unwanted body no longer would have any hold on him.
"But now," he said, "there is much more that I must tell
you, for it concerns your husband, Master Schimmelhorn,
and my sad conscience. It is my fault, not his, that this
Princess Philippa, as they call her, fell in love with him—"

From the courtyard, helicopter rotors beat the air, de-
scending, then settled to a steady, slow thrumming. Humphrey broke off, startled.

"Don'dt vorry!" said Mama Schimmelhorn. "If they
come up, I hide you right avay. I am nodt vorried aboudt
Papa. All der time, he runs avay from home, but alvays I
catch him oder he comes back. You chust keep telling me
der shtory."

Humphrey, now seeming much refreshed but still looking a bit uneasy, took up his tale. He described Gustav-
Adolf's glorious victory; he told about poor Papa Schimmelhorn's despondency over his lost virility, and how, out of

gratitude, he himself had given him the love potion; he described its cataclysmic effects on the Fräulein-Princess-Priestess.

"And now," he said, "my conscience will torment me night and day, at least until he's found. I have heard whispers, Mistress Schimmelhorn, that on this isle there lives a creature, half man, half beast, and old as sin itself. If anything has happened to your husband, never, never shall I forgive myself. Truly I shall remain always saddened and disgraced."

Mama Schimmelhorn dismissed his talk of danger with a shrug. "If tonight they do nodt find him," she said, "tomorrow I vill go oudt vith Gustav-Adolf. He iss a clefer cat, und often he has followed Papa. He vill find him. Now tell me more aboudt der luff potion, how it vorks so fast."

Humphrey obliged her. He told her how Count Cagliostro had brewed the potion for Augustus the Strong, how it worked instantaneously, a mere whiff sufficing, how if Papa Schimmelhorn had added only one drop of the critical ingredient instead of three there probably would have been much less trouble—

"Hah!" exclaimed Mama Schimmelhorn. "Der old goat! It iss a vunder he does nodt add six drops! Und vhat has happened to der potion? It iss all used up?"

"Oh, no," said Humphrey. "He used up less than half of it. He sealed the rest up in a little tube—the sort that can be crumbled 'twixt one's fingers instantly."

"*Ach, ja!* So he can use again later. Maybe vhen ve get home. How shameful! Vhere iss it now?"

"It has been kept safely in the same secret place as I myself."

"Then maybe iss bedter I keep it in my purse"—she smiled—"vhere iss efen safer." Briskly she retrieved the ampule. A calculating gleam was in her eye. "Und does it vork only on vomen?" she enquired.

"It does its dread work on any human being," Humphrey assured her, "and I doubt not also on cherubim and seraphim if they so much as catch a breath of it. All that's needed is that they be looking at the person they must love. Never has any other essence been concocted so powerful, so fearsome, so subtly swift.''

Chust vot der doctor ordered, thought Mama Schimmelhorn. Carefully, she folded the ampule into her handkerchief. Carefully, she stowed it in a pocket of her handbag.

"Dear gentle lady," exclaimed Humphrey, in alarm, "I trust you are not planning to administer this terrible substance *to your husband?* A man of such ardent spirits—"

She snorted. "To Papa? Nefer! I do nodt need. He luffs me now for more than sixty years. Der only trouble iss like I say—he iss an old goat. Anyhow, predty soon ve put a shtop to all der nonsense vith this Fräulein-Prinzessin Vot's-her-name, und I take him by der ear, und he comes back vith me to New Hafen vhere I can lock him in der basement und efery Sunday he must sing hymns in church."

She poured herself another cup of tea and schnapps, and Humphrey a third thimbleful of brandied honey. She sat back in her chair. "Und now," she said, "maybe you tell me more aboudt your life und eferyvhere you haff been all ofer, und all die famous people you haff met."

She sat there with Gustav-Adolf and his little calico both purring on her lap, and she and Humphrey got on famously. She told him about Mrs. Laubenschneider and how she had protected Gustav-Adolf against shpooks und defils, and all about Papa Schimmelhorn's many misbehaviors, and she listened while Humphrey told her of the kings and cardinals, archdukes and alchemists he had encountered, all of whom had tried to use his knowledge to further their own greed and their ambition. He and she saw eye to eye on almost everything, and neither of them paid any heed when the helicopter in the courtyard noisily took off again.

Presently, both she and Humphrey were a little tiddly, and he informed her that he had not enjoyed himself so much since Dr. Dee had introduced him, in a private room of a place called the Swan Tavern, to someone named Ben

Jonson. He sighed nostalgically and, in a thin and reedy voice, sadly sang "Greensleeves" for her, following it up with two or three sentimental songs by Thomas Campion.

Loyally, Humphrey praised Papa Schimmelhorn as a true friend, a man of infinite benevolence, and many times he expressed the devout hope that no evil had befallen him; and every time, she reassured him. After another hour or two, she pressed a fourth thimbleful on him and, when he protested that it was too much, that he might very well become intoxicated, she chuckled and remarked, "Iss all right, Herr Humphrey—you don'dt haff to drife."

Presently they once more heard helicopter rotors beating out a landing. This time, the rotors not only slowed, they stopped completely. There was silence.

"Vell," she said, "I vunder if they find?"

Humphrey yawned. Two or three minutes passed. And suddenly there came a knocking at the door.

"Vot iss?" she demanded, quickly whispering good-night to her little friend and putting him with his chair back into the jar.

"Frau Schimmelhorn," came Mavronides's voice. "We have not found His High—that is, Herr Schimmelhorn. We have combed every inch of Little Palaeon. He has vanished into thin air! But Her Highness the Princess Philippa has returned with us, and she has ordered me to bring you to her."

Quickly, Mama Schimmelhorn tucked Humphrey's jar back in the compartment, pushed the panel closed. "Okay," she called out, "I vill come."

She unbarred the door and joined him.

"She awaits you in the courtyard," said Mavronides.

In the courtyard, the Princess was very much in evidence, and very much distraught. She stood fiercely apart from the small group of men, all of whom were doing their best to hide behind the manly figure of Dr. Rumpler. Her eyes were flashing; her lips were drawn back frighteningly from her fine teeth. She glared at Mama Schimmelhorn as she walked up.

"So *that's* what you have brought me—this old hag!" she almost screamed.

"Don'dt talk to me like dot!" said Mama Schimmelhorn, advancing on her. "I catch you in der belly-button vith der bumbershoot!"

Sarpedon Mavronides uttered a gasp of horror. Little Dr. Nymphenbourg let out a squeak.

The Fräulein whirled tempestuously to confront her business associate. "How can you dare, Gottfried Rumpler? And on the very night when my Prince, my Hero-Prince, has disappeared? How do you *dare* to bring this—this creature to *our* castle, *our* isle?"

She stood there, less than a foot from him, her eyes burning directly into his—and Mama Schimmelhorn, without another word, took two swift steps forward and, holding her breath, with her right hand she snapped the ampule under both their noses.

The Fräulein recoiled. For an interminable instant, she stood there, swaying. Then, clapping hands to forehead, for a moment she rocked wildly back and forth. "Oh, what has *happened?*" came her anguished cry. "Or did I dream? Did spiders spin their magic webs across my eyes? I have been enchained! Enchanted! Oh, Gottfried! *Oh, dearest Gottfried!* It has been a nightmare! I have been mad! *Mad!* What have I *done?*"

Dr. Rumpler's eyes had opened startlingly. It was as though he had never seen his love before. "*My own Philippa!*" he cried out, reaching for her.

Weeping, she threw herself into his arms.

"Philippa! My dear, dear Philippa! Whatever you have done, it does not matter! Nothing matters except that now we are together!"

"It—it must have been that filthy Gaspar Gansfleisch's d-d-doing!" she sobbed. "The beast! And now that poor old man—that Herr Schimmelhorn—is lost! *Lost!* And everyone will say that it's my fault."

"He iss nodt poor," Mama Schimmelhorn said severely.

"He has der goot chob at Heinrich Luedesing's cuckoo-clock factory, und ve safe our money."

The Fräulein turned to her, eyes streaming. "My dear Frau Schimmelhorn, I owe you an apology for what I must have said. Please understand—I was not myself, not my true Swiss self. I—I'm sure I was bewitched."

"It iss all right, shveetheart," Mama Schimmelhorn told her. "I forgiff you. It vas nodt your fault."

She thougt, *Ach, der potion vorks! Lidtle Humphrey vill be pleased.* She snickered to herself. *I should haff safed a lidtle to giff to Papa. Maybe he needs it vhen he finds out he no longer iss a Prince.*

Sarpedon Mavronides had watched his Princess open-mouthed, telling himself that the ways of princesses and priestesses were unfathomable, totally beyond the understanding of simple men. Now, suddenly, she summoned him.

"Sarpedon," she commanded, "by this time some of your footmen should have returned. Take three or four of them, and bring Gaspar Gansfleisch here to me. Oh, he's going to pay for what he's done! Bring him in chains if you have to, but get him here. Then I shall decide what shall become of him—whether we'll throw him to the sharks, or push him through the Door of Sacrifices as Minotaur meat!"

"*Philippa!*" Gottfried Rumpler exclaimed in horror. "We can't do *that!* We Swiss are *civilized!*"

"Dot's der shpirit!" put in Mama Schimmelhorn.

The Fräulein embraced her beloved. "From now on, Gottfried, you shall be my conscience. My only, my one true love, I know I safely can entrust such matters to your judgment!" She turned back to Mavronides. "But bring him anyhow," she said. "I'll think of something civilized to do to him!"

Mavronides beckoned to some servants who had just entered, and went off with them.

The Fräulein came to Mama Schimmelhorn. "Oh, I'm

so glad you understand!'' she said. "You have forgiven me—now tell me that we shall be friends!"

She held out both her hands, and Mama Schimmelhorn took one of them and shook it vigorously. "*Natürlich,*" she replied, "ve girls must shtick togeder. Maybe tomorrow ve haff tea und I vill tell you vot an old goat Papa iss.''

The Fräulein had the grace to blush. "Let us all pray that tomorrow we shall find him, safe and sound," she said. "It is too late to search any more tonight, but we shall start again at daybreak. We—if we have to, we'll even look into the Labyrinth, though— Well, I dare say no more!''

"Pooh!" answered Mama Schimmelhorn. "Don'dt vorry. If you knew Papa as vell as I—ha! Efery time he gets avay iss der same thing . . .''

She went on to regale the Fräulein with several tales of her husband's disappearances, wanderings, misdeeds, and abject returns, and of his invariably broken promises to reform; and the Fräulein listened to her very sympathetically.

While this was going on, Dr. Nymphenbourg, who had been shifting nervously from foot to foot and pulling at the hairs of his well-combed beard, took Gottfried Rumpler by the elbow and drew him tactfully aside.

"Herr Doktor!" he whispered urgently. "Let me warn you! Have nothing—nothing *whatsoever*—to do with this woman, this Princess or whatever, in her delusions, she calls herself. She is a classic case—an extreme schizoid-paranoid! She is a danger to you and to herself! I tell you, she should be committed! Confined!''

Gottfried Rumpler looked at him aghast. "What are you saying?" he roared, seizing him by the shoulders and shaking him thoroughly. Then, recalling that the Fräulein was within hearing distance, he dropped his voice, but not its intensity. "So it is true!" he hissed. "Psychiatrists are all themselves insane. Talking such nonsense!" He whirled, called Herr Grundtli to him. "Herr Grundtli," he barked, "we have no further use for Dr. Nymphenbourg. He is too disturbed. The helicopter will take you back to Crete immediately. See that he is placed on the first commercial flight for Athens. Also, see to it that his fee is paid in full, with a modest bonus to ensure his discretion."

Dr. Nymphenbourg ruffled his feathers, got himself as far out of the Rumpler reach as possible, and muttered something irritated about medical ethics, the seal of the confessional, and his professional reputation.

No one paid him any heed; and Gottfried Rumpler, before he turned back to his Fräulein, whispered one more instruction into Herr Grundtli's ear. "Listen carefully!" he said. "This is of great urgency. You are to get in touch with Brigitte at once. Tell her that—that I shall no longer be able to visit her. If she weeps, ignore it. Simply say that when she returns to Brussels, the settlement we long ago agreed upon shall be paid to her, with a generous bonus. You understand?"

Herr Grundtli, whose attitude toward the upper brass of Swiss banking was rather like that of Sarpedon Mavronides toward princesses, said that he understood perfectly, and that all would be carried out as ordered.

He herded Dr. Nymphenbourg back into the helicopter, followed by the pilots.

Gottfried Rumpler rejoined the Fräulein and Mama Schimmelhorn, and walked them a safe distance from the machine. It started with a roar; its rotors thrashed the air; it rose and cleared the castle walls just as Mavronides and his footmen reappeared.

They came across the courtyard at a run, followed closely by a servant girl. The Fräulein stared at them.

"*Where is he?*" she demanded coldly. "Why have you failed to bring Gansfleisch?"

Mavronides came to a halt before her, bowing apologetically, pale and panting. Beside him the footmen almost genuflected; the little servant girl, disheveled from her run, dropped a deep curtsey.

"Your Highness, he wasn't *there*. He too has disappeared!"

"Then *why* didn't you find him?"

"Highness, we tried! We searched his rooms, and found only great disorder. We searched the battlements. Then we went down to his laboratory—and—and—" He hesitated. "Highness, I don't know how to tell you this—the—*the gold-making machine is also gone!*"

"*What?*" cried the Fräulein.

"It is no longer there," moaned Mavronides, "and we saw tracks upon the floor and in the hallway. I think they are the tracks of what is called a forklift."

"You mean," exclaimed Gottfried Rumpler, "that he has *stolen* it? This is incredible! Where would he take it? How could he get it away from here?"

"*Someone* has surely stolen it, Excellency. But it could not have been Meister Gansfleisch by himself. No, this girl here—her name is Sophia—was all alone in the castle while the rest of us were searching for the Prin—for Herr Schimmelhorn. She was working in the kitchens. She says she heard a helicopter come down here in the courtyard while we were away. Though it seemed much louder, she thought only that we had returned, and did not worry. She says it stayed with its engines idling for a long time—as she was paying no attention, she does not know how long. Then it took off again."

"But *who?*" The Fräulein's face was a mask of anger. "Who could it have *been?*"

"My love," answered Herr Rumpler despairingly, "it could have been anyone with whom this wretched Gansfleisch plotted—a foreign government, or terrorists, or even gangsters from America. What is important is that it is gone. They have escaped. We cannot raise a hue and cry—to do so would be to tell the entire world about our secret! We shall learn who it was only when they start to destroy the world's economies—which we have given them the power to do. My love, all is lost!"

She looked at him, the rage fading from her countenance. She came to him, and took his face between her hands. "No, dear Gottfried!" she declared passionately.

"All is *not* lost—that we must *never* say! We have each other. We are Swiss bankers, you and I! Never fear, we will—as the Americans say—make out. Besides, tomorrow we may find Herr Schimmelhorn. He is a genius, as you know. Perhaps he will think of something."

Gottfried Rumpler's expression cheered up a little. He kissed her tenderly. "Never will we give up!" he told her. "You are right. We will combine our banks! We will become the strongest private bank in Switzerland!"

"And you shall be the father of my sons!" she promised him. "They too will be Swiss bankers!"

"Vell"—Mama Schimmelhorn yawned—"now iss time to go to bed, so don'dt you vorry aboudt der gold-machine. Tomorrow, vith Gustav-Adolf, ve find Papa."

"Take Frau Schimmelhorn to her rooms, Sophia," the Fräulein told the servant girl, "and see if there's anything she needs." Then, after they had said good night, she turned back to Mavronides. "Sarpedon," she said, "see that His Excellency's luggage is taken up to my apartments, and make sure that we are not awakened too early in the morning. You can start searching very well without us, I'm sure. And Sarpedon, when we do find Herr Schimmelhorn, I want you to explain to him. Do it gently and very tactfully, you understand? About the changes that have come about since—since my recovery."

Gottfried Rumpler looked at her, and—temporarily at least—quite forgot that he and she had just lost a device capable of upsetting all the world's financial applecarts.

And Sarpedon Mavronides, though still shaken by the day's events, signed to the footmen to pick up Dr. Rumpler's bags, and followed them.

As for Mama Schimmelhorn, she asked for a little more tea and schnapps, which Sophia presently brought up to her. Then, finding that she wasn't really sleepy, she first tried to wake up Humphrey and tell him the exciting news, found that he was sleeping much too soundly, and finished up by telling Gustav-Adolf the whole story, and informing

him that next day he would have the very responsible job
of finding Papa.

"Dirty old man!" she said. "I tell you, Gustav-Adolf, I
haff already cooked his goose vith die Prinzessin. Tomorrow, if I find him vith anoder naked voman—then vatch
oudt!"

She looked around. Suddenly she saw that, in her absence, someone had brought Papa Schimmelhorn's denims, his polka-dotted shorts, his shoes and socks, and laid
them on the bed. She frowned. She inventoried the closets,
the dresser drawers. "How stranche!" she said. "All his
clothes iss here. I vonder vot he vore?"

And she went to bed worrying, not about her husband's
safety, but what he might be up to with nothing on.

Mama Schimmelhorn had traveled far, and she was
tired. She slept soundly until after eight o'clock, when
Gustav-Adolf woke her, asking to be let out to his catbox.
She opened the door for him, checked on Humphrey just
to make sure he was all right, and took a long and refreshing tub-bath. Then she saw a bell-push by her bed, and
pushed it. Presently, a serving maid appeared, and she
ordered breakfast: bacon, two soft-boiled eggs, croissants,
tea, and fruit juice. With it, the maid brought a message
from the Fräulein, written the night before. She begged
Frau Schimmelhorn not to concern herself unduly; every
effort was being made to find her husband; she and His
Excellency, Herr Doktor Rumpler, would expect her company at luncheon at noon in her apartments. After that, if
Herr Schimmelhorn still had not been found, they would
all join the search.

Mama Schimmelhorn relaxed. She was enjoying herself.
After breakfast, and after she had dressed, she brought
Humphrey out of his compartment, woke him with a tot of
honeyed brandy, and told him everything that had occurred.

As she had foreseen, he was delighted. "Forsooth," he
exclaimed, "there's one problem solved. Perchance this
Switzer—for most of them are men of great good sense—

may wean her from her savage pagan ways. Come, kind and gentle lady, let us drink to it—aye, and to your husband's safe return!''

He raised his thimble. Mama Schimmelhorn raised her teacup. They drank.

''And now,'' said Humphrey, ''pray return me to my jar, for I fain would rest the hours away so that tonight, when you come back perchance with Master Schimmelhorn, I may have strength enough to share your joy and hear the tale of whatever adventures—let's trust they be not misadventures!—have befallen him.''

Reluctantly, she did his bidding; then she whiled the time away by writing postcards to Mrs. Hundhammer, Mrs. Laubenschneider, and several other friends, informing them that Papa had been very bad indeed and that she would confide in them as soon as she came back. To Mrs. Laubenschneider's she added a PS to the effect that her fine flea collar had enabled Gustav-Adolf to kill a rat-defil vithout being hurt.

Niobe came to fetch her, and they set out through the castle's corridors, Niobe eyeing her curiously but not daring to ask questions.

The Fräulein and His Excellency were awaiting her—or at least they were there, sitting close together on the chaise longue, holding hands, absorbed completely in each other.

Vell, vell! True luff! thought Mama Schimmelhorn sardonically as Niobe announced her. *Two lidtle luff birds—so cute!*

The Fräulein and His Excellency awakened to her presence. They rose to greet her. Gottfried Rumpler seated her ceremoniously. Graciously, she accepted a little glass of wine.

Luncheon proceeded smoothly while she regaled them with stories of her travels and extraordinary experiences with Papa, quite well aware that they were much too busy playing little lovers' games under the table to listen to her.

Finally, dessert was served and eaten. Coffee was served and sipped. Mama Schimmelhorn sat back in her chair.

"You haff heard noding aboudt this Gaspar Gansfleisch?" she enquired.

For a moment, their faces fell. They replied that they had not.

"Und you haff nodt found Papa?"

They looked at her. Solemnly, with infinite regret, they shook their heads.

She stood. "Okay," she said, "Papa ve can find. I vill get Gustav-Adolf, und ve all go togeder."

"Dear Frau Schimmelhorn," replied the Fräulein hesitantly, "there is only one place on the entire island we have not searched—that is the Labyrinth of the Minotaur. No one has ever entered it, and—and survived, or at least survived with his sanity. If Herr Schimmelhorn has really entered it—oh, it rends my heart to have to tell you this!—there is no hope that we will find him still alive. None, none!"

"You don'dt know Papa like I know," Mama Schimmelhorn told her. "I get Gustav-Adolf. He vill know right avay if Papa iss inside."

The Fräulein and her lover exchanged glances. Each conveyed the message that perhaps they'd better humor her.

"Of course," the Fräulein said. "I'll have Ismail bring the station wagon." Picking up the phone, she gave her orders. "Dr. Rumpler will escort you to your turret and bring you back."

Minutes later, accompanied by Sarpedon Mavronides, they were driving to the mound of the Labyrinth, to the Door of Sacrifices; and if Papa Schimmelhorn could have seen them, he would have realized that the processions he and the Princess had led in their gold and ivory chariot had been much more picturesque.

They dismounted in front of the great bronze door. Mama Schimmelhorn put Gustav-Adolf on the ground. "You are a brafe, clefer cat," she told him. "Now you must find Papa."

Gustav-Adolf looked up at her. In Cat, he growled,

"You go find him! The old bastard ain't been around fer two whole days. Let him get lost!"

"Shniff at der door!" ordered Mama Schimmelhorn. "Don'dt just shtand there saying 'Meow!'"

Gustav-Adolf shrugged. "Oh, what th' hell!" he muttered. "Okay, I'll give it just one try."

He sniffed carefully around the edges of the door. Abruptly, hoisting his tail, he turned around.

"*Mrrrow!*"

"So!" said Mama Schimmelhorn. "Papa iss inside! Open der door und ve get him oudt."

Nobody seemed at all anxious to.

"You are shcared of der vot-you-call-it Minotaur?" she sneered, brandishing her umbrella. "Vell, I go in myself!"

Gottfried Rumpler, his manhood challenged, stood forward. "Frau Schimmelhorn," he declared, "we shall *all* go in."

"My Gottfried!" whispered the Fräulein. "You are a true hero, an Arnold von Winkelried, a William Tell! I am proud of you. Sarpedon, the key!"

Sarpedon Mavronides produced it. With no enthusiasm, he unlocked the door and pushed it open.

Mama Schimmelhorn strode into the chamber. "Vell," she commented, "anyvay iss nice und cool inside."

They stood there with her. The Fräulein called out loudly in archaic Greek, asking the Minotaur to harken to their pleas, to come forth and release the poor old man who, in all innocence, had blundered into his retreat.

There was no reply; and after a few minutes Mama Schimmelhorn announced that she was moving forward. "All ve haff to do iss follow Gustav-Adolf," she declared. "He vill know vhere."

"B-but, Frau Schimmelhorn," His Excellency put in, "how can we find our way out again?"

She looked him up and down. "For a shmart banker, Herr Rumpler, you are shtupid. I bring a shpool of thread." She gave it to him. "You tie it here, und vhen ve vant to come oudt again ve haff no trouble."

The Fräulein, reminded of Theseus and Ariadne, flushed and said nothing.

They walked cautiously into the Labyrinth, peering into its branching passages. Suddenly, Mama Schimmelhorn halted.

"*Listen!*" she hissed.

They stopped. They listened. From the bowels of the Labyrinth, the discordant music that had so often terrified the peasantry of Little Palaeon was sounding, getting louder.

And over it, echoing from wall to wall, they heard the sound of massive footsteps, approaching threateningly.

Held there by Mama Schimmelhorn, they stood their ground. It was impossible to tell from where the footsteps came. But they were coming nearer, nearer—

Abruptly, the Fräulein screamed. "Look, *look!*" she cried. Their eyes followed her wildly pointing finger to a passage entrance where an enormous figure loomed. "There he *is!* There is the Minotaur! He—he has poor Herr Schimmelhorn! *He has him in his claws!*"

XI.

Gone But Not Forgotten

When Papa Schimmelhorn dropped his spear at his first sight of the Minotaur, it was by no means out of fear. It was out of pure astonishment, for he realized instantly that he had seen the Minotaur before—the Minotaur or his twin brother—during his captivity on Beetlegoose Nine. He had been shown a picture of him in full color, in a book very simply written for men and backward children and entitled *Strange Beings of Other Star Systems*. The memory brought with it quite as clearly a recollection of the description accompanying the illustration: *More than ten feet tall, incredibly long lived, horrendous in appearance but dedicated solely to esthetic ideals and pursuits.*

"But—but you are nodt a Minotaur!" he cried out in the Beetlegoosian tongue, much relieved. "*You are a Jekemsyg!*"

The shouted words echoed through the Labyrinth, and at once the Minotaur stopped his roaring; he dropped his enormous hands; he goggled at his uninvited guest. "How's this? How's this?" he rumbled in the same language. "It's unbelievable! You speak a civilized—well, *almost* a civilized tongue, that of the big women's planet!"

"*Ja*," said Papa Schimmelhorn, "Mama und me und Gustav-Adolf vas kidsnatched by die big vomen. I tell you all aboudt—"

"Oh, you must! You must!" The Minotaur was quite excited. "I'm terribly pleased. Why, I haven't heard that language spoken for—let me see, more than four thousand five hundred of your years."

"You mean you are here so long?" Papa Schimmelhorn was incredulous. "Und all alone? How sad! All dot time vithoudt efen a lady Jekemsyg!"

The Minotaur's expression changed. His features were indeed taurine, but anyone should have been able to tell that he was the product of independent evolution, and not the offspring of a pliant queen and an amorous bull. Now he smiled, exhibiting his carnivorous teeth.

"My dear fellow," he rumbled, "I've not been at all lonely. My wife's been with me. I just haven't let the natives here know about her. You see— By the way, you're dressed the way they used to dress when we first arrived, but you aren't one of them, I hope?"

"*Nein,*" answered Papa Schimmelhorn. "I am a Shviss, und now I liff in der United Shtates. It iss a long vay avay."

"Well—" The Minotaur shook his head. "They're awfully primitive and dreadfully uncouth. At first, I tried to get into communication with them, but all they did was run away and bring me human sacrifices. Imagine that! It took them centuries to understand that we Jekemsyg don't eat other intelligent beings, even when they aren't *very* intelligent. They took me for some sort of godling, apparently a fertility god judging by the way they behaved. My wife would have been hideously embarrassed; that's why she's kept out of sight." He looked down at his own impressive masculine equipment. "I don't usually go around this way," he added, "and my wife does frown on it, but it really does something for the natives, and after all they've kept us in provisions all these years."

"Gotts from Oudter Shpace!" marveled Papa Schimmelhorn. "Herr von Däniken should only know aboudt!"

"You'd think that after nearly five thousand years they could learn that we're just *people*, and not gods at all, wouldn't you? But I'm afraid they're hopeless. After we landed, and they started building that Labyrinth to keep us in—believe me, we welcomed it!'' He sighed. ''I suppose you've had your supper, haven't you?''

Papa Schimmelhorn nodded.

''Well then, if you aren't in a hurry, why don't we just go back into the ship? I'll get some clothes on, and you can meet my wife, and we'll drink some of the local wine—I got a fresh supply just yesterday—and you can tell me all about yourself, and perhaps answer a few questions about this barbarous world, and you might also like to hear my story.''

Papa Schimmelhorn thought of his now undoubtedly highly irritated Princess, and declared that he was in no hurry, none at all, and that he would very much like to hear the story. ''Vhy did you come?'' he asked. ''Und vhy haff you shtayed so long?''

''We came because I needed solitude—because I yearned for a new milieu, for inspiration, for what I thought would be the pristine innocence of primitive societies.'' Again, the Minotaur sighed. ''Instead, I found only brutal savagery. But it has not stopped me from working, no indeed! Allow me to introduce myself. I am Zongtur; my wife is Xorxan.''

''I am Papa Schimmelhorn, but you chust call me Papa.''

''I am delighted.'' The Minotaur bowed. ''Yes, I have worked here,'' he went on. ''I have composed two thousand and nineteen symphonies, almost thirty thousand concerti and shorter pieces, any number of magnificent operas on the most tragic and romantic themes, and songs innumerable. My latest and greatest symphony was being played when you came in, electronically of course. It takes seven of your years—naturally with intermissions. Would you like to hear it?''

''Maybe some oder time,'' Papa Schimmelhorn said politely. ''But vhy did you shtay so long?''

''I hadn't intended to,'' the Minotaur replied, ''but something happened to our spaceship after we came down.

When we tried to take off again, it just wouldn't run. All our auxiliaries work. The lights and all the other electric gadgets go on, and the security devices and all that, so we know it's not the power plant. But when I turn on the ignition, nothing happens. The drive doesn't respond at all. It's really very irritating—it was the latest model, and quite expensive, and it was still under warranty.''

"You haff nodt fixed it?"

"My dear, er, Papa''—the Minotaur looked down at him in stark surprise—"I am an artist, a composer! I am not a scientist or a spaceship engineer. And all I have is the owner's manual, which I can barely understand. Goodness only knows when we can get away!"

"Maybe I can fix,'' suggested Papa Schimmelhorn.

"*You* aren't a spaceship technician? Surely not! Not on *this* planet!"

"*Nein,*" admitted Papa Schimmelhorn. "I am chust a chenius. Vhen ve get back inside der ship, I tell you vhat I haff infented.''

He and the Minotaur conversed pleasantly all the rest of the way, until finally they reached what looked like a stainless steel door behind the limestone wall. His new friend opened it and bowed him in, and he saw that it was furnished very cozily, with several strange musical instruments in the background and a number of holographic portraits of Jekemsyg family groups here and there.

"And this is my wife Xorxan,'' said the Minotaur proudly as she entered. "My dear, this gentleman comes from Switzerland, a planet far from here, and he speaks the language of the big women's world fluently! It's astonishing. His name is Papa Schimmelhorn, but he wants us just to call him Papa.''

Compared to her husband, Xorxan was petite. She was scarcely eight and a half feet tall; instead of huge, hooked horns, she had dainty little nubbins; and Papa Schimmelhorn was relieved to see that she had only two breasts and that they were where breasts ought to be. She wore a glossy garment of lavender and silver, cut very much like the lounging pajamas favored by vamps in 1920ish films.

"I am so glad you came," she said, offering him her hand, the claws of which were neatly manicured. "We haven't had a caller for simply years and years. Do take your helmet off and stay awhile." She waved him to a seat, to which he climbed, and hung his helmet up for him. "I'll pour some wine. It's a native vintage, but years old and really quite acceptable. We can talk while Zongtur's dressing." She looked a little askance at Papa Schimmelhorn's goatskin miniskirt. "Well," she said, "different peoples do have different customs, don't they?"

"*Ja, ja,*" agreed Papa Schimmelhorn, "und iss like I alvays say—die different customs make life more inderesting."

They chatted, comparing the climates of Earth and Jekem, until Zongtur returned, now decently attired in a beautifully tailored pearl-gray jumpsuit over which he wore his jeweled belts and pouches.

He accepted a glass of wine from his spouse. "To your health!" he said, and drank. "And now, please tell us your whole story. I can hardly wait. . . ."

So Papa Schimmelhorn filled them in on his background and accomplishments, telling them about how he vas a chenius only in der subconscience, and how he had infented der *gnurrpfeife* vhich brought gnurrs from der voodvork out, and a time machine that looked chust like a hobbyhorse, and a steam-driven device using a small black hole that had opened the way into a parallel universe. To dramatize his recital, he demonstrated his cuckoo watch, explaining that it employed really advanced electronics which he, its inventor, could not consciously understand.

Xorxan clapped her hands delightedly, with a sound rather like that of a dolphin beating the water with its tail; and her husband exclaimed in astonishment that Papa Schimmelhorn's mind worked just the way his did. "My dear sir," he said, "you, like myself, are a true artist! With all my advanced degrees in musicology, with all my centuries of study at our most prestigious institutions, had it not been for my subconscious, I never could have written my greatest works."

"I think it's wonderful!" said Xorxan. "Do tell us more."

So Papa Schimmelhorn told them the whole story of his kidnapping, and of how he had not only restored the lost virility of the tiny men of Beetlegoose Nine, but also liberated them; and they murmured their approval, agreeing that female chauvinism, which they had seen in action during their stay there, was every bit as bad as its male counterpart.

"But tell me," said Zongtur, refilling all around, "after such adventures, what are you doing *here?*"

Papa Schimmelhorn decided that it would not be really politic to tell them the entire story, not about Niki and Emmy and his tempestuous wrestlings with the Princess, so he gave them, if not a General Admission, at least a Parental Guidance version of his saga, finally explaining that the Princess had made him an honorary Prince to reward him for contriving the gold-making machine, but that the success had gone to her head and she had demanded that he forthwith challenge the Minotaur himself to mortal combat—something he was much too civilized to do. He also told them how, trying to hide from her, he had inadvertently stumbled into the very Labyrinth he was trying to avoid.

"Well," remarked Zongtur, "it's certainly lucky you didn't break in through the front door. I would have had to turn up the protective field, the one that keeps the wigglies out, and that would have been most unpleasant for you."

"Die vigglies?" asked Papa Schimmelhorn.

Xorxan shuddered. "The place is full of them! Some are long and slithery; others buzz and fly around, or creep on all sorts of horrid legs. And they all bite or sting."

"But the field does keep them out beautifully," Zongtur added. "And it also works very well on the natives, almost as well as my music. All I have to do is turn it up high enough, and none of them, especially those who don't live on this island, will come near the place. Sometimes, in the old days, some of them would try breaking in, but it always drove the poor things mad. Quite often, when they've been threatened by invaders, I've had to come to their assistance. I dare say that's another reason they bring me sacrifices. Don't you think so, Xorxan?''

"I'm sure it is," she said. "Thank goodness it's only the drive that's broken down, so that the field's kept working. Besides, I don't know what we would have done without lights, or hot water, or the freezer."

"Well," Zongtur growled, "it certainly took those natives long enough to find out that we didn't want our sacrifices at the door with their throats cut and all the hair on. It was several centuries before I could stop doing my own cleaning and skinning and butchering and freezer wrapping—imagine that!—and then we only managed to get the idea over to them by turning down the music and the field whenever they brought things all cut up and wrapped."

They discussed the difficulties of living in a spaceship buried in the center of a Labyrinth on Little Palaeon; and then they told him all about Jekem, their home planet, where the average lifetime was seventy to a hundred thousand Earth-years, and artists and philosophers were the aristocracy. Papa Schimmelhorn learned that they had had space travel for so long that ordinary people took it in their stride; he learned that they were unaggressive, fighting no wars but taking excellent care of themselves when the circumstances warranted. He heard a great deal about their arts, their universities, their philosophies and theologies. From Xorxan, he learned that male and female Jekemsyg all participated, that she herself was a performing artist and therefore rather more frustrated here on Earth than Zongtur was. He also learned that they had pets on Jekem, mostly cats imported from the big women's planet.

"And we do get awfully homesick," Xorxan told him, "especially when we think that we may never go home again. For a while, before it became obvious that they'd destroy themselves first, we thought the peoples of this planet might advance enough to develop interstellar travel, and either be able to fix our drive for us or at least relay a message to the JSSA—"

"Der JSSA? Vot iss?"

"The Jekem Spaceship Association. They have an excellent emergency service, but there's no way for us to get in touch with them from a planetary surface, not at this distance."

"Papa here thinks that maybe *he* could fix our drive," said Zongtur a little dubiously.

"Well, I don't see why he couldn't, because he certainly is a genius—and an artist too. Zongtur, why don't you take him back into the engine room and show it to him, and I'll come with you and bring the wine."

"First, let me show him the control room," Zongtur said. "Maybe it'll give him some idea of how things work, and anyhow we'll have to go there to find the owner's manual."

The ship was heavily compartmented, and they passed through several bulkheads dividing more of the living quarters before reaching the control room. It was impressive in its simplicity. There were two huge seats before a panel of manual switches, readouts, video screens. There were several gadgets that made no sense at all. No lights blinked. No dials registered.

"Everything's automatic these days," declared Zongtur. "Most of those switches are never used, and if they have to be the computer tells us how. The thing simply runs itself—when it is running, that is. You just tell it to give you a look at the right star charts, and tell it where to go, and it takes you there. Then, when you reach a planet, it lets you know if it's safe to land—if the air is breathable and all that sort of thing, and if the indigenous life-forms have advanced enough to be really dangerous."

He picked up the owner's manual and began thumbing through it. "Luckily, everything's explained very simply," he told Papa Schimmelhorn. "So I'll probably be able to translate it even if I don't understand it. I do hope I get all the terms right."

Finally they reached the engine room, and it was immediately apparent that, whether the drive worked or not, the ship itself was very much alive.

"There's some sort of power plant—atomic, I suppose—that keeps things going." Zongtur pointed at a group of four massive ovoids reaching from floor to ceiling. "It's just the drive itself that's shot."

The drive stood all alone in the middle of the compartment, and it did not share the austere design characteristics of the rest. Instead, it looked more as though it had been conceived and brought into being by Papa Schimmelhorn himself. Twice as big as the gold-making machine had been, it possessed mysterious moving parts, equally mysterious crystalline transparencies showing highly complicated, presumably electronic assemblies. Built into it were several enormous solenoids, apparently fashioned of ceramic wire.

Papa Schimmelhorn gazed at it ecstatically, and his subconscious at once reared up on its hind legs and whispered in his ear, *Chum, this is going to be duck soup!*

There were benches along the wall, and he clambered up on one of them, letting his legs dangle and forgetting all about his goatskin skirt. He motioned to Zongtur and his wife to join him.

"It iss beaudtiful!" he told them. "Nefer haff I seen a dingus except mein own vhich iss so—how do you say it?"

"Esthetically satisfying?" suggested Zongtur.

"*Ja!* Und mein subconscience says if noding's missing I can fix—maybe efen if. *Ach*, I am so glad I came! Vhere are die tools?"

"Tools? Well, there's some sort of kit that came with it when we bought it, but the salesman said we'd never need it. It should be somewhere around. . . ."

He began rummaging in boxes and storage lockers, and finally found the kit stashed in a closet with what appeared to be spare parts for something.

"Is this it?" he asked.

Papa Schimmelhorn opened it, and his subconscious told him instantly that it was what he needed.

"Okay, Herr Zongtur," he said cheerfully. "You read der book, und translate so maybe I can undershtand, und I vill take apart."

"Take it *apart?* But—but can you get it back *together?*"

He assured them that of course he could.

For several hours, then, while Zongtur and Xorxan translated, he worked happily away, dismantling the cosmic-ray converter, reducing the black-hole simulacrum to its component parts, and adorning the deck around the drive with a neatly arranged row of miscellaneous hickuses.

Occasionally, he grunted with satisfaction as some unsuspected function was revealed, or cried out joyfully at the cleverness of the design, holding up a part or two and exclaiming that even he could never have contrived it quite as well.

Gradually, as he worked, his hosts' fears were lulled, for it was obvious that, at least when it came to taking things apart, he really knew what he was doing.

Presently, Xorxan began to sing snatches from a few light songs of her husband's composition—she explained that singing them in full would take much too long—and at around three A.M. she prepared a snack for all of them, of goat's-milk cheese, and the best sausage of Little Palaeon, fresh fruit, and wine.

It was almost daybreak when Papa Schimmelhorn, with a shout of triumph, held up a convoluted metal-and-ceramic object for their inspection.

"Only look!" he bellowed. "Ho-ho-ho! Chust vun lidtle vire inside comes loose. Maybe vhen they put it in somevun iss thinking of his lidtle lady Jekemsyg, *nicht wahr?*"

"Then you *can* fix it?" gasped Zongtur.

"*Nein,*" laughed Papa Schimmelhorn. "I do nodt fix. Ve chust throw avay, und chump anoder vire across die socket terminals."

"*Throw it away?*"

"Vith it, der designer vas maybe nodt so shmart. Vithoudt it, if you vant, you can go ten times as fast."

"My goodness!" Xorxan was impressed. "That would be seventy times the speed of light instead of only seven. We could get home *much* sooner."

"You're sure it'll work?" Zongtur asked.

"*Ja, ja!* But after breakfast, anyvay, I fix it so if you are shcared or do nodt like you can put back."

While Xorxan prepared their breakfast, he fastened the wire firmly back in place, then jumped another wire across the terminals. Point by point, he showed Zongtur how to put it back the way it was. "But," he added, "I think you do nodt haff to. You ask der computer. It vill undershtand."

They breakfasted merrily, Papa Schimmelhorn with an excellent appetite, and the two Jekemsyg elated at the prospect of perhaps finally leaving Little Palaeon for home. Afterward, Papa Schimmelhorn took a short nap, declaring that he really wasn't very tired, and then spent the rest of the morning putting the drive back together again.

"Und now ve test," he announced.

They returned to the control room. Zongtur sat himself down in one of the two chairs. He turned the computer on. In his own language, he told it what he wanted. The computer answered him in the same tongue.

"Vot does it say?" asked Papa Schimmelhorn.

"It says, *All systems are go!*" answered Zongtur.

He snapped an order. Abruptly, the earth shook. The ship's entire hull started to struggle against the earth and stone that held it. Just as suddenly, it stopped. The computer spoke again.

"I—I can't believe it! It—it says our drive is now ten times as efficient as it was before!"

"Of course," said Papa Schimmelhorn.

"Oh, how can we *ever* thank you?" Zorxan bent down and kissed him with her nose. "At last we can go home! At last my Zongtur's work will get the recognition it deserves! I can just hear the critics now!" Her countenance lit up. "Why don't you come with us? You can stay thirty or forty years and then we'll bring you back."

"I am sorry," Papa Schimmelhorn told her. "I luff to

see your planet, but I must predty soon go home to Mama—if die Prinzessin iss nodt too angry und lets me go. But I haff a lidtle friend, only so high. . . ." Briefly, he told them of Humphrey and his plight. "All he vants iss to get to oudter shpace, so from der body his shpirit can be free. Maybe vith you he gets a ride?"

"Of course," Zorxan said sympathetically. "Just bring him to us here before we leave. And now, surely you'll stay to lunch? We can't let you hurry off like that after all you've done for us!"

"I shtay for lunch. You are a goot cook, chust like Mama. Maybe someday I come to Jekem und visit you."

Xorxan hustled them back into the dining room. "We really must celebrate! I'll open up a bottle of Jekem wine— it's almost our last one." She busied herself preparing luncheon in the adjoining kitchen while Papa Schimmelhorn told Zongtur about his doubts and trepidations regarding his own return to the Princess.

"I think," said Zongtur, "that you won't need to worry. If she's in love with you—and especially when she hears who we really are, and sees our ship take off—well, somehow I don't think you'll have any problem after that."

"Take off?" Papa Schimmelhorn was astonished. "But how—how do you take off before they shofel all die rock und shtone und eferything avay?"

"No problem," Zongtur answered. "The ship'll simply push it all aside."

At lunch, they talked about each other's planets, and about the big women's world, and other curious places the Jekemsyg had visited. They ate roast lamb, and finished with a wonderful dessert Xorxan had made from her own recipe. They drank the famous wine of Jekem, which privately Papa Schimmelhorn didn't think was very good.

Then, just as they were finishing, a buzzer shrilled and on the wall one of seven red lights went on.

"Well!" said Zongtur. "It's the main door, where they leave the sacrifices. I wonder what they want."

"I can imachine!" Papa Schimmelhorn told him unhappily. "It iss die Prinzessin chasing me!"

Zongtur patted him gently on the back to reassure him. "Just come with me," he said, handing him his helmet. "We'll meet them, and I'll explain everything. . . . Darling," he called to Xorxan, "turn on my symphony, one of the more dramatic passages, but not too loudly—at least not at first."

The well-ordered lives of eminent Swiss bankers are seldom disturbed by such creatures as Minotaurs, or even by their close facsimiles. Therefore it speaks well for the efficacy of Humphrey's love potion that Gottfried Rumpler's only thought, on first seeing Zongtur, was for the safety of his Philippa, just as hers was for his own. Wishing that he had brought his Sig-Neuhausen, he tried to shield her with his body. She tried to do the same for him. The maneuver simply brought them a little closer to the Minotaur. Sarpedon Mavronides, who had lived all his life knowing that the Minotaur was there but who had never seen him, was frozen in his tracks by sheer terror. Only Mama Schimmelhorn kept her head.

Just as her husband had, she recognized the Jekemsyg immediately. "Vot nonsense!" she exclaimed. "He iss *nodt* a Minotaur. He iss from der planet Jekem, far avay. They are very cifilized, und I have met maybe his relatifes on Beetlegoose. Und he does *nodt* haff Papa in die claws."

In this, of course, she was quite correct, for Zongtur had simply taken Papa Schimmelhorn's arm companionably.

The moment of first recognition came and went. Her eyes narrowed. "But he does nodt haff der pants on!" she remarked severely. "Maybe he iss a dirty old man Jekemsyg?" She became aware of her husband's strange attire. "Und vot iss? Papa in der Greeker monkey-suit? Und vithoudt undervear, chust der lidtle shkirt?" She advanced upon him, umbrella at the ready. "Der Jekemsyg vithout der pants on und you vithoudt der undervear! Come here at vunce. I lend my shawl so you are decent.

Chust vait till ve get back home. *This* time, I teach a lesson.''

It had taken Papa Schimmelhorn only a few moments to recover from his original shock, and then he had taken in the whole situation at a glance. He saw his wife, black dress, black bumbershoot, and all. With a sinking heart, he beheld his Princess clinging to Gottfried-Rumpler and looking up at him with an expression now only too, too familiar. He realized that he no longer was a Prince with princely privileges, and he knew at once that Mama Schimmelhorn had met Humphrey, had confiscated the leftover love potion, and had used it to maximum effect. *Vell,* he thought, brightening up, *maybe iss for der best. Odervise, vith only der lidtle shkirt to cofer me, und Mama here* . . . He shuddered at the thought. *Anyvay, I am now off der hook vith die Prinzessin.*

Obediently, with a simpering smile, he came to Mama Schimmelhorn, took the shawl she thrust at him, and wrapped himself modestly.

Before he could say anything, Zongtur spoke up. ''Madame,'' he rumbled in Beetlegoosian, ''I am Zongtur, the composer. As I know you are aware, I am a native of the planet Jekem, and I have been marooned on this savage isle for nearly five thousand of your years.''

''Vell,'' snapped Mama Schimmelhorn, ''you at least could put der pants on. On Jekem people do nodt go around like dot. Your vife vould nodt like.''

Zongtur admitted that she was quite correct—that his wife strongly disapproved. Then he explained that much against his will he had gone along with what the natives of Little Palaeon expected, with what seemed to turn them on.

Mama Schimmelhorn eyed her husband. Shrewdly, she eyed Dr. Rumpler and the Fräulein. ''I am chust here vun day,'' she said, ''but already I undershtand. I do nodt haff anoder shawl or I vould lend. Maybe you can open der bumbershoot und hold in front.''

She held it out to him, and he accepted it.

"Und now, if you chust vait, I translate so eferybody knows vot you are saying."

Swiftly, she outlined what she had learned about the Jekemsyg. Zongtur began rumbling. She translated. "He says you vill get tired, shtanding here. He says vhy don'dt ve all go back inside his house, vhich iss a spaceship, und haff some vine, und ve meet his vife?"

The Fräulein and her lover, staring open-mouthed, were hesitant. "Are—are you sure it's *safe?*" Dr. Rumpler asked. "Even—even if they're not Minotaurs at all but, as you say, creatures from some other world, still they are enormous, and—and did you see those *teeth?*"

Mama Schimmelhorn scoffed. "Papa has been inside since yesterday," she said.

"*Ja,*" put in Papa Schimmelhorn, "und Frau Xorxan iss a goot cook und very nice to me. They are goot people, chust like us Shviss."

Again, Zongtur rumbled.

"He says," translated Mama Schimmelhorn, "dot now Papa has fixed der shpace-drife, he und his vife vill leafe for Jekem maybe this efening oder tomorrow morning, und they vould like to haff you as der guests chust vunce before they go. He says it iss to thank you for so many years of der hospitality und sacrifices."

The Fräulein looked up at the Doktor. "Oh, my Gottfried!" she cried out to him. "My love! My dear, dearest love! This is my duty as the Princess—*our* duty now. I'm sure they are completely law-abiding, for Frau Schimmelhorn vouches for them. And if anything did happen—well, it would happen to both of us. We would die together!" She turned to Mama Schimmelhorn. "Tell him we would be honored," she declared.

Ordering Sarpedon Mavronides to stay behind and guard the door, she moved bravely forward, Dr. Rumpler holding her hand protectively.

The small procession retraced the steps Papa Schimmelhorn and Zongtur had followed the day before. Once again, Xorxan came forward and was introduced. Once again, the frightening music was turned completely off. Once more, having returned Mama Schimmelhorn's umbrella, Zongtur donned his jumpsuit. Xorxan served wine. They chatted. Gradually, they relaxed. Gottfried Rumpler began to wonder about the possibilities of a profitable trade developing between Earth and Jekem; and the Fräulein's quick mind started speculating on the changes the departure of the Minotaur would bring to Little Palaeon, and the best ways to handle them.

Would it be possible, she asked, for the people of the island to witness the departure? They would hold a splendid ceremony. It would start a completely new tradition.

Zongtur replied that they had no objection, just as long as it did not delay them. "In fact," he said to Papa Schimmelhorn, "I don't see how they can possibly miss seeing us take off—not when we burst through all that stone and rubble over us."

Mama Schimmelhorn was kept busy translating. On the few occasions when her husband tried to help her, she invariably corrected him, and after a while he gave it up, only exchanging a few asides occasionally with Zongtur or Xorxan.

All in all, they got along beautifully, though the Doktor could not conceal his disappointment when Zongtur told him, as tactfully as possible, that at least for the next few millennia trade and cultural contacts between Earth and Jekem would be inadvisable, the peoples of Earth—present company of course excepted—being, well, too retarded. Finally, Zongtur presented Dr. Rumpler with a recording of his latest symphony (which no instrument on Earth could play), and gave the Fräulein a portable device which, he assured her, would set up the sort of anti-wiggly field that had protected Little Palaeon over the years, and showed her exactly how to use it. Xorxan gave Papa Schimmelhorn a holograph of the three of them, taken the night before, which showed the little goatskin skirt quite startlingly, and which Mama Schimmelhorn confiscated immediately on their return. Then the two Jekemsyg escorted them back

the way they'd come, again terrifying poor Mavronides,
who had never dreamed that the Labyrinth contained more
than one Minotaur.

At the door, Papa Schimmelhorn fortunately remembered about Humphrey. "Almost I forget," he said to
Zongtur, "mein lidtle friend. . . ."

"Bring him here in about an hour," Zongtur told him.
"We'll be happy to take him with us. I'll be here at the
door."

They said good-bye. They locked the door behind them.
As they climbed into the station wagon, much to the relief
of poor Ismail, the Fräulein hung back for a quick word
with Mavronides. "Listen carefully, Sarpedon!" she whispered. "A great event is about to happen here on Little
Palaeon. Our Minotaur, the demigod who has protected us
for all these years, will soon return to his own domain.
From there, he will continue to watch over us. There will
be certain changes in the sacrifices, but our rites and
ceremonies will continue unaltered. However, Little Palaeon
will no longer be shut off from the outer world as it has
been. We will admit carefully selected visitors. And
Sarpedon, tell the people also that the Minotaur, in his
unfathomable wisdom, has decided to take our great Prince
August with him, together with this old woman who is
related to him. Is that all clear?"

"It is clear, Highness," Mavronides replied dutifully.

"Then tell them to assemble around the Mound of the
Labyrinth after dark has fallen, to keep vigil until *he* takes
leave of us. Tell them there will be singing and dancing,
food and drink. *He* does not want us to be saddened by his
going, but instead to celebrate him loyally. You understand?"

"I understand, Highness. I shall arrange everything."

She joined the others in the station wagon. "Frau
Schimmelhorn," she said softly, "when we reach the
castle I would like a word or two with you in private,
before you go to freshen up or anything."

The station wagon rolled into the castle courtyard, and
as soon as it had stopped and they had all dismounted,

Mama Schimmelhorn ordered her husband to go up to his turret, put on his trousers, and get back down where she could keep an eye on him. Then she followed the Fräulein into a small private drawing room, where she was graciously shown to a Louis XIV couch.

The Fräulein sat down next to her. Gently, she put a hand on the stiff black material of her dress; gently, she touched Mama Schimmelhorn's hand with her own. "Frau Schimmelhorn," she said, "you are a woman of wisdom and experience. I have concealed nothing from you, and you have been kindly and forgiving. Now there is one more favor I must ask of you." She blushed. "You will understand that under the—the circumstances, my people here on Little Palaeon will wonder what happened to their Prince. I have instructed Sarpedon Mavronides to tell them that he is leaving with the Minotaur, that he is being taken to the domain of the gods as a reward for his heroism."

Mama Schimmelhorn covered the Fräulein's hand with hers. "Don'dt vorry, Prinzessin Philippa," she said. "Ve vomen are more sinned against than sinning, I alvays say. I know you are a goot Shviss girl, und shmart. Right avay after supper, Papa und I und Gustav-Adolf fly avay in der helicopter. But chust you vait till I get der old goat back to New Hafen! Ha!"

The Fräulein thanked her, promising that someday she would visit her, and for several minutes they exchanged pleasantries; then they returned to the courtyard just as Papa Schimmelhorn, now in his best denims, reentered it.

Gottfried Rumpler was waiting for them there, looking as though he'd been clobbered squarely between the eyes.

"Gottfried! My love, my adored!" Anxiously the Fräulein ran to him. "What is *wrong?*"

He mopped his brow. Without a word, he handed her a sheet of paper.

She looked at it. "It is a radiogram!" she whispered. "From—from Moscow! B-but we know no one there."

"Read it, dear Philippa," said Dr. Rumpler dismally. "It is addressed to you."

I HAVE ARRIVED IN TRIUMPH! (she read aloud). MY
GOOD FRIENDS BROUGHT ME HERE THIS MORNING.
AT LAST I AND MY GREAT INVENTION ARE APPRECI-
ATED. THEY WILL MAKE ME AN ACADEMICIAN! I WILL
HAVE A DACHA AND A LIMOUSINE! DOWN WITH SWISS
IMPERIALISM! LONG LIVE THE REVOLUTION!

It was signed, GASPAR GANSFLEISCH.

The Fräulein dropped the paper. For an instant, her eyes
darted desperately, as though hoping for some last-minute
rescue. "Do you realize what this *means?*" she moaned.

"Only too well, *too* well!" replied the Doktor.

"Vot iss?" asked Papa Schimmelhorn, coming up to
them. "Vot happens to Meister Gassi?"

"Yesterday evening, while everyone was searching for
you," said Gottfried Rumpler, "a helicopter landed here.
The servant girl who heard it said it stayed for a long time.
We were searching too, in our own helicopter, and we did
not hear it over the sound of our engines and our rotors.
When we returned, Gaspar Gansfleisch had disappeared.
So had your gold-making machine." He picked up the
radiogram and handed it to Papa Schimmelhorn. "Read
that!"

Papa Schimmelhorn read it twice, his lips moving. Then
he threw it down again and roared with laughter. "*Ach!
Ach!*" he bellowed. "Meister Gassi could nodt sell his
soul to der Defil, so he has defecated to die Russians!
Ho-ho-ho-ho-*ho!*" Red-faced, convulsed with merriment,
he held his splitting sides. "*Ach*, predty soon inshtead of
der hot place, I think maybe he gets inside a cold vun!"

Gottfried Rumpler seized him by the shoulders and tried
to shake him. "My God, man! Are you mad? Don't you
understand what this *means?* Your machine *works*. It turns
lead into *gold!*"

"Don't you *realize?*" the Fräulein added hysterically.
"He has given *them* the power to buy the world! To
shatter all the world's economies! Don't you *see? We're
doomed!*"

"*Nein, nein!*" said Papa Schimmelhorn, trying hard to stop laughing. "Vunce, lidtle Phil—vunce, Fräulein Prinzessin, I try to tell you. Remember? Alvays I put der dial at only tvelve? Vhy? Because iss vun or two adchustments I haff nodt made. I do nodt know how to make die explanations, but if it iss turned too high, der ray gets vider—first chust a lidtle, then a lidtle more, then a lot. Vhen ve go to maybe fifty, ve shtop making gold, und der ray is vide I think vun hundred oder two hundred feet. Vhen ve turn to eighty, it iss a mile almost—und now der machine vorks differently. Now it"—again he burst out laughing—"now for a vhile it makes *gold* into *lead!* Und then—then it melts! I think Meister Gassi und die Russians are so greedy they find out der hard vay."

"Let us pray," said Gottfried Rumpler, "that you are right."

"Don'dt vorry," said Papa Schimmelhorn.

"Anyvay," put in Mama Schimmelhorn, "der gold machine iss gone forefer. So now ve lose der money for der shteeple!"

"Certainly not," the Fräulein told her. "Herr Schimmelhorn built the machine, and it worked. The fact that we failed to guard it was not his fault. Gottfried and I would have no business reputation if we did not keep our promises. The money shall be released to your account." She turned to Dr. Rumpler. "Dear Gottfried, I feel that what Herr Schimmelhorn has said is true—the traitor Gansfleisch and his Russian masters will never profit by his treachery! As for the machine, we do not need it, you and I. We are Swiss bankers—we can turn *anything* into gold! Besides, there's Little Palaeon—now that the Minotaur is gone, there will be the tourist trade to consider."

XII.

Hot Line from Moscow

Fräulein von Hohenheim apologized to Mama Schimmelhorn for not inviting her to dinner, pleading the ceremonies that had to be so hastily arranged, and Mama Schimmelhorn patted her hand and told her not to worry—she understood. They exchanged farewell good wishes, during which Papa Schimmelhorn was pointedly ignored except by Dr. Rumpler, who shook his hand in some embarrassment, complimented him on his pioneering alchemy, and said that he expected a photo of the steeple when completed. Then the Schimmelhorns repaired to the turret to do their packing and to give Humphrey a report on the happenings of the day.

Papa Schimmelhorn brought him out of his compartment and seated him again on his little chair; and he was not at all surprised when Mama Schimmelhorn greeted him by name. He gave the homunculus, who looked very tired and worried, a thimbleful of his honeyed brandy to cheer him up. Then, with frequent corrections and emendations from his wife, he reported the doings of the previous day.

Humphrey listened in wonderment, crying out occasionally that neither Ariel nor twisted Caliban could tell him of such wonders. "No, only you, sweet Master Schimmelhorn, could so inflame my hopes!" he finally cried. "Oh, tell me—tell me truly! This Minotaur—this Jekemite whom you have succored from his age-long shipwreck—does he indeed make plans to soar again into the empyrean? To cruise the vasty realms between the stars? Those realms from which I came, where I was free?''

"*Ja, ja!* This efening he vill leafe, und so right avay I take you in der jar up to der mound, because he says he vill take you vith him.''

Anxiously, poor Humphrey pleaded with him to say again that it was true, and when he was assured that indeed it was, he was so overcome that for some moments he fell to weeping. Mama Schimmelhorn patted him on the head, consoling him.

"Soon you vill be inside der spaceship,'' she promised him, "but Papa does nodt take you there. Papa''—she glared at her husband—"vill shtay right here inside der turret, vhere iss no naked vomen, und do der packing. I myself vill take you to der Jekemsyg.''

"Pray, do not be too harsh with him, dear gentle lady!'' begged Humphrey. "He is full of vital spirits, and truly noble in his beneficence!'' He dried his eyes with an infinitesimal handkerchief, and blew his nose. "But still it matters not who takes me there. It is enough to think that soon this wretched husk, this artificial body that's held me in its terrible toils so many years, will wither, crumble, and scatter to the fair winds of space. Aye, 'twill vanish like next-day's dandelions! Good Master Schimmelhorn, I owe it all to you! How, how can I reward you?''

Papa Schimmelhorn was on the point of asking him to repeat the formula for the love potion, which he had inconveniently forgotten. However, he caught his wife's eye in time. "You haff already done enough, lidtle Herr Humphrey. If it has not been for you—'' He caught Mama Schimmelhorn's eye again, and broke off. "Don'dt vorry. It iss all right.''

While he and Humphrey said good-bye with many expressions of regret, affection, and esteem, Mama Schimmelhorn phoned the Fräulein, told her that she had a final present for the Jekemsyg, and asked to borrow Ismail and the station wagon for the run up to the mound. Then Humphrey made his farewells to her and to Gustav-Adolf, who obligingly rubbed against him, purring. "And now, good friends," he said, "once more you can return me to that jar, that now no longer loathsome jar. Forever, farewell!"

Mama Schimmelhorn obeyed him; she made sure the stopper was in tightly; she placed the jar in Papa Schimmelhorn's carpetbag together with the flask of honeyed brandy. "Get all your shtuff togeder," she commanded. "I come right back."

She picked up the carpetbag, and a moment later the door closed behind her.

Papa Schimmelhorn was depressed. He felt that he had lost a friend and ally. Even Gustav-Adolf looked at him askance, muttering sullenly in Cat. Nor was he completely comforted when, a few minutes later, Sarpedon Mavronides knocked on the door to say good-bye to him, to wish him well, and to present him with a memento of his short reign over Little Palaeon, one of the huge conchs that had brayed at his investiture and at the various ceremonies in which he had taken part.

"One must accept the ups and downs of life with philosophy," Mavronides declared. "Throughout history, men have risen suddenly and then as suddenly have been cast down." He quoted solemnly from Grecian tragedy about the fall of princes. "You must not blame Her Highness, who is infallible and therefore blameless."

"Of course nodt, Herr Zorba," said Papa Schimmelhorn. "It vas nodt her fault." Ruefully, he recalled the nights in the Princess's bedroom. "I had a goot time vhile it lasted."

Mavronides departed, having promised to come and visit in New Haven if the tourist business permitted it; and Papa Schimmelhorn busied himself getting his things together until his wife came back, which she did just in time for dinner.

The servant girls who brought it set the table, and waited on them silently and courteously. It was a meal

over which great pains had been taken, and Mama
Schimmelhorn tipped the girls a Swiss franc each. But she
never said a word while they were eating, and Papa
Schimmelhorn was relieved, just as they were finishing, to
hear the helicopter drop down into the courtyard.

The trip back to New Haven was not a happy one for
him. All the way, on Gottfried Rumpler's jet, which—
with Herr Grundtli—had been waiting for them on Crete,
he did not dare to say a word to the pretty pussycat now
serving as its stewardess. That night, Mama Schimmelhorn
and Gustav-Adolf had a cabin to themselves, and the next
day they sat stiffly across the aisle from him, telling Herr
Grundtli about Papa's sins and failings.

Therefore it was with considerable relief that, when
their airport cab finally brought them to their door, and
after he had lugged their bags up the front stoop and into
the living room, he found Little Anton awaiting them.
Neither he nor Mama Schimmelhorn was in the least surprised that Little Anton had burgled his way in, for they
were thoroughly familiar with the talents that had made
him so successful as, among other things, a smuggler.
Mama Schimmelhorn was delighted. She had been disappointed when he had been unable to accompany her on her
mission, and—as she mistakenly believed him to be an
upright, religiously inclined young man—she looked forward eagerly to having him as an audience. She insisted
that he stay with them for at least a day or two.

Little Anton told her that he would happily stay to
dinner, which he insisted on having sent in from a Chinese
restaurant, but that any longer visit would have to be
postponed until he returned from Montreal, where he was
bound that very night on business for Pêng-Plantagenet.
He promised he'd be back very shortly.

"Okay," she said regretfully, "you phone die Chinesers,
und aftervards I call Mrs. Hundhammer und der pastor,
und Mrs. Laubenschneider, und giff them der goot news."
She glared at Papa Schimmelhorn. "Put der shtuff avay,"

she ordered, "und be useful for a chanche. Set der table so Lidtle Anton can sit down to dinner."

Obediently, he did what he was told. The phone calls were made. Dinner arrived—a very good one because of Little Anton's expertise and Chinese connections.

They ate, and all through the meal Little Anton listened to a highly biased account of what had happened on Little Palaeon. Knowing his great-uncle, he was able to read between the lines, and at times it was all he could do not to burst out with "*Whee-whee-ew!*" Whenever he could, he winked at Papa Schimmelhorn to encourage him.

Then, after supper, the Hundhammers and Mrs. Laubenschneider arrived to hear the glad tidings from Mama Schimmelhorn's own lips, and Papa Schimmelhorn was exiled to the basement. When Little Anton tried to join him there, she put her foot down firmly, and so, until it was time to leave and catch his flight, he had to suppress his curiosity and listen to pious ejaculations and devout rejoicings over a steeple destined to be the highest in New Haven.

It was not until three days later, on his way back, that he was able to hear Papa Schimmelhorn's rather more detailed and dramatic story; and during those three days, Mama Schimmelhorn relaxed her disciplinary measures only once. In recognition of the fact that he had indeed succeeded in making lead into gold, and that consequently he deserved at least some of the credit, she allowed him to attend a celebratory service on the Sunday, at which Pastor Hundhammer delivered a homily on how virtue, as exemplified by church steeples, could surprisingly burgeon forth from unlikely soil, and how even in the most unregenerate of sinners there lurked—even if it was unintentional and hard to find—the impulse to be of some service to mankind. As his congregation knew Papa Schimmelhorn very well indeed, having on more than one occasion had to fend him off their wives and daughters, their sisters and their cousins and their aunts, the *Amens* with which his words were greeted were passionately sincere—and none resounded more impressively than the deep bass *Amen* uttered by Papa Schimmelhorn himself.

Otherwise, he remained in Coventry, fiddling around in his basement workshop, sometimes comforting himself with his assorted clocks or with the dulcet tones of his cuckoo watch. He thought about the Princess, sighing occasionally and reminding himself of Sarpedon Mavronides's philosophical consolations. He thought about Miss Niki and Miss Emmy, and how they had sported in the waves. And he worried about his gold-making machine and what Meister Gansfleisch and the Russians might have done with it. Waiting for Little Anton to come back, he carefully prepared a packet of the mutated catnip for him to smuggle somehow to poor Ismail.

Little Anton returned on schedule, and Mama Schimmelhorn welcomed him joyfully.

"*Ach,*" she said to him, "I haff now a full schedule. Pastor Hundhammer makes me Chairvoman of der Church Committee for der new shteeple, so I am busy, busy, busy. Most of der time I vill be avay, und maybe you can keep der eye on Papa so ve have no monkeyshines vith more naked vomen."

Little Anton promised her faithfully that he would indeed keep an eye on his great-uncle, and hinted that he would guide him tactfully into the paths of innocence; and the moment she left the house he fetched Papa Schimmelhorn up out of the basement. He poured out two glasses of Bristol Milk.

"Very well, Papa," he said, sitting down. "Tell me all."

Papa Schimmelhorn was only too ready to oblige him. He felt rather more optimistic than he had, for that morning Gustav-Adolf had not only brought him a freshly caught mouse as a peace offering, but had actually purred for him again.

He told his story simply and dramatically, leaving out none of the important details; and for the first time, Little Anton heard the whole truth about Niki and Emmy, Meister

Gansfleisch and Twitchgibbet, the dreadful episode of the concoction that took der lead out of der pencil, Humphrey and the love potion, the Princess—(*"Ach Gott!"* exclaimed the ex-Prince regretfully. "Nefer haff I known such a voman!")—his investiture as her consort and the pagan practices of Little Palaeon, then her insistence that he fight the Minotaur, and finally, how he had at once recognized the dreaded demigod as only a Jekemsyg.

Little Anton was entranced. "Well," he commented, "at least, except for my dear great-aunt, you came out smelling like a rose—as they say here in America. It's too bad, though, that you never can remember any of your own devices so that you can duplicate them. Pêng-Plantagenet would be pleased as punch to make you a millionaire for that gold-maker of yours."

Papa Schimmelhorn's face fell. "Dot iss vun reason I am vorried, Lidtle Anton," he confided, holding his glass out to be refilled. "Maybe Meister Gassi has more sense than I beliefed. On Lidtle Palaeon, I vas sure he vould turn der dial up too high und wreck eferything, but vot iff I am wrong? If die Russians haff der gold, because I cannodt made der machine again, eferyvun blames me."

For a moment, Little Anton frowned, thinking hard. Then suddenly he almost dropped his glass, leaped to his feet. "My word!" he cried excitedly. "Why didn't I put two and two together? Flying down here I read something in the paper. Wait just a second and I'll get it—I have it in my room!"

He rose. In half a minute he was back with the Montreal *Star*. "I think we've solved your problem. Listen! It's in a column—*Hot Line from Moscow*."

> *Official spokesmen here*—he read—*announced today that the vigilance of Soviet security authorities had "totally frustrated a Western-capitalist-imperialist plot against Russia's artistic and cultural heritage by trapping a secret CIA*

infiltrator before he could accomplish his nefarious purpose."

The infiltrator, they declared, had posed as an eminent scientist and defector from the Free World.

They categorically denied persistent reports that such an agent, before his apprehension, succeeded in penetrating the Kremlin itself, destroying innumerable art objects made of precious metal, and burning down an architectural treasure, a Kremlin building dating back to Ivan the Terrible.

"I have a feeling," remarked Little Anton, smiling, "that we have found your Meister Gansfleisch, and that we can guess what's going to happen to him."

Papa Schimmelhorn heaved a great sigh of relief. "I am so glad," he said. "Now iss off my mind. Odervise I feel guilty all my life."

He sat back in his chair. "*Ja*," he said, "Lidtle Anton, iss true I nefer can remember how I make mein dinguses, so I can make vun time only. But—" He peered into his glass abstractedly. "But maybe der luff potion—*ach*, I did nodt infent it, so if I try . . ." He licked his chops. He felt an old familiar tingle. His whiskers quivered. He raised his glass. "Ve drink a toast!" he boomed. "Ve drink to— But you do nodt know her? You haff nodt met lidtle Tilda Blatnik? *Ach*, Lidtle Anton—such a predty pussycat!"